Winx Club 8

Magic in the Air

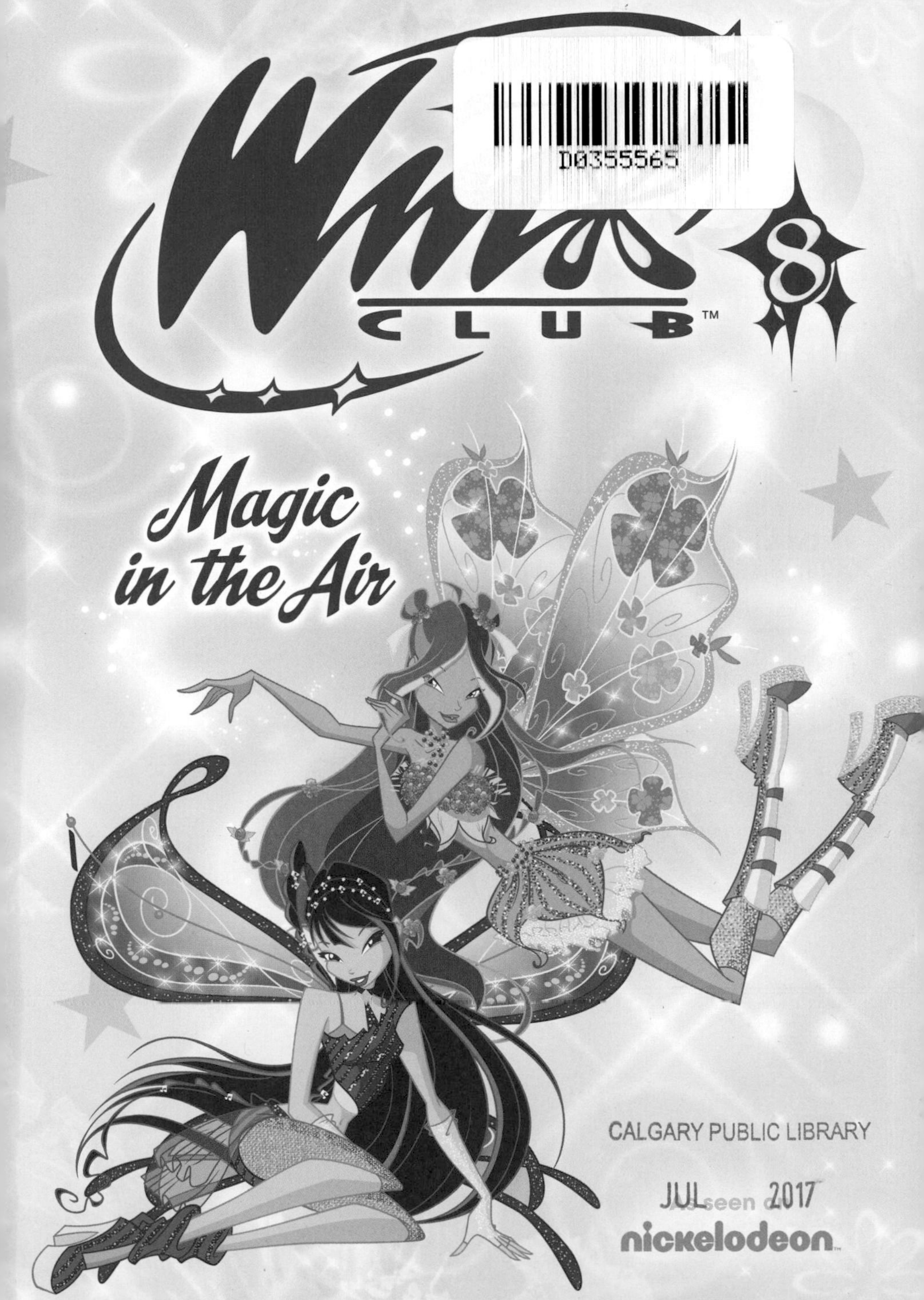

As seen on
nickelodeon

Winx Club
Volume 8

Winx Club ©2003–2013 Rainbow S.r.l. All Rights Reserved.
Series created by Iginio Straffi www.winxclub.com

Designer • Fawn Lau
Letterer • John Hunt
Editor • Amy Yu

This volume contains material that was originally published in
Italian in Issues 67 and 73 of *Winx Club* magazine.

The stories, characters and incidents mentioned in this
publication are entirely fictional.

Printed in China

Published by VIZ Media, LLC
P.O. Box 77010
San Francisco, CA 94107

10 9 8 7 6 5 4 3 2 1
First printing, July 2013

www.vizkids.com

www.viz.com

Table of Contents

Volume 8

Caught in the Web

Magic in the Air

Meet the Winx Club

Raised on Earth, **BLOOM** had no idea she had magical fairy powers until a chance encounter with Stella. Intelligent and loyal, she is the heart and soul of the Winx Club.

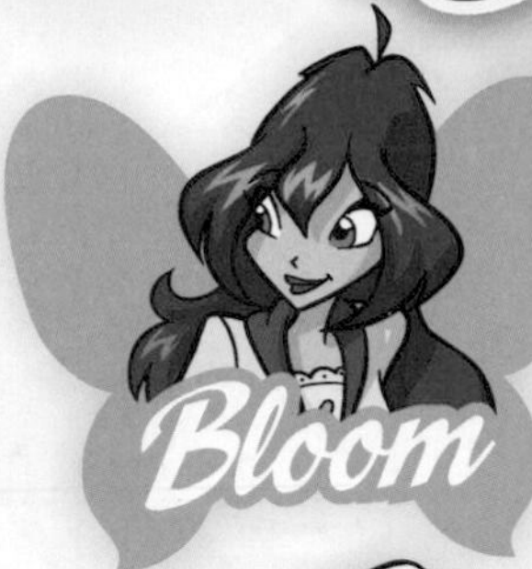
Bloom

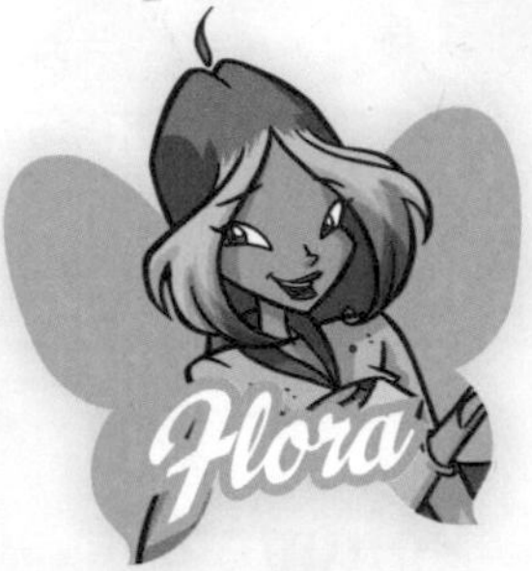
Flora

FLORA draws her fairy powers from flowers, plants and nature in general. Sweet and thoughtful, she tends to be the peacemaker in the group.

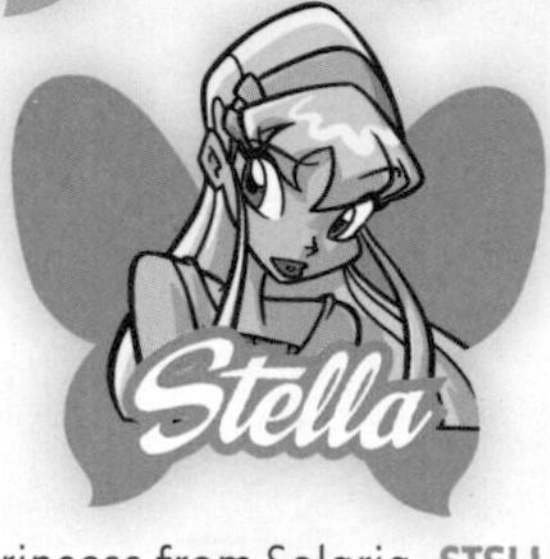
Stella

A princess from Solaria, **STELLA** draws her fairy power from sunlight. Optimistic and carefree, she introduces Bloom to the world of Magix.

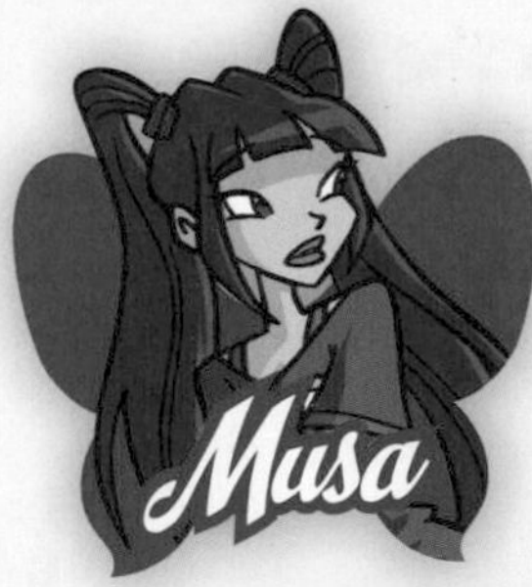
Musa

MUSA draws power from the music she plays. She has a natural talent for investigating, and she's got a keen eye for details.

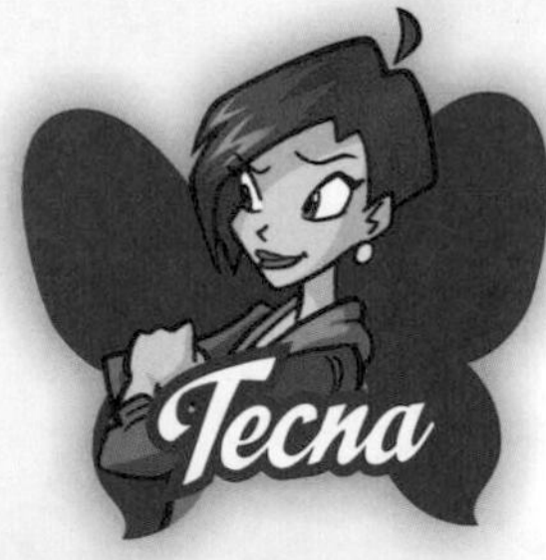
Tecna

Self-confident and a perfectionist, **TECNA** has a vast knowledge of science, which enables her to create devices that can get her and her friends out of trouble.

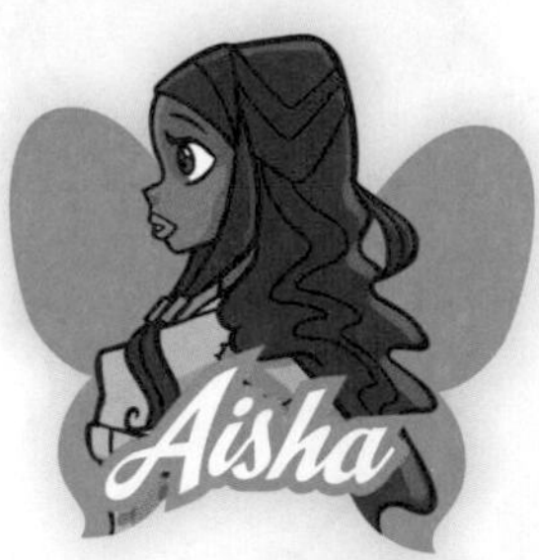
Aisha

Strong and fearless, **AISHA** is able to control the properties of liquids like water. She joined the Winx Club after they saved her from some powerful nightmares.

Their Friends

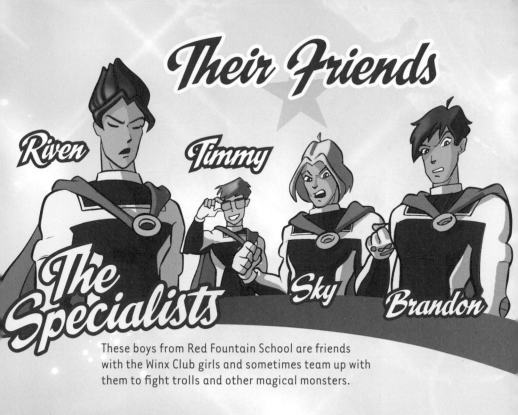

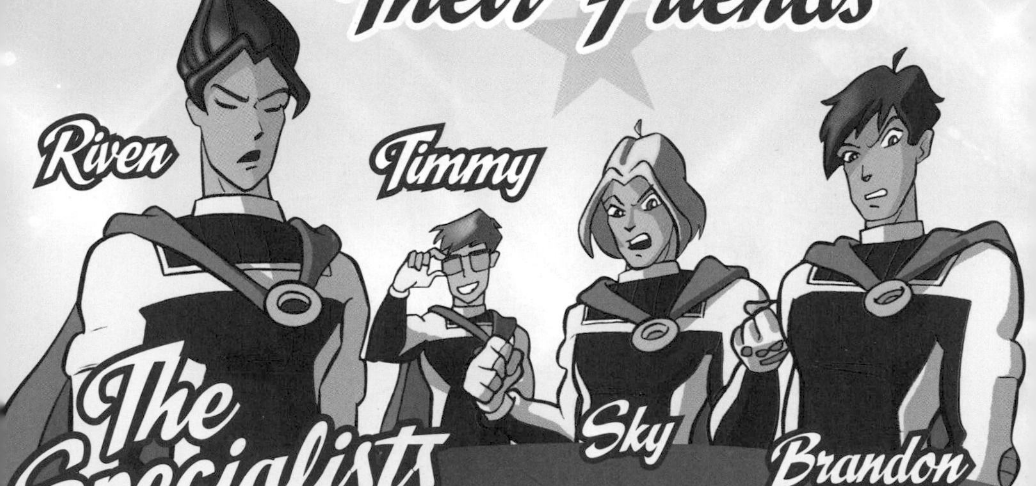
Riven
Timmy
Sky
Brandon

The Specialists

These boys from Red Fountain School are friends with the Winx Club girls and sometimes team up with them to fight trolls and other magical monsters.

Their Foes

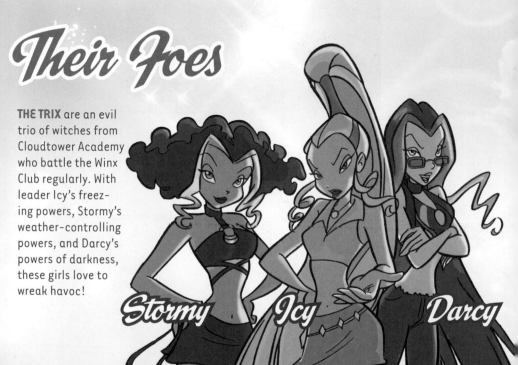

THE TRIX are an evil trio of witches from Cloudtower Academy who battle the Winx Club regularly. With leader Icy's freezing powers, Stormy's weather-controlling powers, and Darcy's powers of darkness, these girls love to wreak havoc!

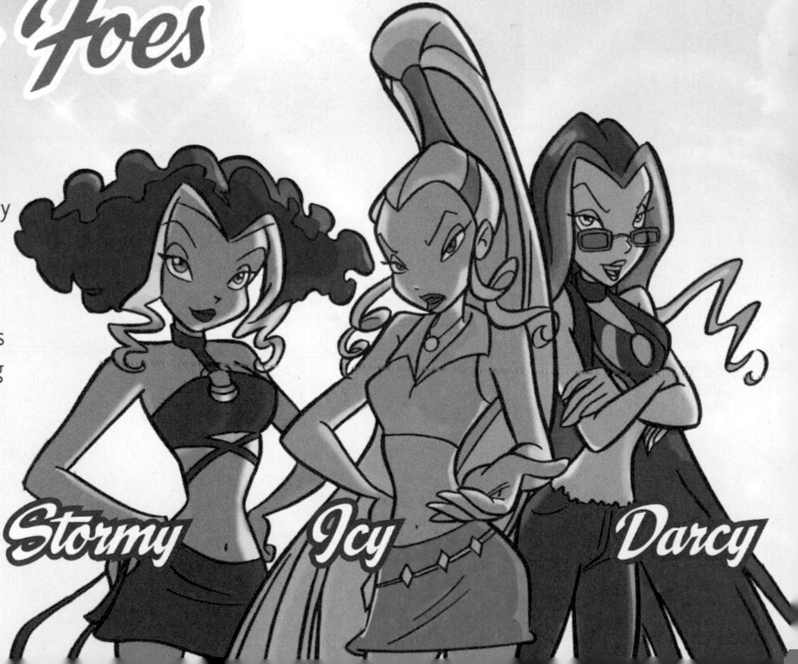
Stormy
Icy
Darcy

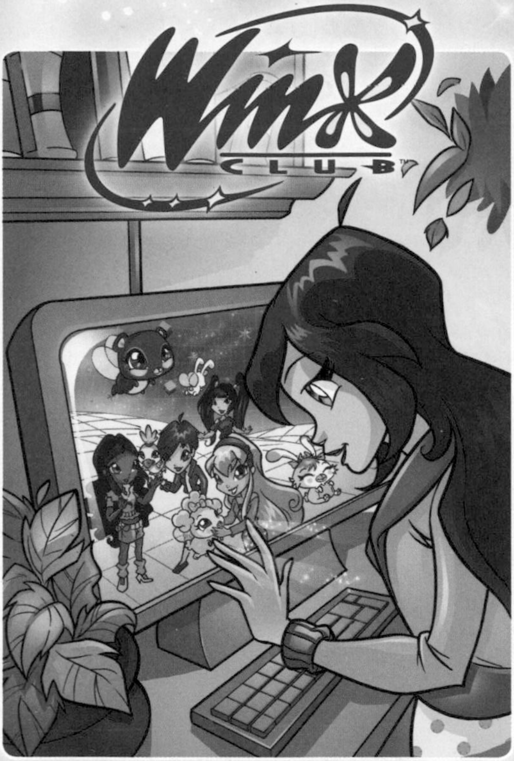
Winx
CLUB

Caught in the Web

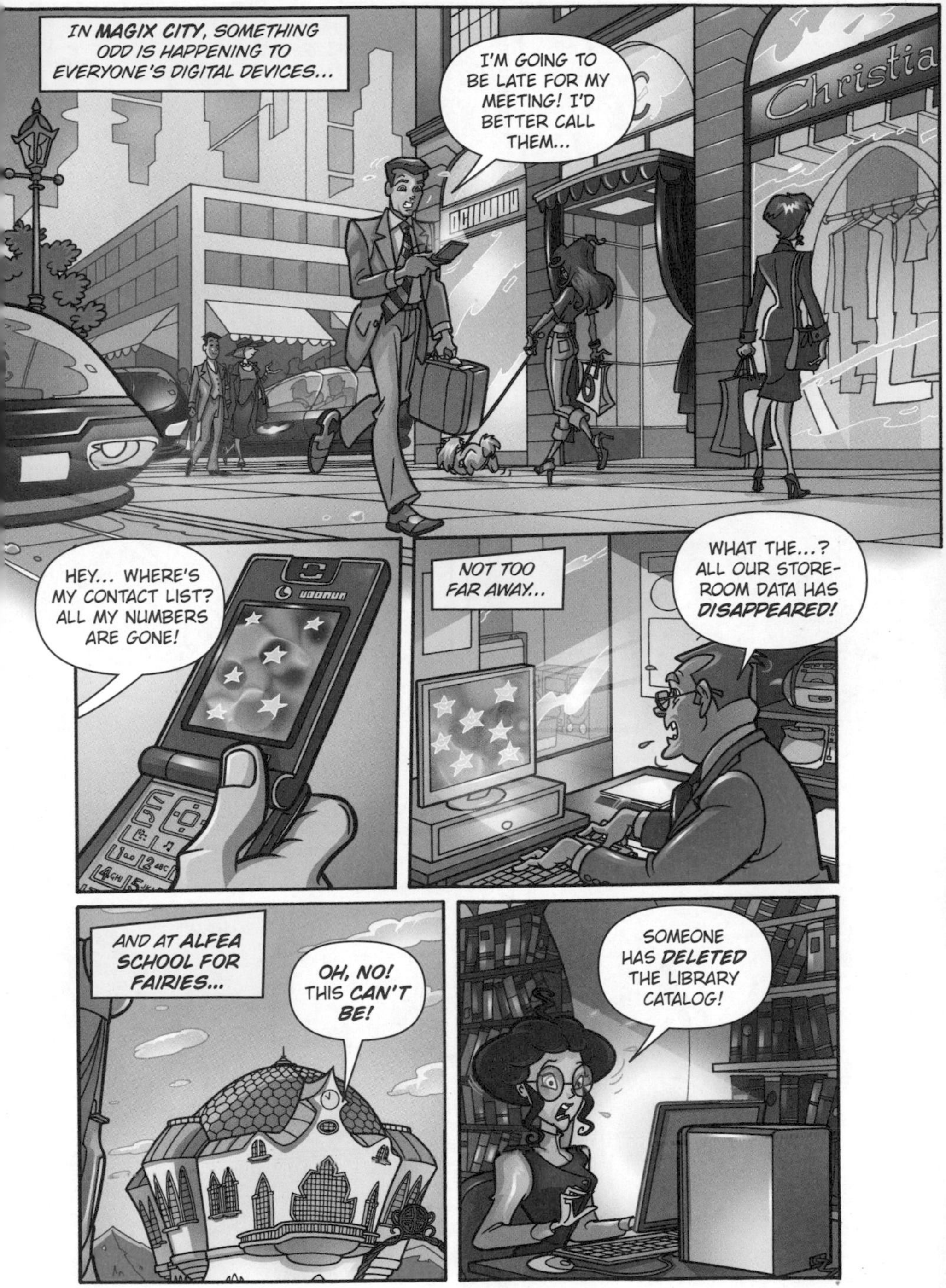
IN MAGIX CITY, SOMETHING ODD IS HAPPENING TO EVERYONE'S DIGITAL DEVICES...
I'M GOING TO BE LATE FOR MY MEETING! I'D BETTER CALL THEM...
HEY... WHERE'S MY CONTACT LIST? ALL MY NUMBERS ARE GONE!
NOT TOO FAR AWAY...
WHAT THE...? ALL OUR STORE-ROOM DATA HAS DISAPPEARED!
AND AT ALFEA SCHOOL FOR FAIRIES...
OH, NO! THIS CAN'T BE!
SOMEONE HAS DELETED THE LIBRARY CATALOG!

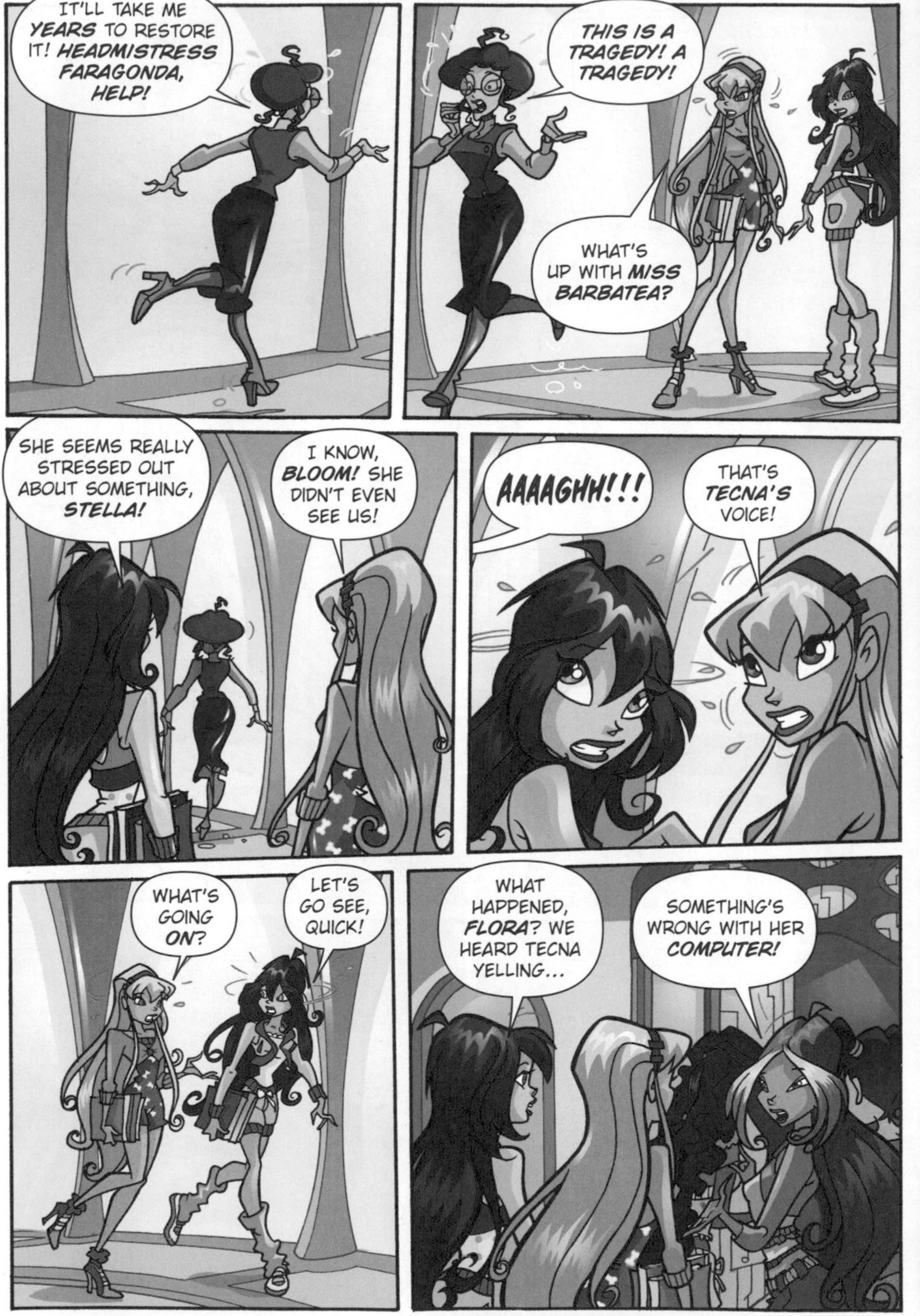
IT'LL TAKE ME YEARS TO RESTORE IT! HEADMISTRESS FARAGONDA, HELP!
THIS IS A TRAGEDY! A TRAGEDY!
WHAT'S UP WITH MISS BARBATEA?
SHE SEEMS REALLY STRESSED OUT ABOUT SOMETHING, STELLA!
I KNOW, BLOOM! SHE DIDN'T EVEN SEE US!
AAAAGHH!!!
THAT'S TECNA'S VOICE!
WHAT'S GOING ON?
LET'S GO SEE, QUICK!
WHAT HAPPENED, FLORA? WE HEARD TECNA YELLING...
SOMETHING'S WRONG WITH HER COMPUTER!

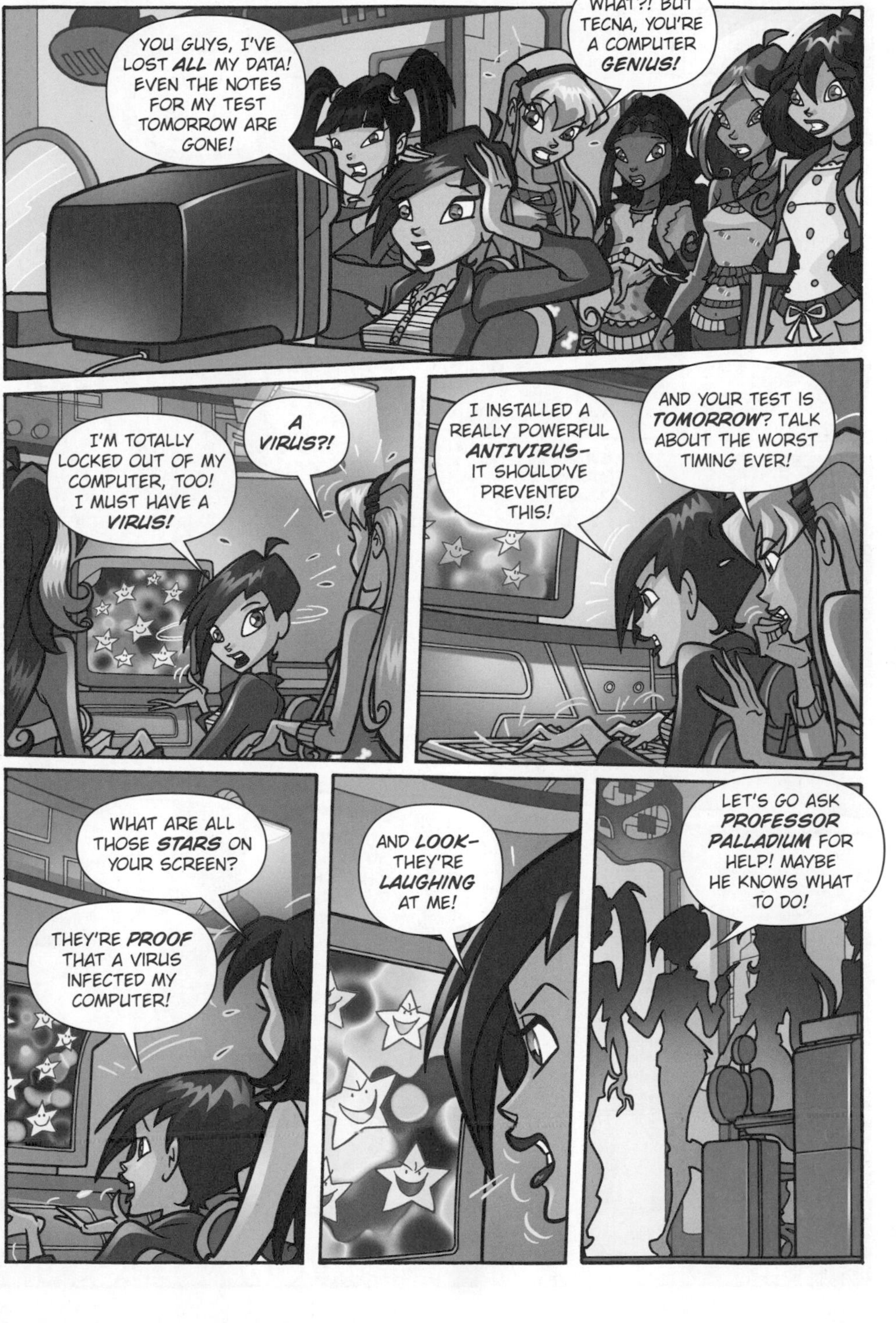
YOU GUYS, I'VE LOST ALL MY DATA! EVEN THE NOTES FOR MY TEST TOMORROW ARE GONE!
WHAT?! BUT TECNA, YOU'RE A COMPUTER GENIUS!
I'M TOTALLY LOCKED OUT OF MY COMPUTER, TOO! I MUST HAVE A VIRUS!
A VIRUS?!
I INSTALLED A REALLY POWERFUL ANTIVIRUS- IT SHOULD'VE PREVENTED THIS!
AND YOUR TEST IS TOMORROW? TALK ABOUT THE WORST TIMING EVER!
WHAT ARE ALL THOSE STARS ON YOUR SCREEN?
THEY'RE PROOF THAT A VIRUS INFECTED MY COMPUTER!
AND LOOK- THEY'RE LAUGHING AT ME!
LET'S GO ASK PROFESSOR PALLADIUM FOR HELP! MAYBE HE KNOWS WHAT TO DO!

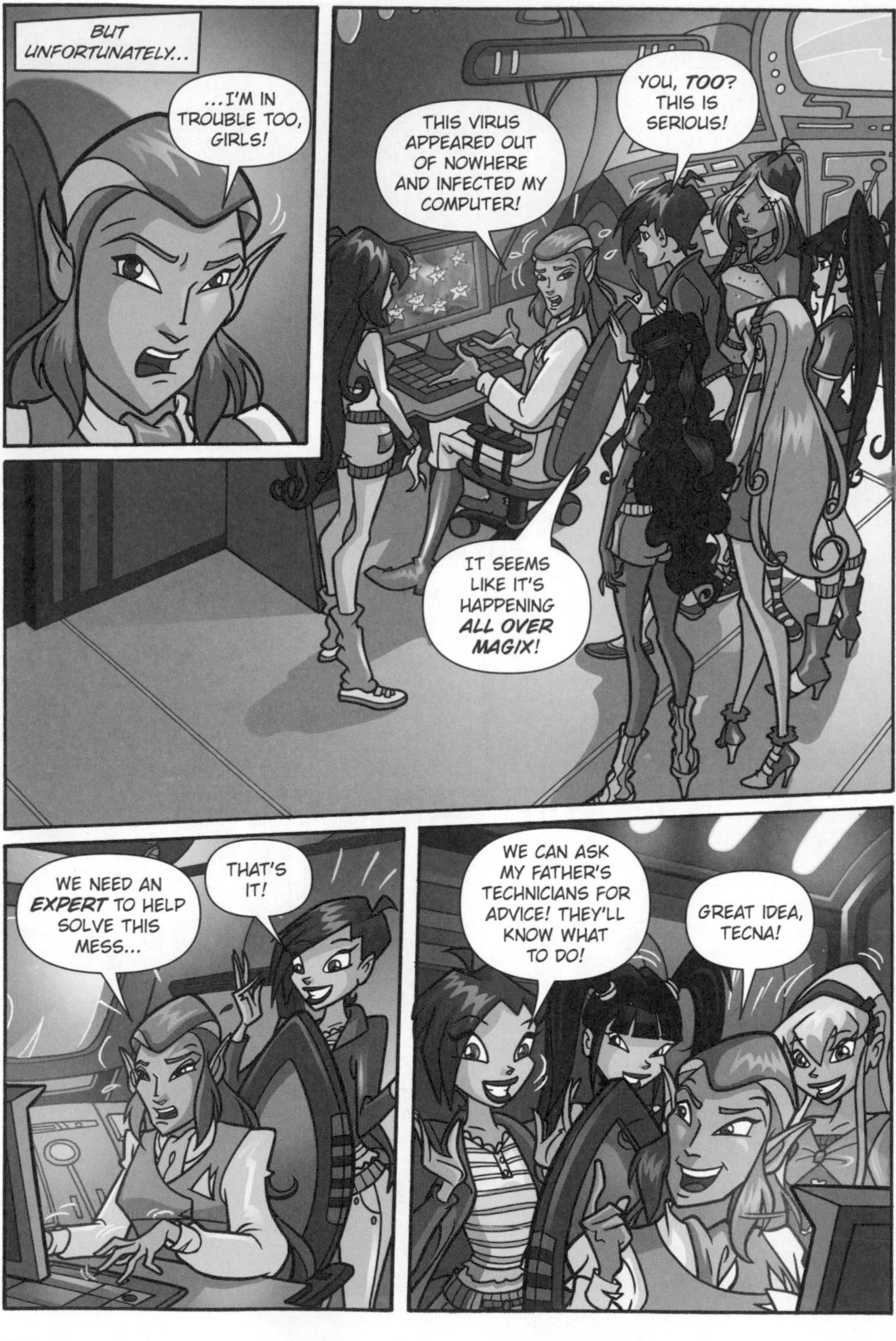
BUT UNFORTUNATELY...
...I'M IN TROUBLE TOO, GIRLS!
THIS VIRUS APPEARED OUT OF NOWHERE AND INFECTED MY COMPUTER!
YOU, *TOO*? THIS IS SERIOUS!
IT SEEMS LIKE IT'S HAPPENING *ALL OVER MAGIX*!
WE NEED AN *EXPERT* TO HELP SOLVE THIS MESS...
THAT'S IT!
WE CAN ASK MY FATHER'S TECHNICIANS FOR ADVICE! THEY'LL KNOW WHAT TO DO!
GREAT IDEA, TECNA!

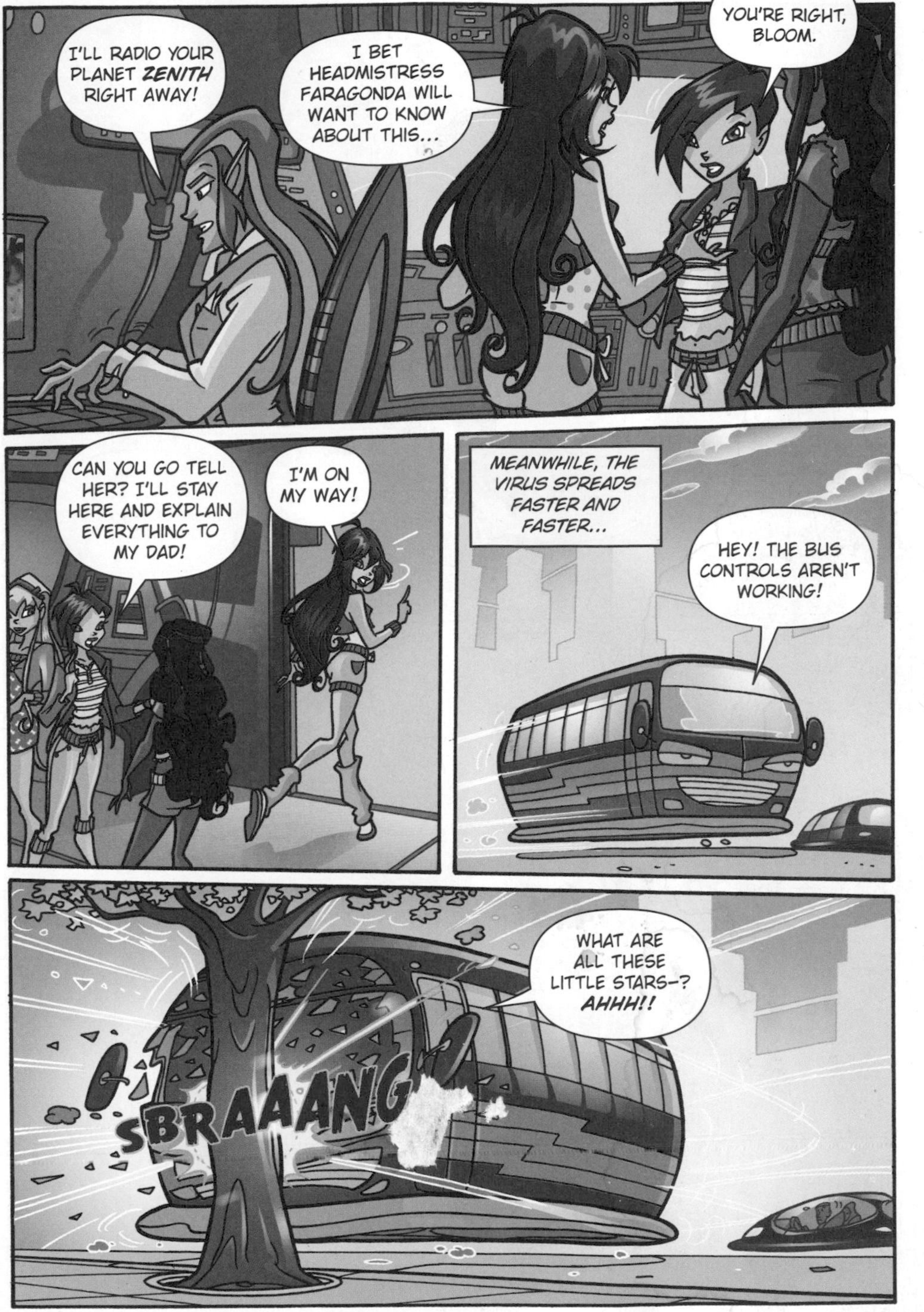
I'LL RADIO YOUR PLANET *ZENITH* RIGHT AWAY!
I BET HEADMISTRESS FARAGONDA WILL WANT TO KNOW ABOUT THIS...
YOU'RE RIGHT, BLOOM.
CAN YOU GO TELL HER? I'LL STAY HERE AND EXPLAIN EVERYTHING TO MY DAD!
I'M ON MY WAY!
MEANWHILE, THE VIRUS SPREADS FASTER AND FASTER...
HEY! THE BUS CONTROLS AREN'T WORKING!
WHAT ARE ALL THESE LITTLE STARS–? ***AHHH!!***
SBRAAANG

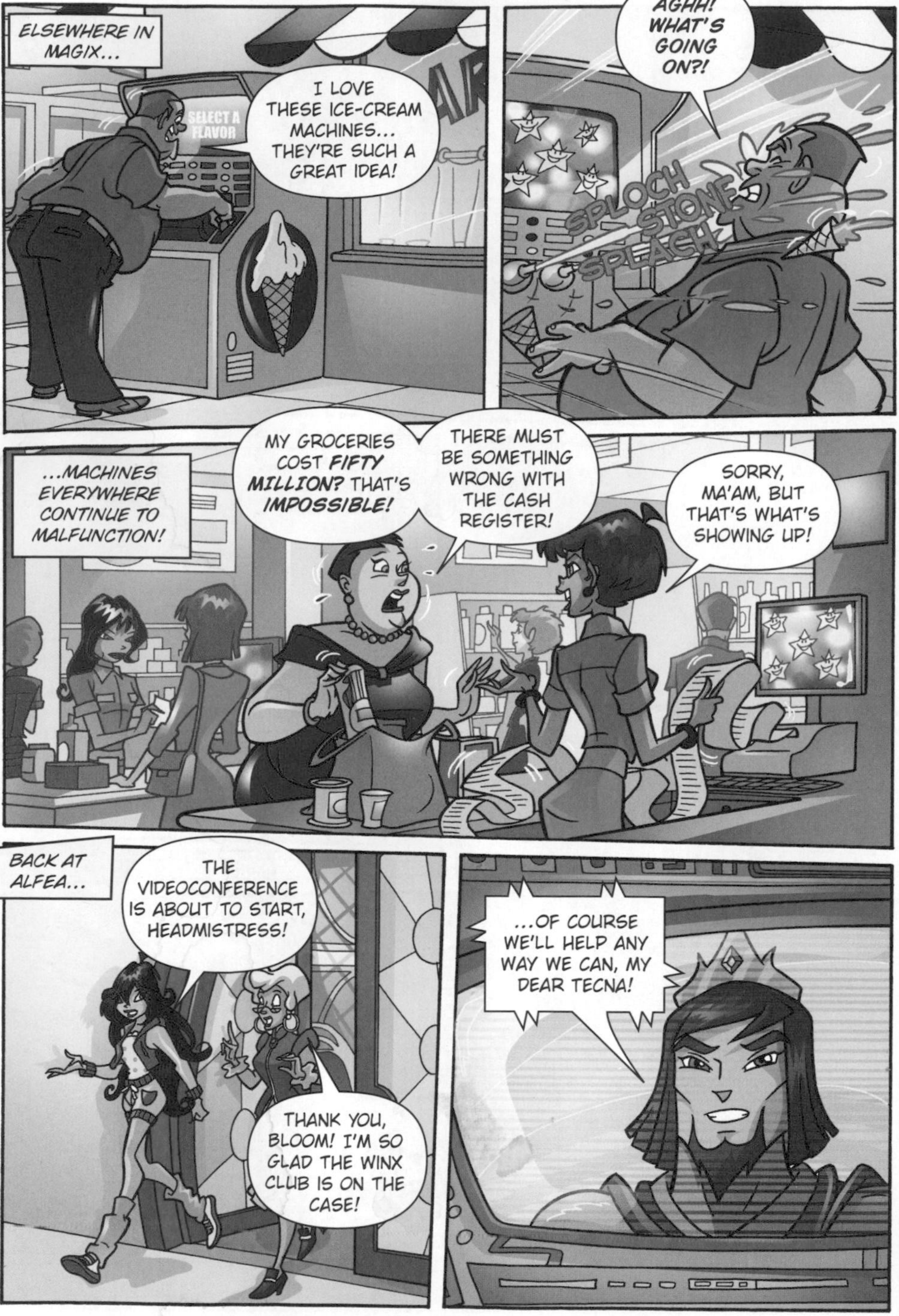

ELSEWHERE IN MAGIX...
SELECT A FLAVOR
I LOVE THESE ICE-CREAM MACHINES... THEY'RE SUCH A GREAT IDEA!
AGHH! WHAT'S GOING ON?!
SPLOCH STONE SPLACH
...MACHINES EVERYWHERE CONTINUE TO MALFUNCTION!
MY GROCERIES COST FIFTY MILLION? THAT'S IMPOSSIBLE!
THERE MUST BE SOMETHING WRONG WITH THE CASH REGISTER!
SORRY, MA'AM, BUT THAT'S WHAT'S SHOWING UP!
BACK AT ALFEA...
THE VIDEOCONFERENCE IS ABOUT TO START, HEADMISTRESS!
THANK YOU, BLOOM! I'M SO GLAD THE WINX CLUB IS ON THE CASE!
...OF COURSE WE'LL HELP ANY WAY WE CAN, MY DEAR TECNA!

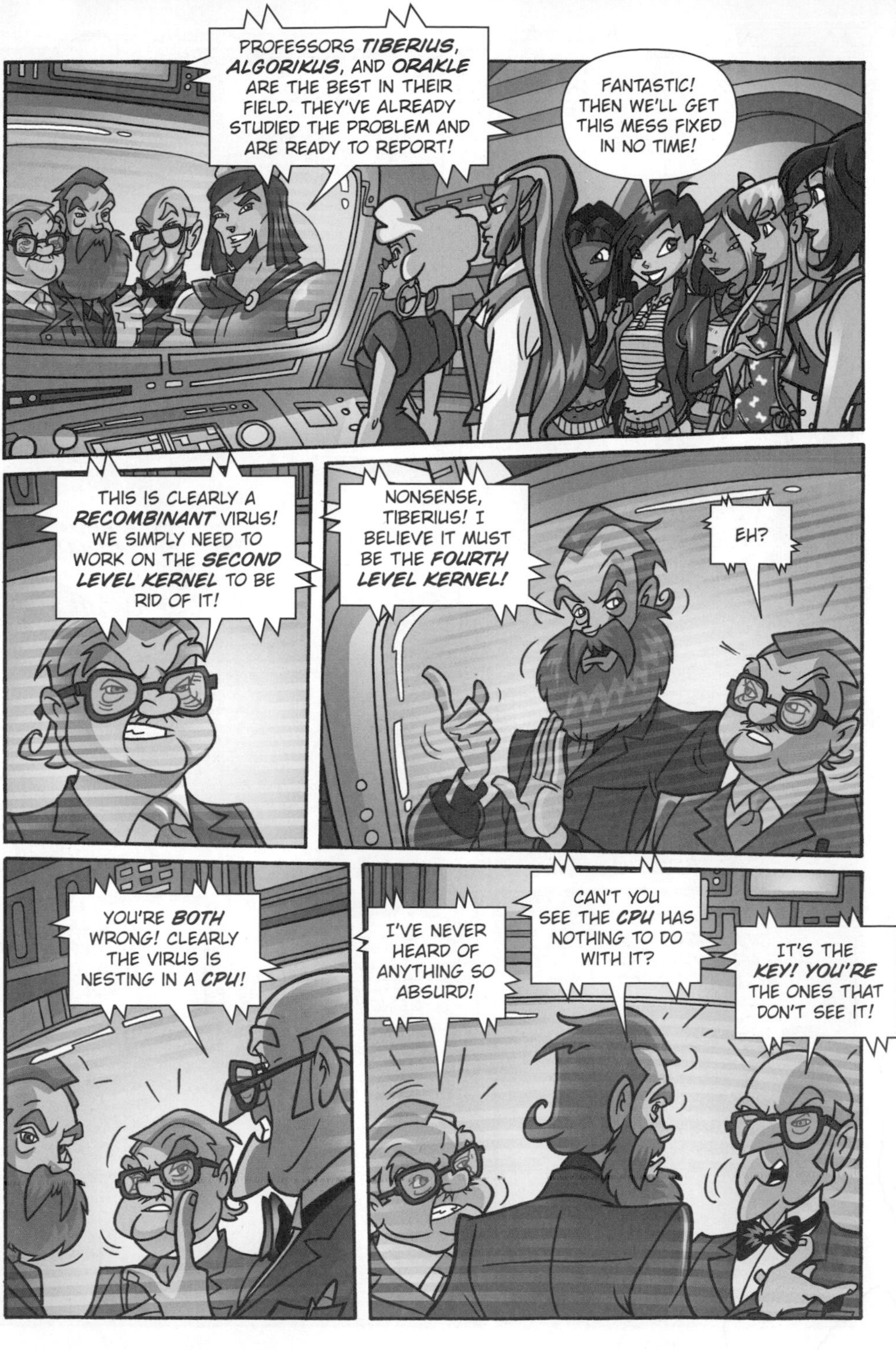
PROFESSORS TIBERIUS, ALGORIKUS, AND ORAKLE ARE THE BEST IN THEIR FIELD. THEY'VE ALREADY STUDIED THE PROBLEM AND ARE READY TO REPORT!
FANTASTIC! THEN WE'LL GET THIS MESS FIXED IN NO TIME!
THIS IS CLEARLY A RECOMBINANT VIRUS! WE SIMPLY NEED TO WORK ON THE SECOND LEVEL KERNEL TO BE RID OF IT!
NONSENSE, TIBERIUS! I BELIEVE IT MUST BE THE FOURTH LEVEL KERNEL!
EH?
YOU'RE BOTH WRONG! CLEARLY THE VIRUS IS NESTING IN A CPU!
I'VE NEVER HEARD OF ANYTHING SO ABSURD!
CAN'T YOU SEE THE CPU HAS NOTHING TO DO WITH IT?
IT'S THE KEY! YOU'RE THE ONES THAT DON'T SEE IT!

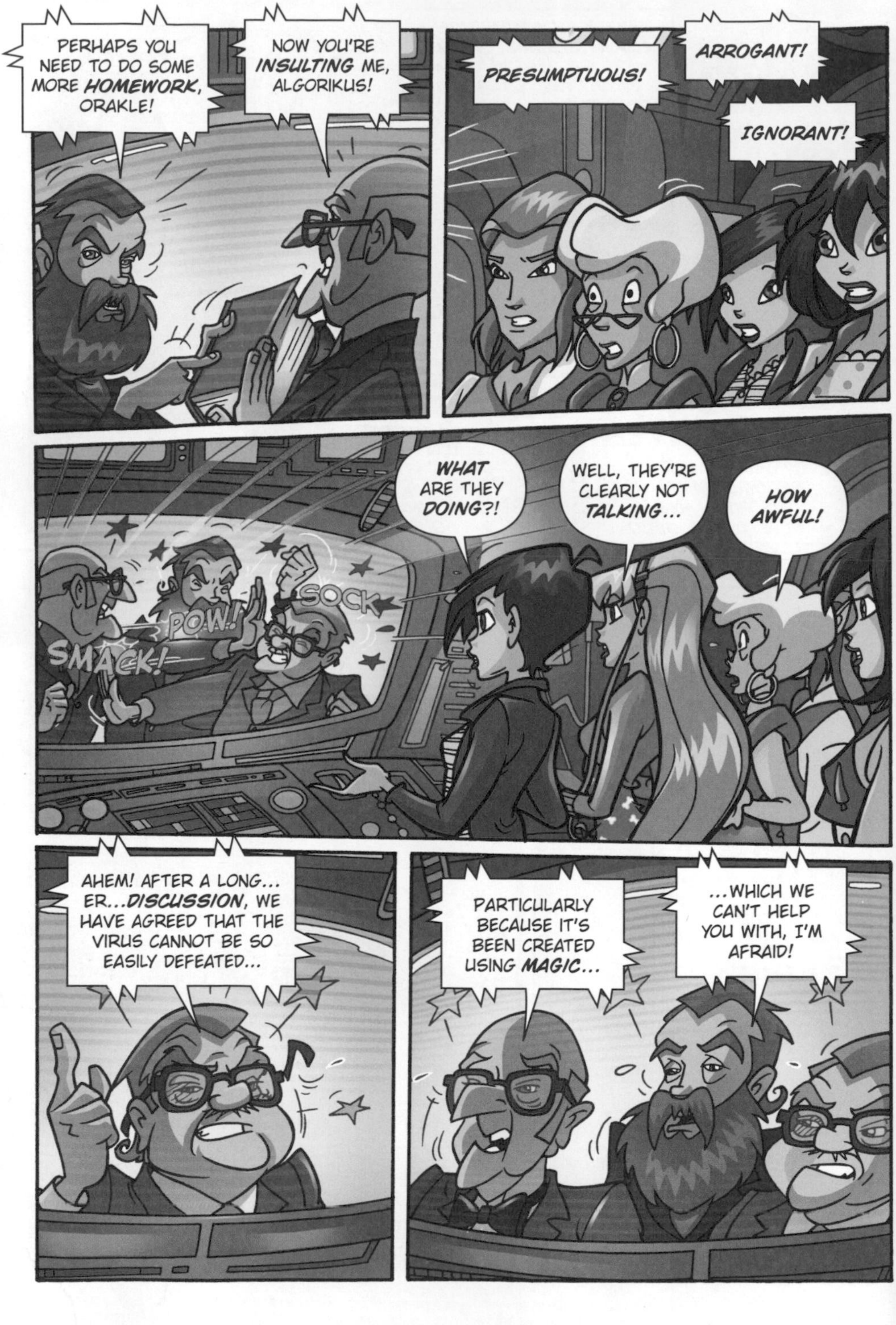

PERHAPS YOU NEED TO DO SOME MORE HOMEWORK, ORAKLE!
NOW YOU'RE INSULTING ME, ALGORIKUS!
PRESUMPTUOUS!
ARROGANT!
IGNORANT!
SMACK!
POW!
SOCK
WHAT ARE THEY DOING?!
WELL, THEY'RE CLEARLY NOT TALKING...
HOW AWFUL!
AHEM! AFTER A LONG... ER...DISCUSSION, WE HAVE AGREED THAT THE VIRUS CANNOT BE SO EASILY DEFEATED...
PARTICULARLY BECAUSE IT'S BEEN CREATED USING MAGIC...
...WHICH WE CAN'T HELP YOU WITH, I'M AFRAID!

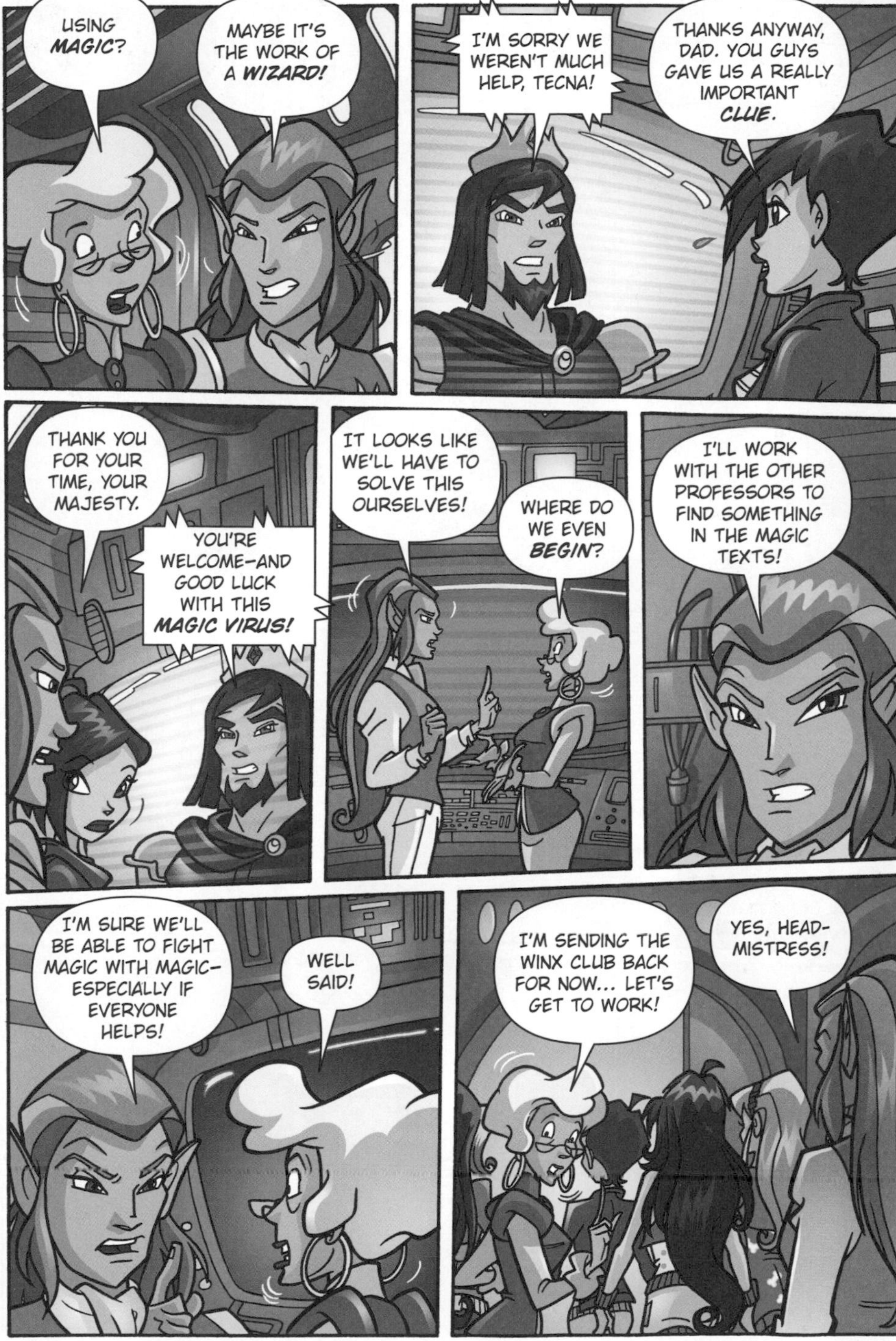
USING MAGIC?
MAYBE IT'S THE WORK OF A WIZARD!
I'M SORRY WE WEREN'T MUCH HELP, TECNA!
THANKS ANYWAY, DAD. YOU GUYS GAVE US A REALLY IMPORTANT CLUE.
THANK YOU FOR YOUR TIME, YOUR MAJESTY.
YOU'RE WELCOME—AND GOOD LUCK WITH THIS MAGIC VIRUS!
IT LOOKS LIKE WE'LL HAVE TO SOLVE THIS OURSELVES!
WHERE DO WE EVEN BEGIN?
I'LL WORK WITH THE OTHER PROFESSORS TO FIND SOMETHING IN THE MAGIC TEXTS!
I'M SURE WE'LL BE ABLE TO FIGHT MAGIC WITH MAGIC—ESPECIALLY IF EVERYONE HELPS!
WELL SAID!
I'M SENDING THE WINX CLUB BACK FOR NOW... LET'S GET TO WORK!
YES, HEAD-MISTRESS!

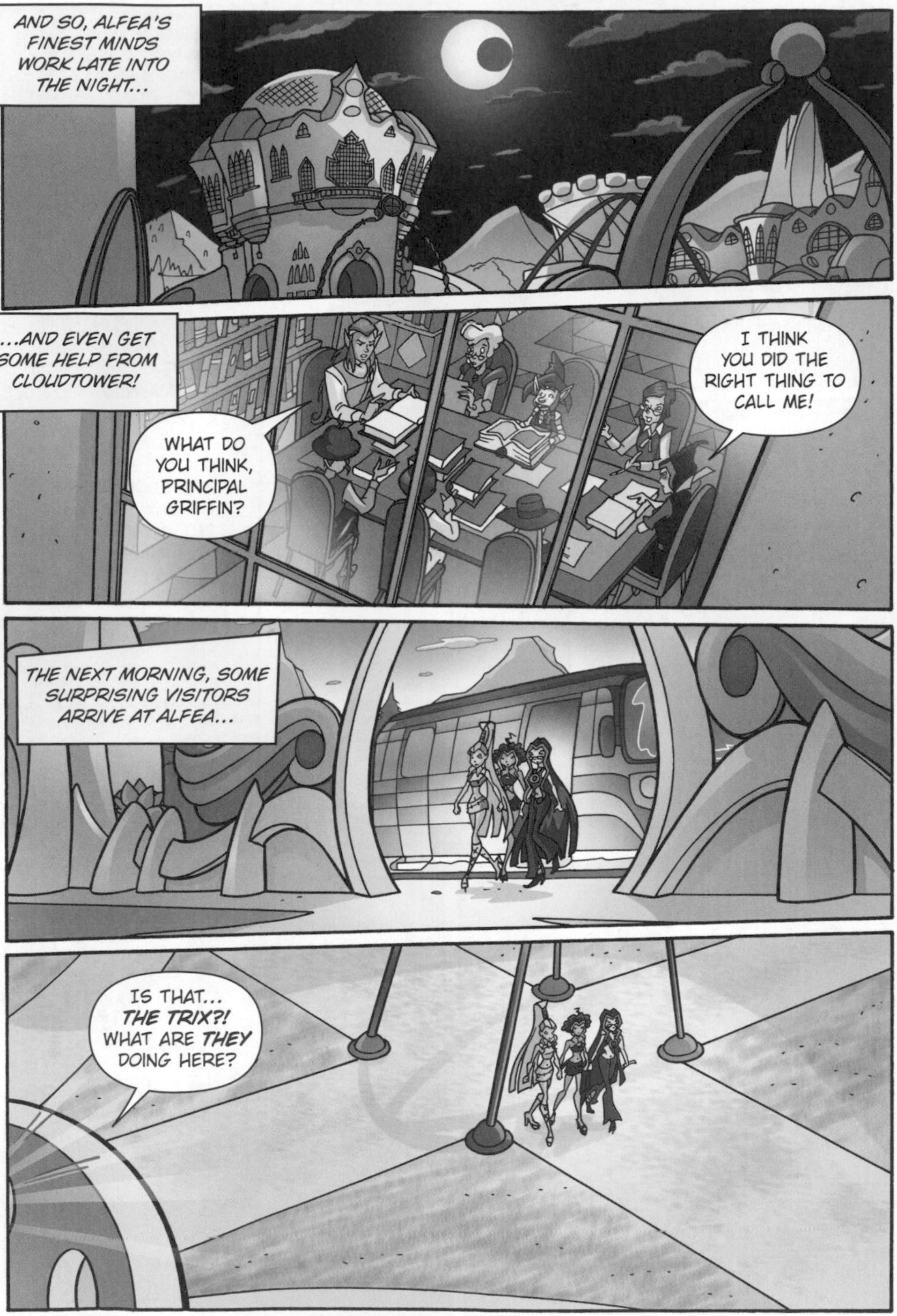

AND SO, ALFEA'S FINEST MINDS WORK LATE INTO THE NIGHT...
...AND EVEN GET SOME HELP FROM CLOUDTOWER!
WHAT DO YOU THINK, PRINCIPAL GRIFFIN?
I THINK YOU DID THE RIGHT THING TO CALL ME!
THE NEXT MORNING, SOME SURPRISING VISITORS ARRIVE AT ALFEA...
IS THAT... **THE TRIX?!** WHAT ARE **THEY** DOING HERE?

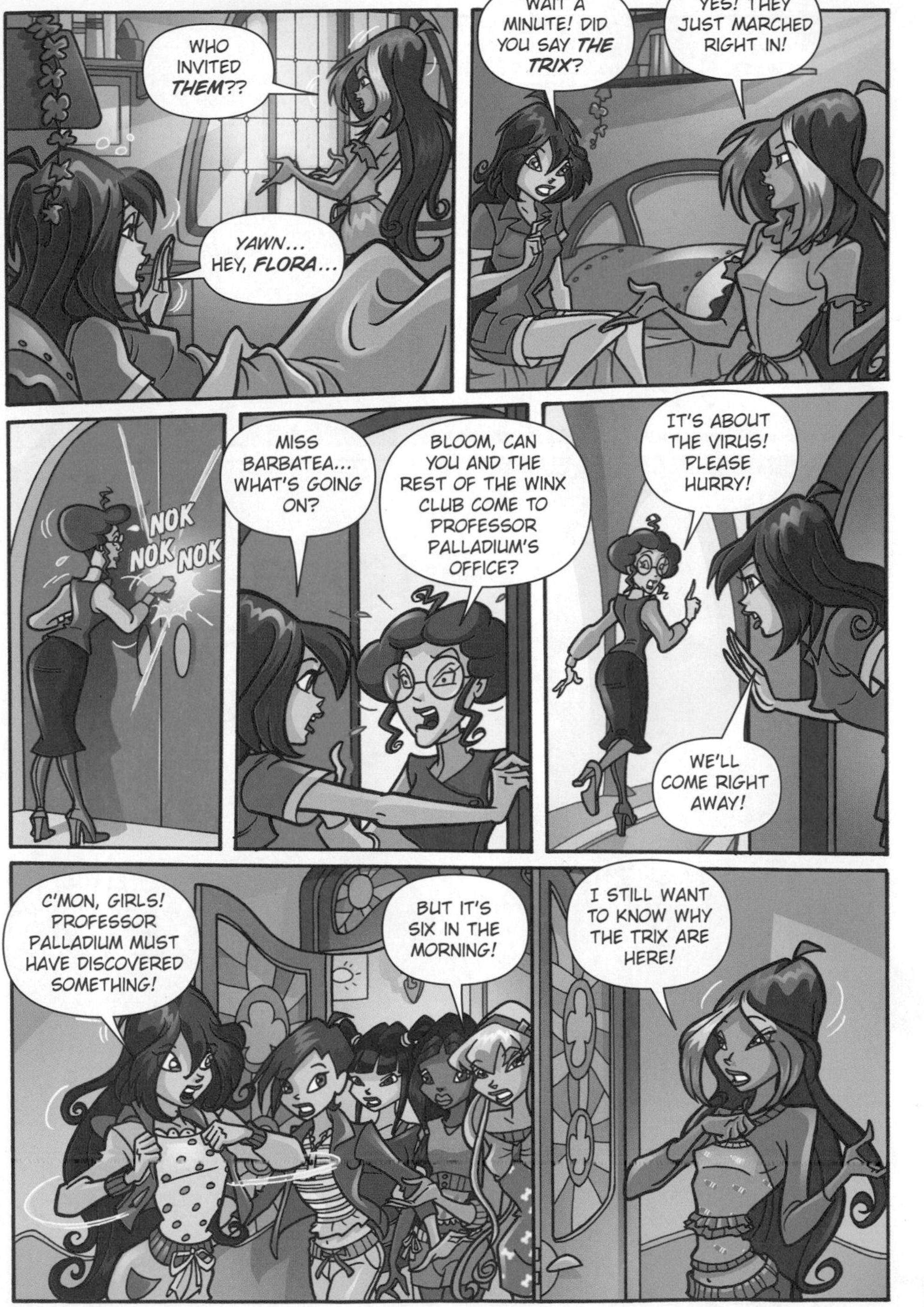
WHO INVITED *THEM*??
YAWN... HEY, **FLORA**...
WAIT A MINUTE! DID YOU SAY ***THE TRIX***?
YES! THEY JUST MARCHED RIGHT IN!
NOK NOK NOK
MISS BARBATEA... WHAT'S GOING ON?
BLOOM, CAN YOU AND THE REST OF THE WINX CLUB COME TO PROFESSOR PALLADIUM'S OFFICE?
IT'S ABOUT THE VIRUS! PLEASE HURRY!
WE'LL COME RIGHT AWAY!
C'MON, GIRLS! PROFESSOR PALLADIUM MUST HAVE DISCOVERED SOMETHING!
BUT IT'S SIX IN THE MORNING!
I STILL WANT TO KNOW WHY THE TRIX ARE HERE!

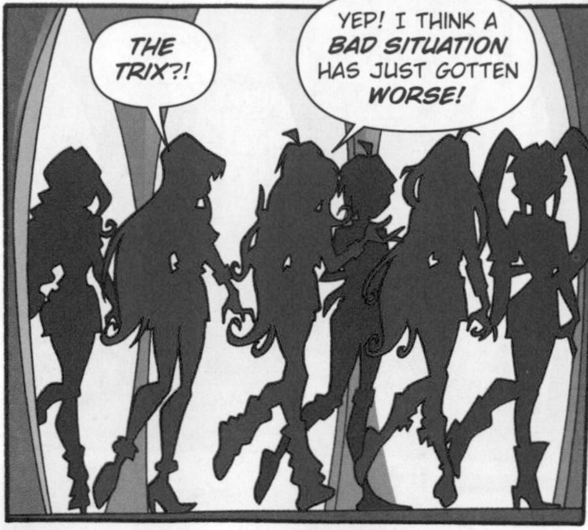
THE TRIX?!
YEP! I THINK A BAD SITUATION HAS JUST GOTTEN WORSE!

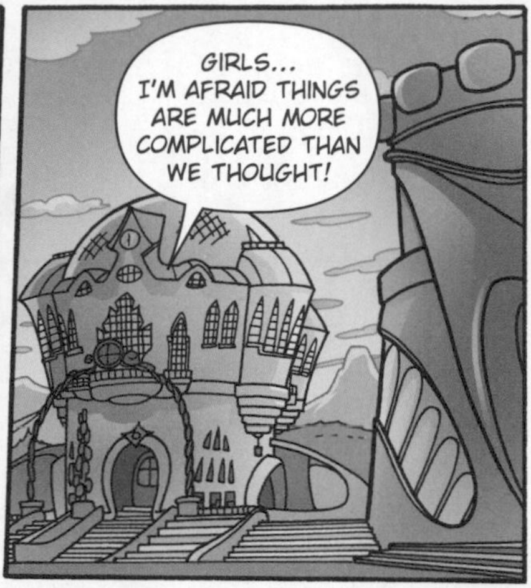
GIRLS... I'M AFRAID THINGS ARE MUCH MORE COMPLICATED THAN WE THOUGHT!

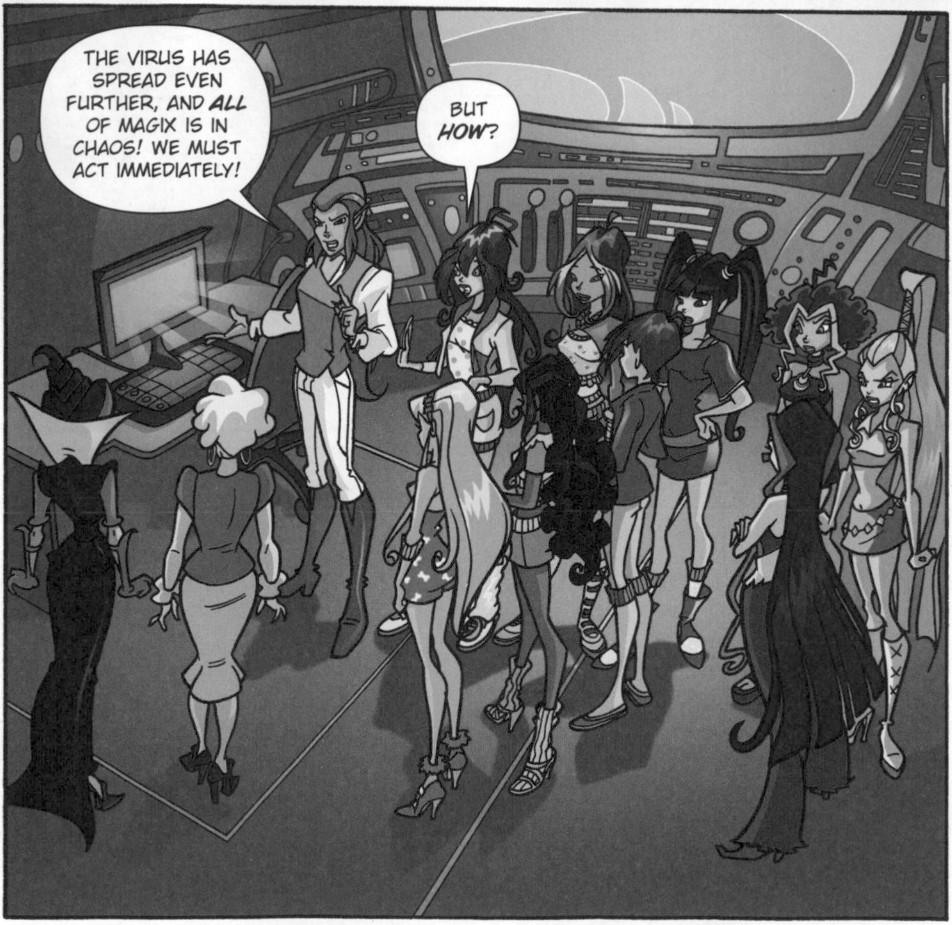
THE VIRUS HAS SPREAD EVEN FURTHER, AND ALL OF MAGIX IS IN CHAOS! WE MUST ACT IMMEDIATELY!
BUT HOW?

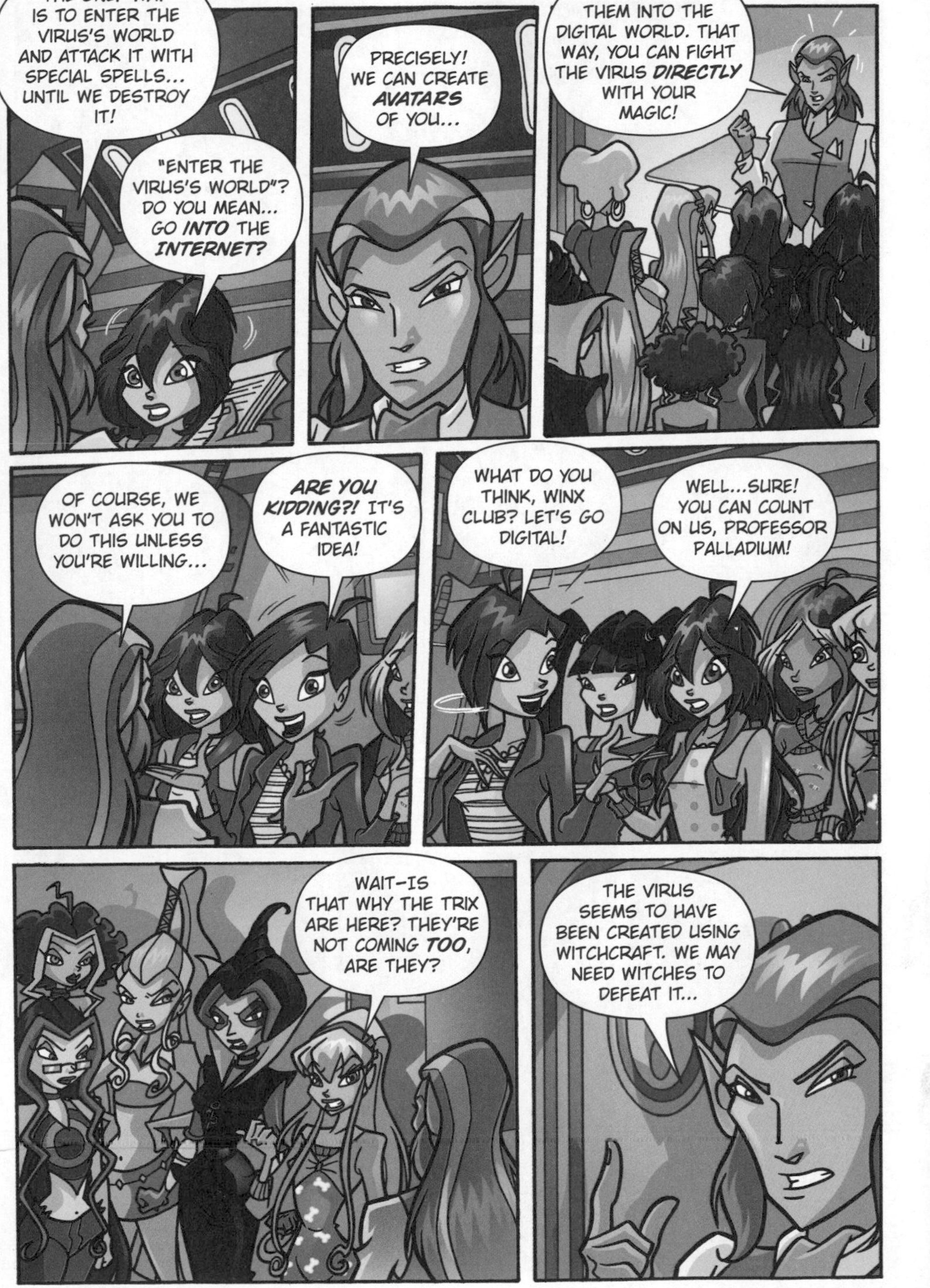
THE ONLY WAY IS TO ENTER THE VIRUS'S WORLD AND ATTACK IT WITH SPECIAL SPELLS... UNTIL WE DESTROY IT!
"ENTER THE VIRUS'S WORLD"? DO YOU MEAN... GO INTO THE INTERNET?
PRECISELY! WE CAN CREATE AVATARS OF YOU...
...AND SEND THEM INTO THE DIGITAL WORLD. THAT WAY, YOU CAN FIGHT THE VIRUS DIRECTLY WITH YOUR MAGIC!
OF COURSE, WE WON'T ASK YOU TO DO THIS UNLESS YOU'RE WILLING...
ARE YOU KIDDING?! IT'S A FANTASTIC IDEA!
WHAT DO YOU THINK, WINX CLUB? LET'S GO DIGITAL!
WELL...SURE! YOU CAN COUNT ON US, PROFESSOR PALLADIUM!
WAIT–IS THAT WHY THE TRIX ARE HERE? THEY'RE NOT COMING TOO, ARE THEY?
THE VIRUS SEEMS TO HAVE BEEN CREATED USING WITCHCRAFT. WE MAY NEED WITCHES TO DEFEAT IT...

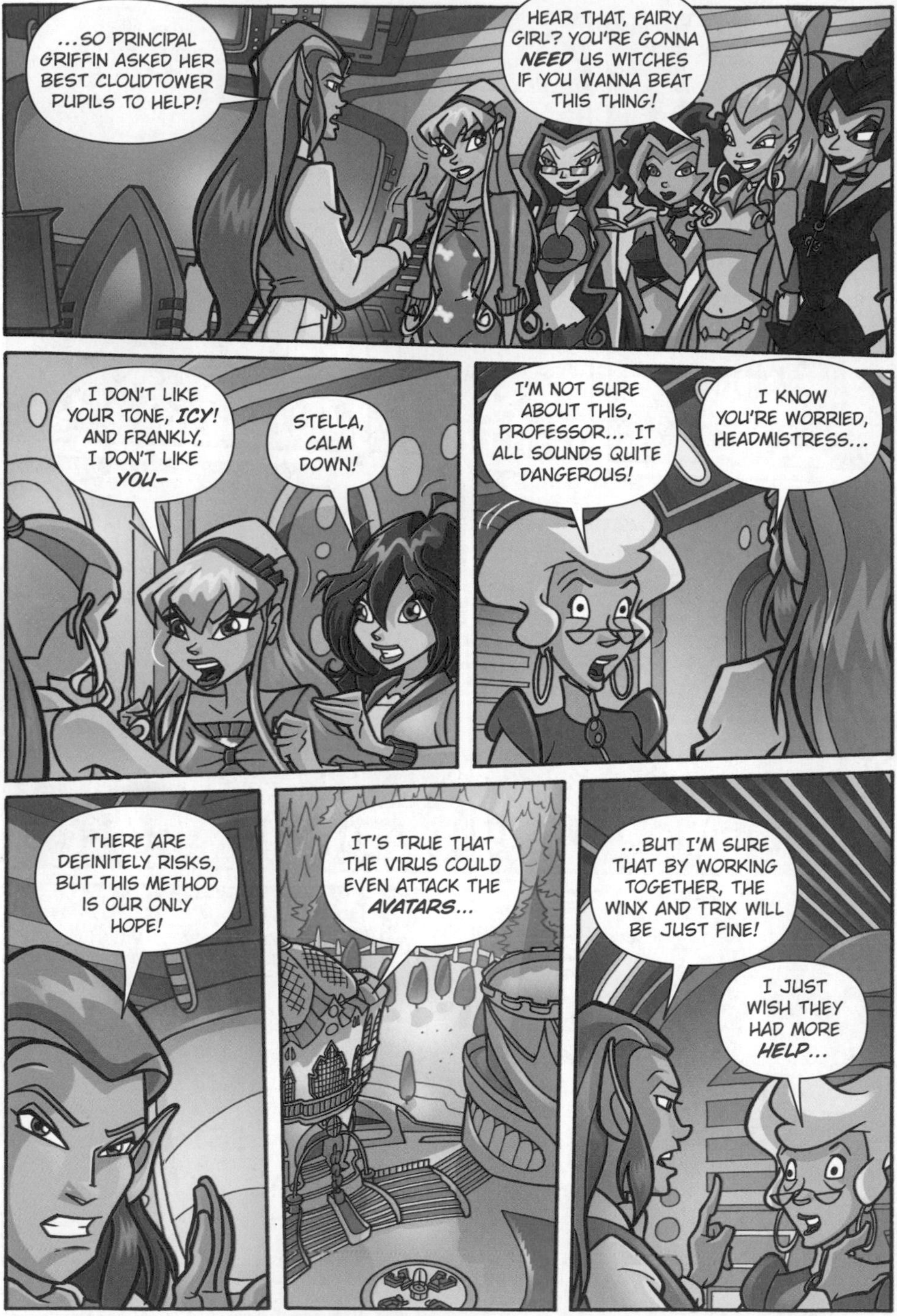
...SO PRINCIPAL GRIFFIN ASKED HER BEST CLOUDTOWER PUPILS TO HELP!
HEAR THAT, FAIRY GIRL? YOU'RE GONNA **NEED** US WITCHES IF YOU WANNA BEAT THIS THING!
I DON'T LIKE YOUR TONE, **ICY**! AND FRANKLY, I DON'T LIKE **YOU**-
STELLA, CALM DOWN!
I'M NOT SURE ABOUT THIS, PROFESSOR... IT ALL SOUNDS QUITE DANGEROUS!
I KNOW YOU'RE WORRIED, HEADMISTRESS...
THERE ARE DEFINITELY RISKS, BUT THIS METHOD IS OUR ONLY HOPE!
IT'S TRUE THAT THE VIRUS COULD EVEN ATTACK THE **AVATARS**...
...BUT I'M SURE THAT BY WORKING TOGETHER, THE WINX AND TRIX WILL BE JUST FINE!
I JUST WISH THEY HAD MORE **HELP**...

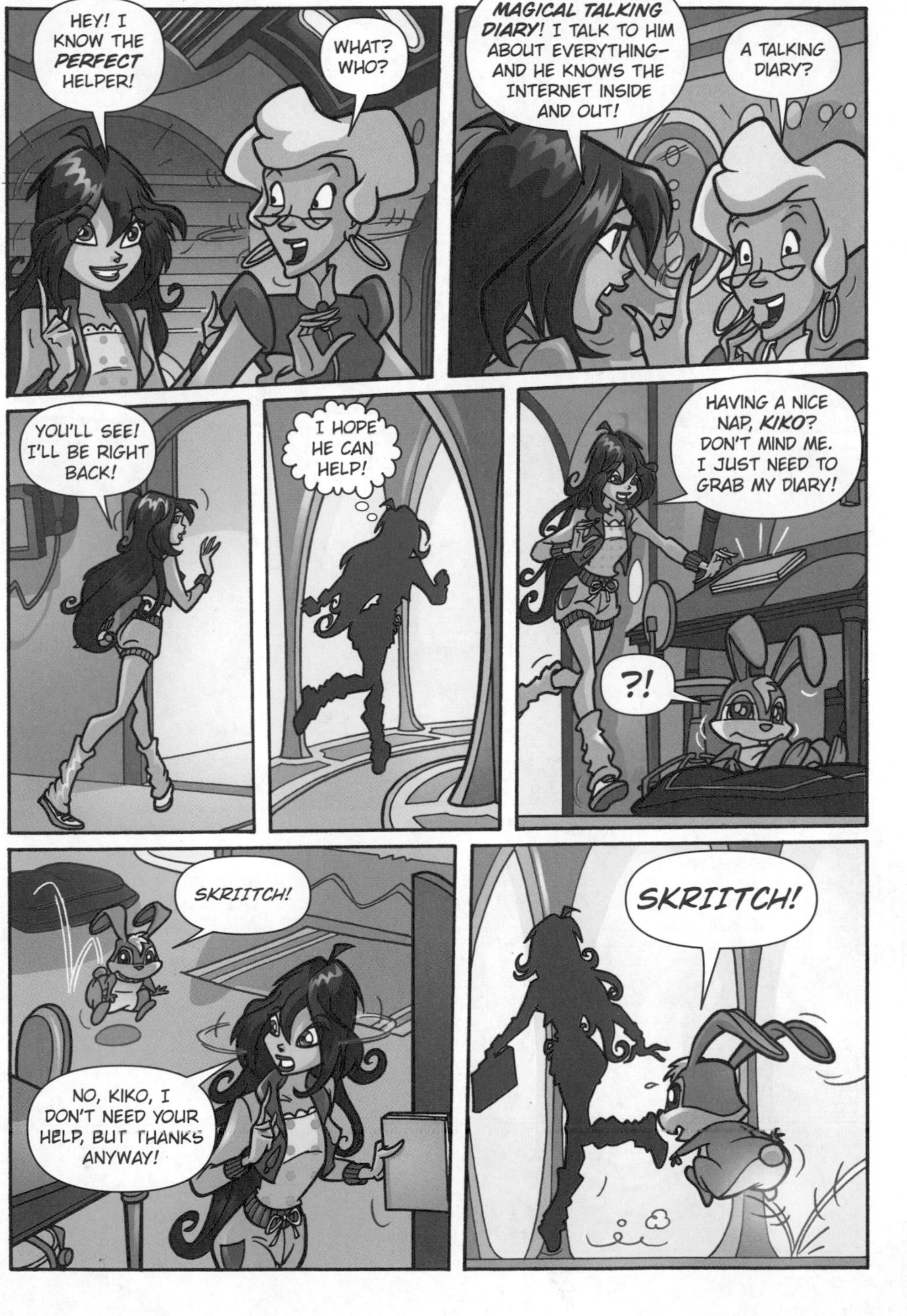
HEY! I KNOW THE PERFECT HELPER!
WHAT? WHO?
MY MAGICAL TALKING DIARY! I TALK TO HIM ABOUT EVERYTHING– AND HE KNOWS THE INTERNET INSIDE AND OUT!
A TALKING DIARY?
YOU'LL SEE! I'LL BE RIGHT BACK!
I HOPE HE CAN HELP!
HAVING A NICE NAP, KIKO? DON'T MIND ME. I JUST NEED TO GRAB MY DIARY!
?!
SKRIITCH!
NO, KIKO, I DON'T NEED YOUR HELP, BUT THANKS ANYWAY!
SKRIITCH!

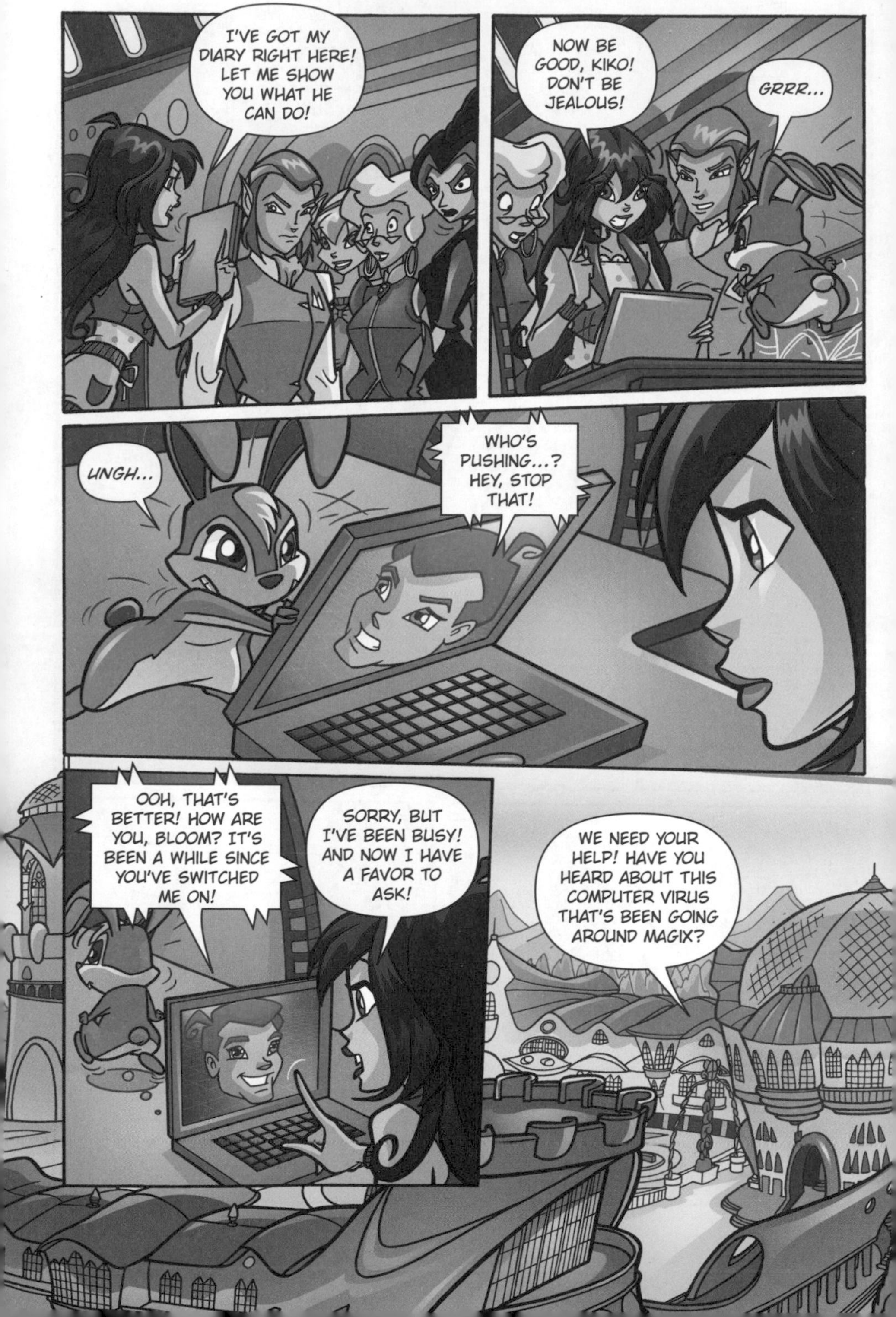
I'VE GOT MY DIARY RIGHT HERE! LET ME SHOW YOU WHAT HE CAN DO!
NOW BE GOOD, KIKO! DON'T BE JEALOUS!
GRRR...
UNGH...
WHO'S PUSHING...? HEY, STOP THAT!
OOH, THAT'S BETTER! HOW ARE YOU, BLOOM? IT'S BEEN A WHILE SINCE YOU'VE SWITCHED ME ON!
SORRY, BUT I'VE BEEN BUSY! AND NOW I HAVE A FAVOR TO ASK!
WE NEED YOUR HELP! HAVE YOU HEARD ABOUT THIS COMPUTER VIRUS THAT'S BEEN GOING AROUND MAGIX?

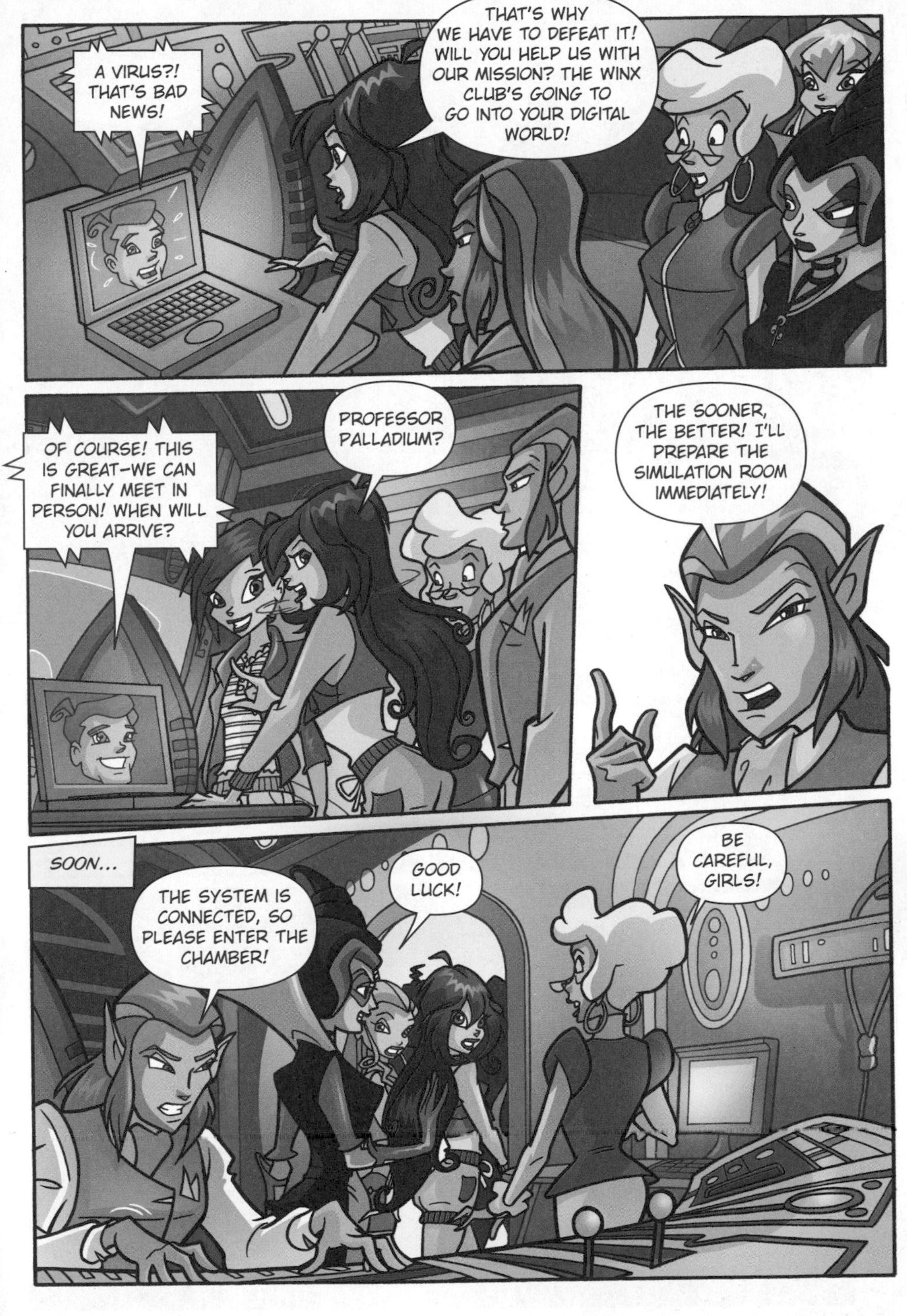
A VIRUS?! THAT'S BAD NEWS!
THAT'S WHY WE HAVE TO DEFEAT IT! WILL YOU HELP US WITH OUR MISSION? THE WINX CLUB'S GOING TO GO INTO YOUR DIGITAL WORLD!
OF COURSE! THIS IS GREAT—WE CAN FINALLY MEET IN PERSON! WHEN WILL YOU ARRIVE?
PROFESSOR PALLADIUM?
THE SOONER, THE BETTER! I'LL PREPARE THE SIMULATION ROOM IMMEDIATELY!
SOON...
THE SYSTEM IS CONNECTED, SO PLEASE ENTER THE CHAMBER!
GOOD LUCK!
BE CAREFUL, GIRLS!

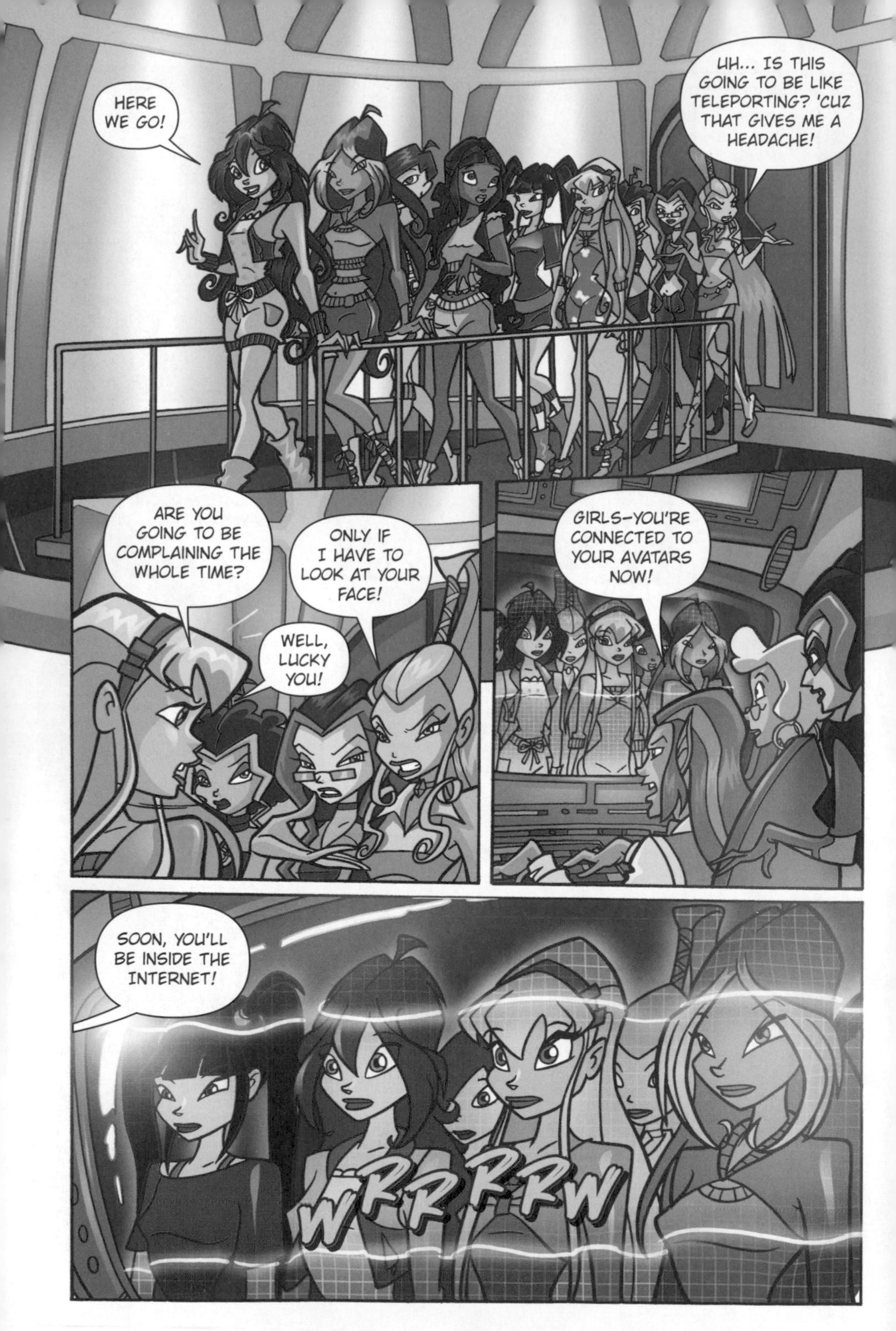
HERE WE GO!
UH... IS THIS GOING TO BE LIKE TELEPORTING? 'CUZ THAT GIVES ME A HEADACHE!
ARE YOU GOING TO BE COMPLAINING THE WHOLE TIME?
ONLY IF I HAVE TO LOOK AT YOUR FACE!
WELL, LUCKY YOU!
GIRLS—YOU'RE CONNECTED TO YOUR AVATARS NOW!
SOON, YOU'LL BE INSIDE THE INTERNET!
WRRRRRW

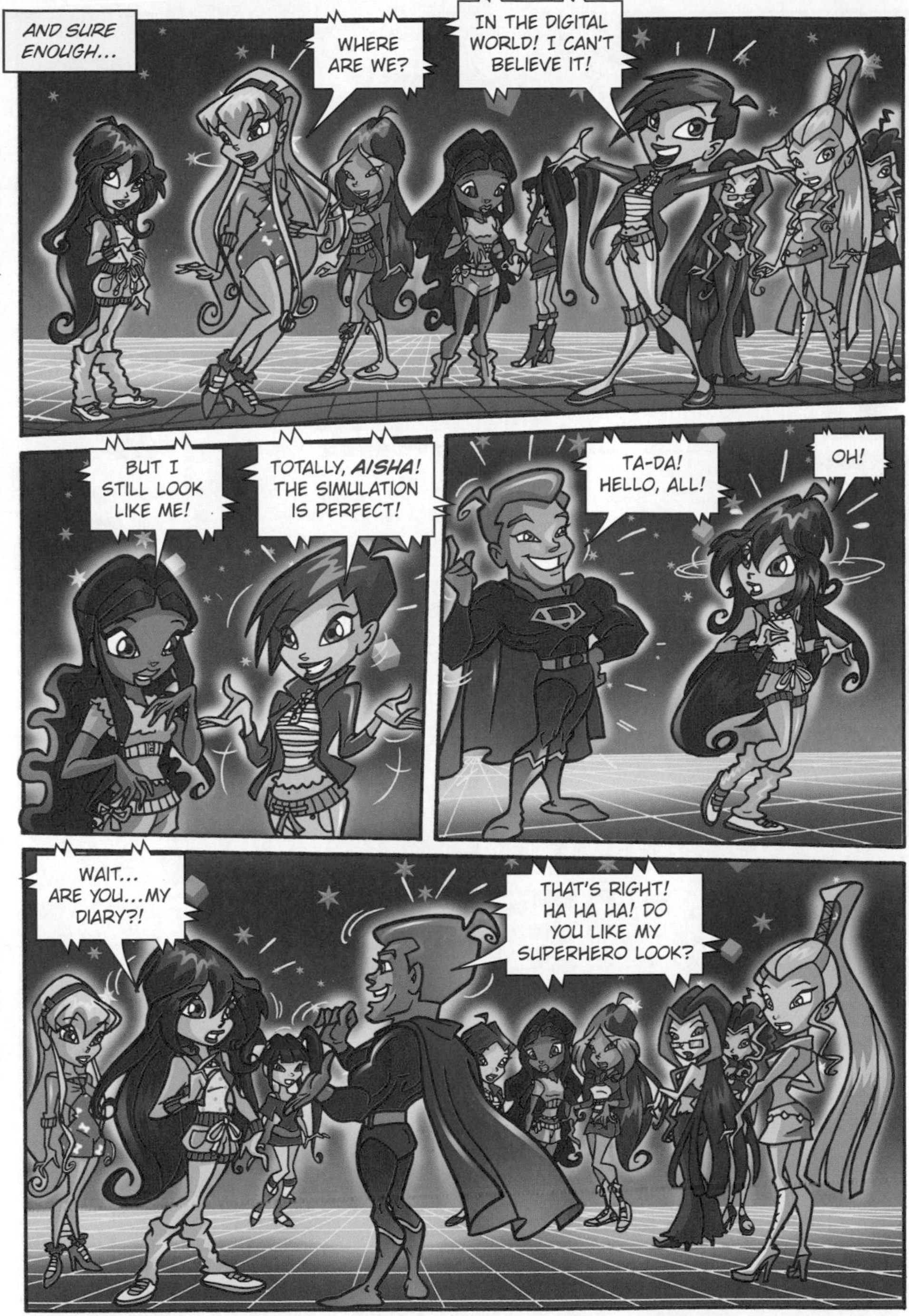
AND SURE ENOUGH...
WHERE ARE WE?
IN THE DIGITAL WORLD! I CAN'T BELIEVE IT!
BUT I STILL LOOK LIKE ME!
TOTALLY, AISHA! THE SIMULATION IS PERFECT!
TA-DA! HELLO, ALL!
OH!
WAIT... ARE YOU...MY DIARY?!
THAT'S RIGHT! HA HA HA! DO YOU LIKE MY SUPERHERO LOOK?

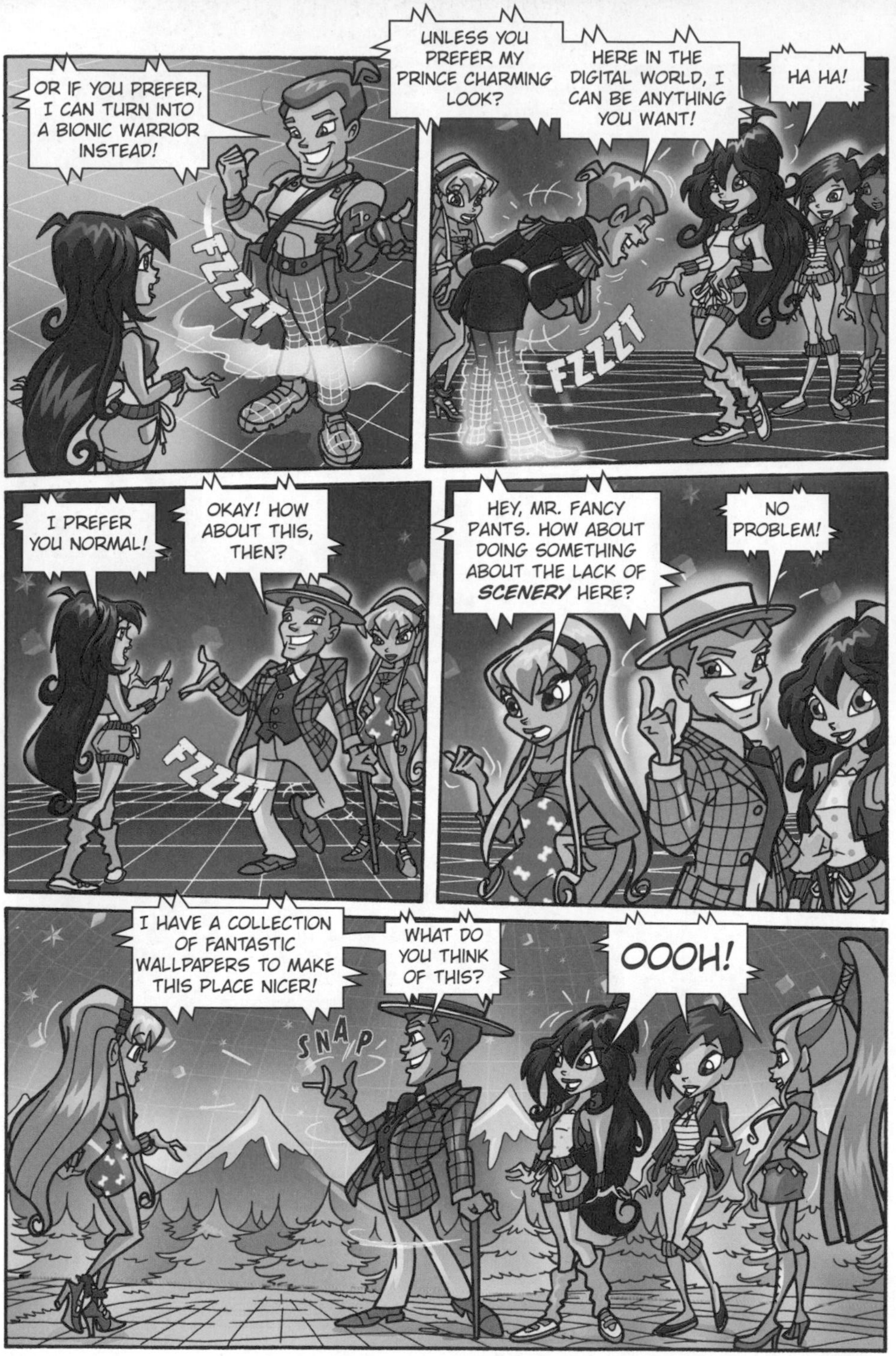
OR IF YOU PREFER, I CAN TURN INTO A BIONIC WARRIOR INSTEAD!
FZZZT
UNLESS YOU PREFER MY PRINCE CHARMING LOOK?
HERE IN THE DIGITAL WORLD, I CAN BE ANYTHING YOU WANT!
HA HA!
FZZZT
I PREFER YOU NORMAL!
OKAY! HOW ABOUT THIS, THEN?
FZZZT
HEY, MR. FANCY PANTS. HOW ABOUT DOING SOMETHING ABOUT THE LACK OF *SCENERY* HERE?
NO PROBLEM!
I HAVE A COLLECTION OF FANTASTIC WALLPAPERS TO MAKE THIS PLACE NICER!
SNAP
WHAT DO YOU THINK OF THIS?
OOOH!

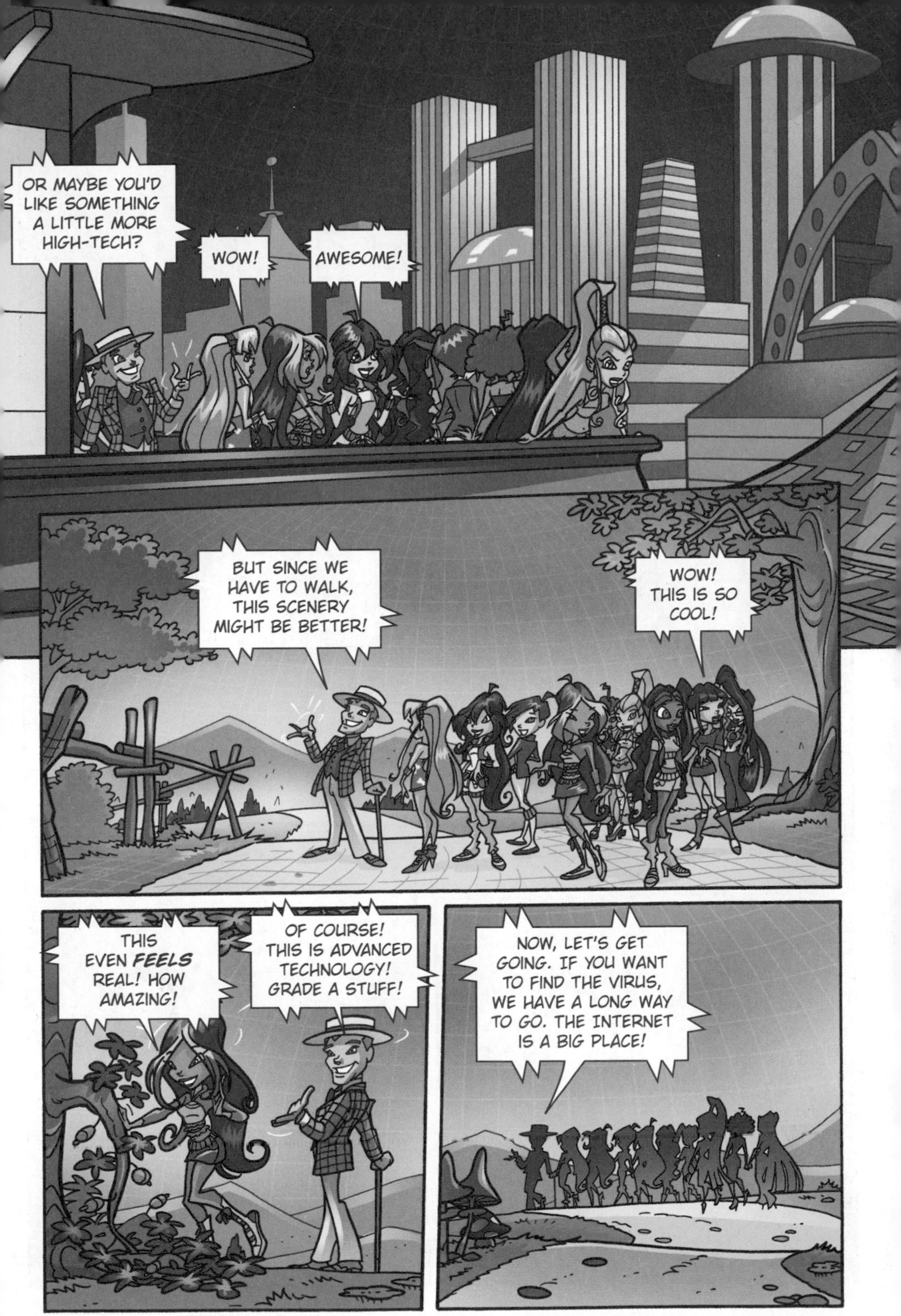
OR MAYBE YOU'D LIKE SOMETHING A LITTLE MORE HIGH-TECH?
WOW!
AWESOME!
BUT SINCE WE HAVE TO WALK, THIS SCENERY MIGHT BE BETTER!
WOW! THIS IS SO COOL!
THIS EVEN *FEELS* REAL! HOW AMAZING!
OF COURSE! THIS IS ADVANCED TECHNOLOGY! GRADE A STUFF!
NOW, LET'S GET GOING. IF YOU WANT TO FIND THE VIRUS, WE HAVE A LONG WAY TO GO. THE INTERNET IS A BIG PLACE!

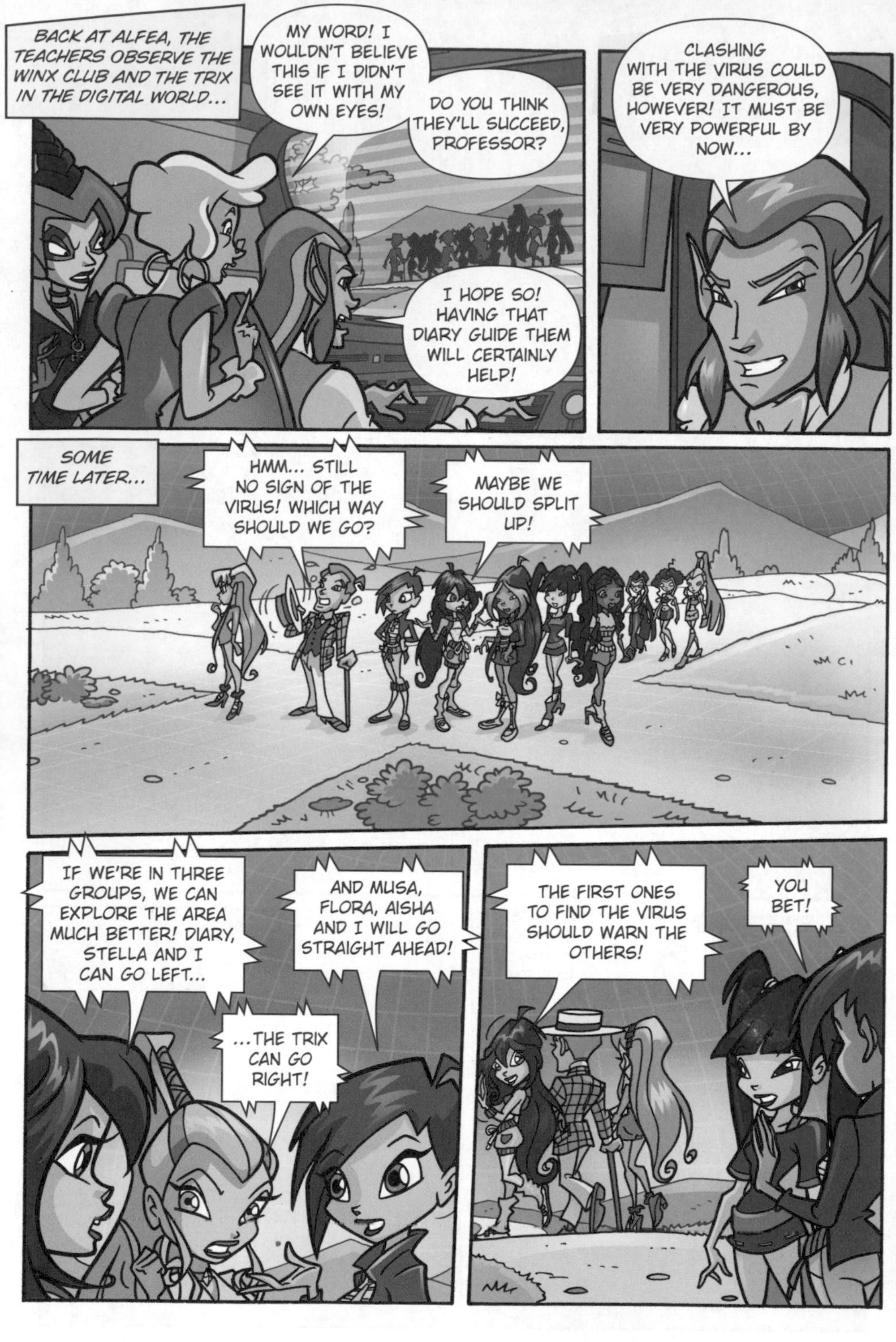
BACK AT ALFEA, THE TEACHERS OBSERVE THE WINX CLUB AND THE TRIX IN THE DIGITAL WORLD...
MY WORD! I WOULDN'T BELIEVE THIS IF I DIDN'T SEE IT WITH MY OWN EYES!
DO YOU THINK THEY'LL SUCCEED, PROFESSOR?
I HOPE SO! HAVING THAT DIARY GUIDE THEM WILL CERTAINLY HELP!
CLASHING WITH THE VIRUS COULD BE VERY DANGEROUS, HOWEVER! IT MUST BE VERY POWERFUL BY NOW...
SOME TIME LATER...
HMM... STILL NO SIGN OF THE VIRUS! WHICH WAY SHOULD WE GO?
MAYBE WE SHOULD SPLIT UP!
IF WE'RE IN THREE GROUPS, WE CAN EXPLORE THE AREA MUCH BETTER! DIARY, STELLA AND I CAN GO LEFT...
AND MUSA, FLORA, AISHA AND I WILL GO STRAIGHT AHEAD!
...THE TRIX CAN GO RIGHT!
THE FIRST ONES TO FIND THE VIRUS SHOULD WARN THE OTHERS!
YOU BET!

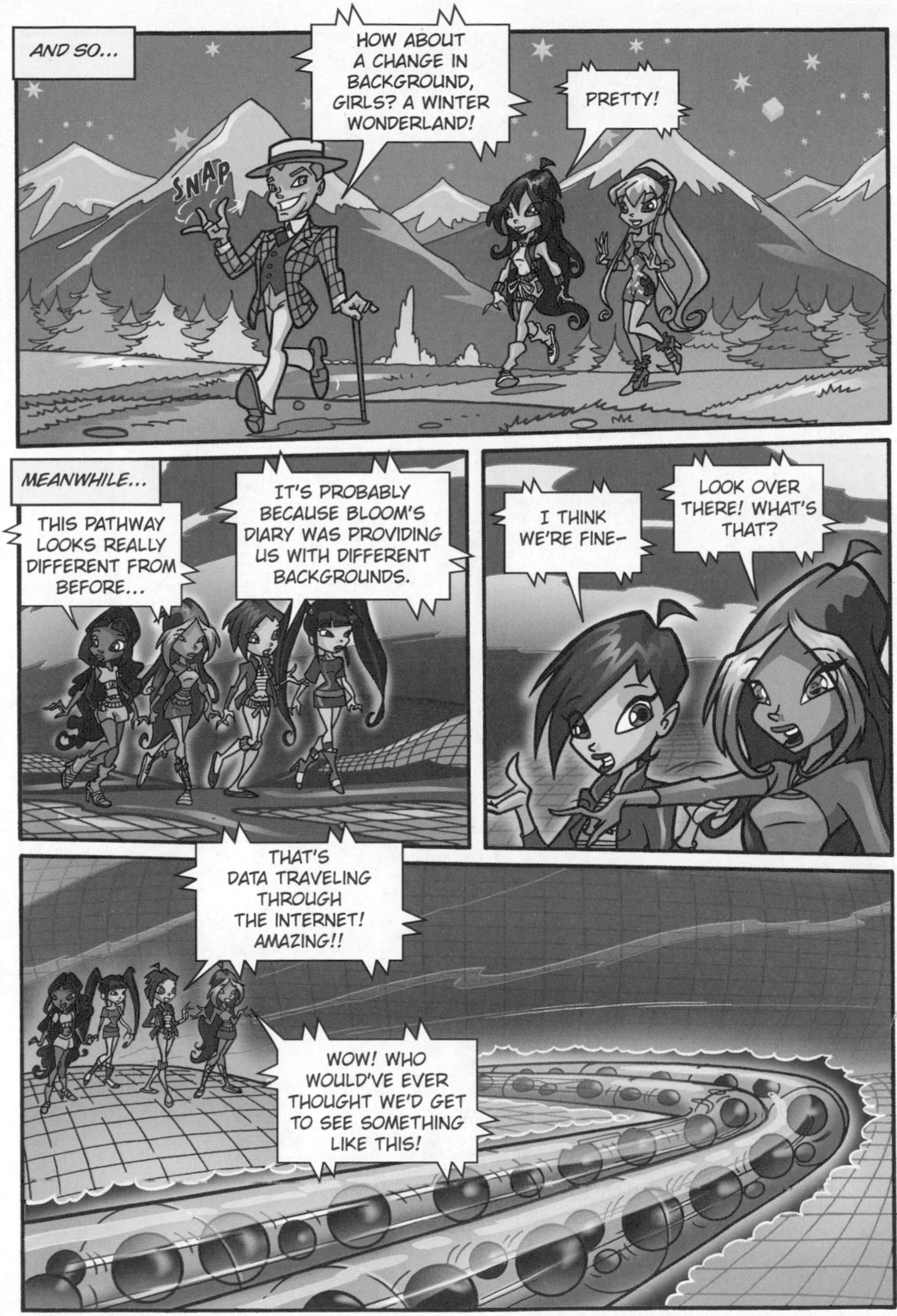
AND SO...
HOW ABOUT A CHANGE IN BACKGROUND, GIRLS? A WINTER WONDERLAND!
PRETTY!
SNAP
MEANWHILE...
THIS PATHWAY LOOKS REALLY DIFFERENT FROM BEFORE...
IT'S PROBABLY BECAUSE BLOOM'S DIARY WAS PROVIDING US WITH DIFFERENT BACKGROUNDS.
I THINK WE'RE FINE-
LOOK OVER THERE! WHAT'S THAT?
THAT'S DATA TRAVELING THROUGH THE INTERNET! AMAZING!!
WOW! WHO WOULD'VE EVER THOUGHT WE'D GET TO SEE SOMETHING LIKE THIS!

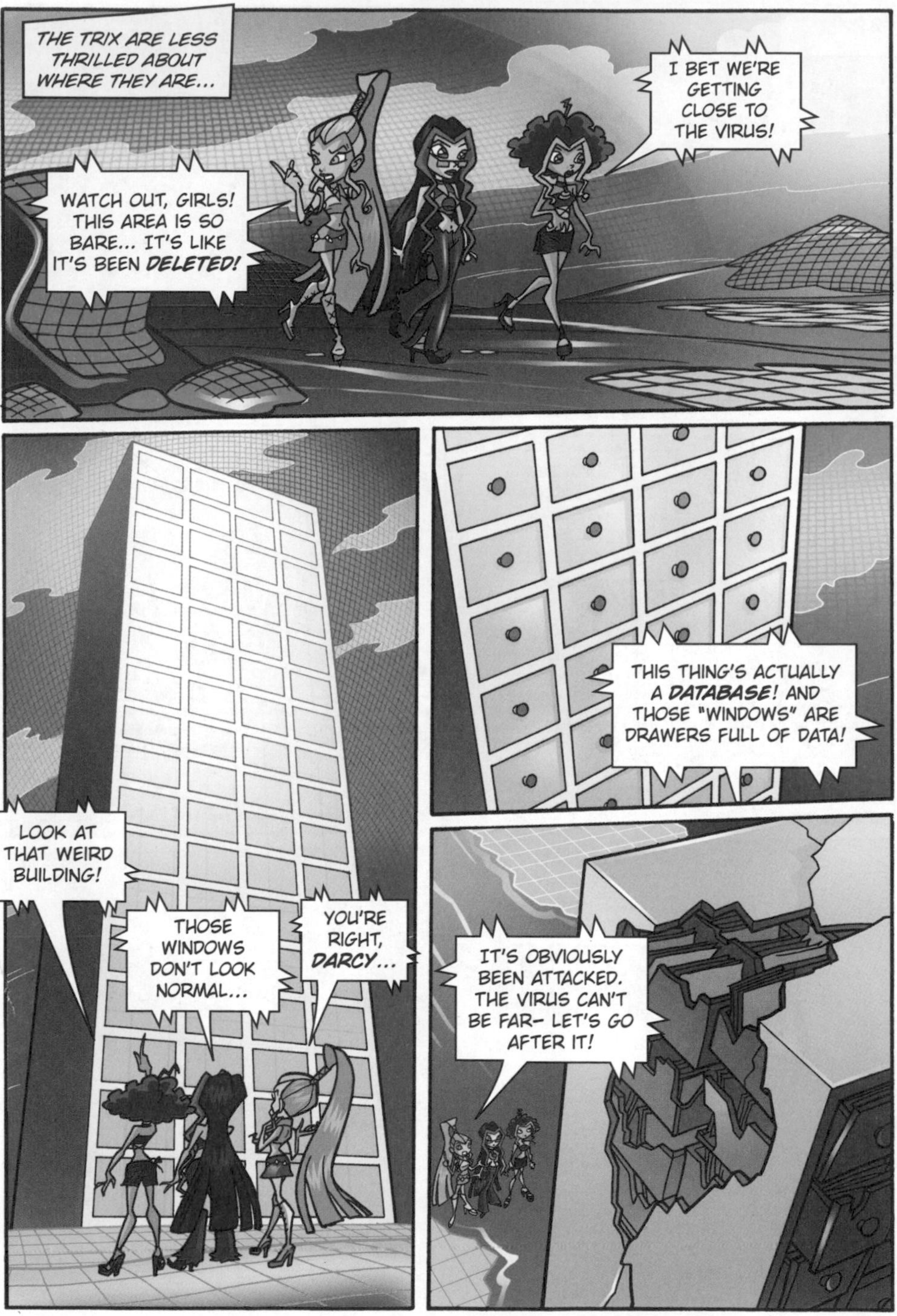
THE TRIX ARE LESS THRILLED ABOUT WHERE THEY ARE...
I BET WE'RE GETTING CLOSE TO THE VIRUS!
WATCH OUT, GIRLS! THIS AREA IS SO BARE... IT'S LIKE IT'S BEEN DELETED!
LOOK AT THAT WEIRD BUILDING!
THOSE WINDOWS DON'T LOOK NORMAL...
YOU'RE RIGHT, DARCY...
THIS THING'S ACTUALLY A DATABASE! AND THOSE "WINDOWS" ARE DRAWERS FULL OF DATA!
IT'S OBVIOUSLY BEEN ATTACKED. THE VIRUS CAN'T BE FAR– LET'S GO AFTER IT!

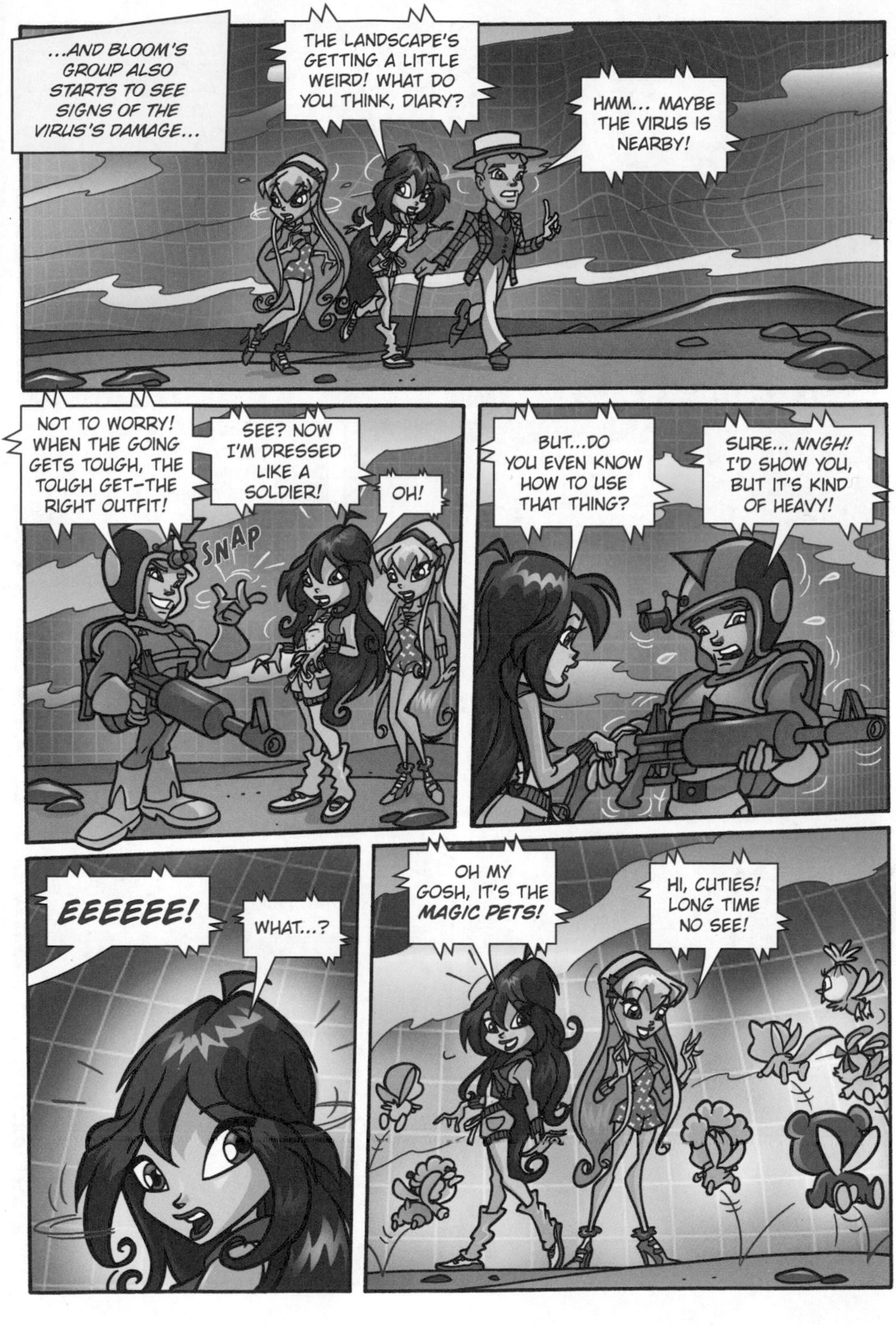

...AND BLOOM'S GROUP ALSO STARTS TO SEE SIGNS OF THE VIRUS'S DAMAGE...
THE LANDSCAPE'S GETTING A LITTLE WEIRD! WHAT DO YOU THINK, DIARY?
HMM... MAYBE THE VIRUS IS NEARBY!
NOT TO WORRY! WHEN THE GOING GETS TOUGH, THE TOUGH GET—THE RIGHT OUTFIT!
SEE? NOW I'M DRESSED LIKE A SOLDIER!
SNAP
OH!
BUT...DO YOU EVEN KNOW HOW TO USE THAT THING?
SURE... *NNGH!* I'D SHOW YOU, BUT IT'S KIND OF HEAVY!
EEEEEE!
WHAT...?
OH MY GOSH, IT'S THE ***MAGIC PETS!***
HI, CUTIES! LONG TIME NO SEE!

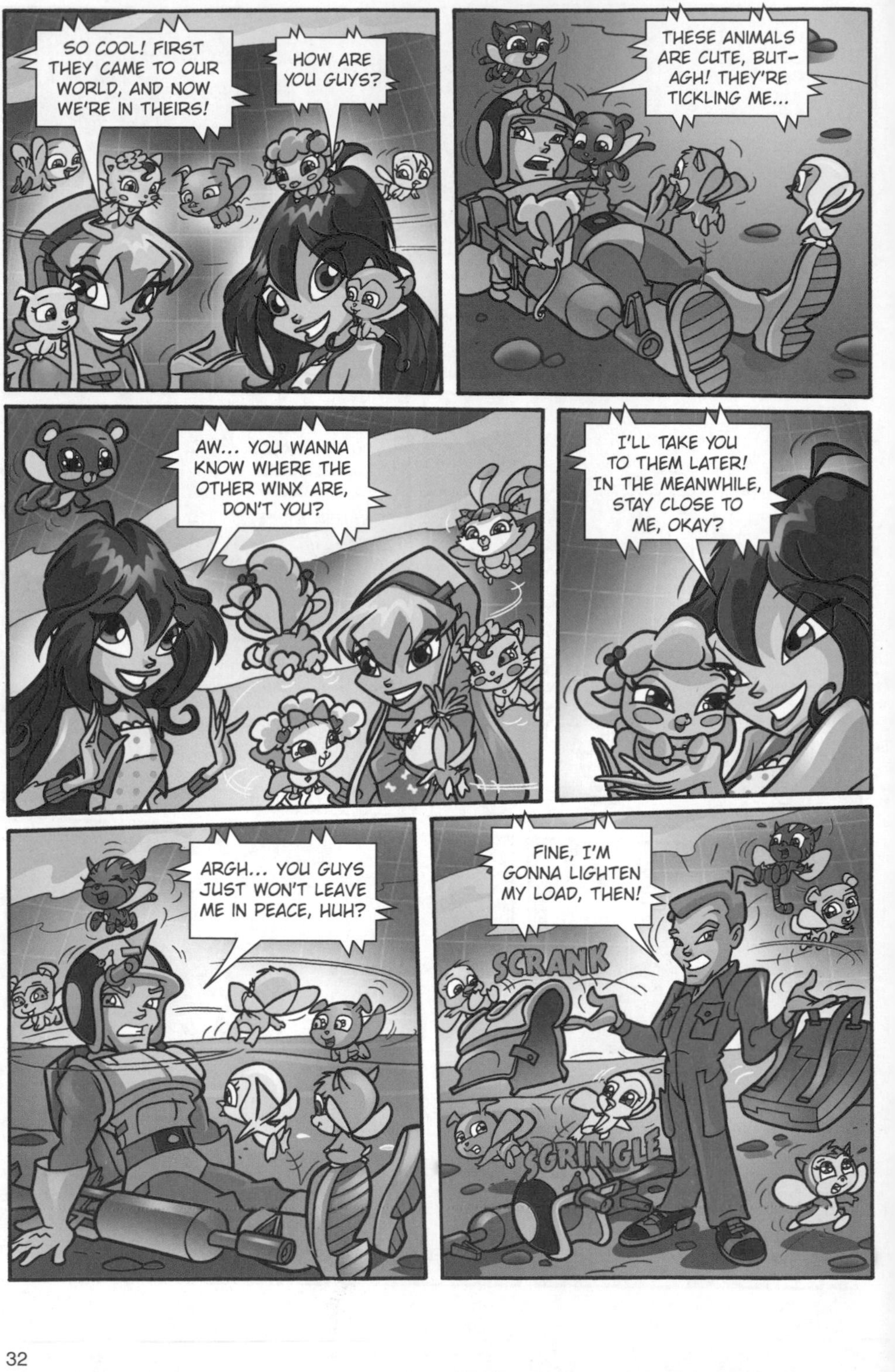
SO COOL! FIRST THEY CAME TO OUR WORLD, AND NOW WE'RE IN THEIRS!
HOW ARE YOU GUYS?
THESE ANIMALS ARE CUTE, BUT– AGH! THEY'RE TICKLING ME...
AW... YOU WANNA KNOW WHERE THE OTHER WINX ARE, DON'T YOU?
I'LL TAKE YOU TO THEM LATER! IN THE MEANWHILE, STAY CLOSE TO ME, OKAY?
ARGH... YOU GUYS JUST WON'T LEAVE ME IN PEACE, HUH?
FINE, I'M GONNA LIGHTEN MY LOAD, THEN!
SCRANK
SGRINGLE

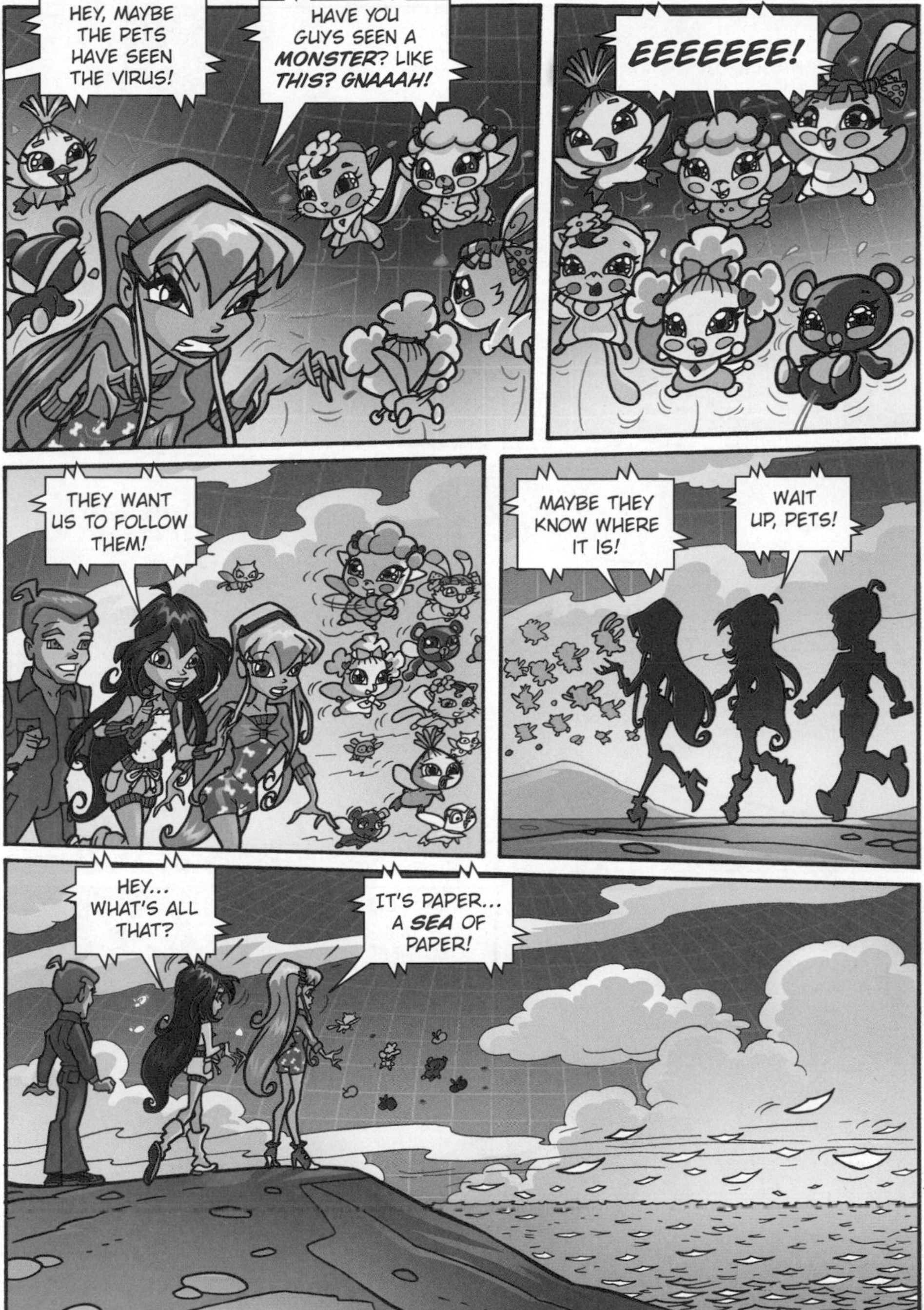
HEY, MAYBE THE PETS HAVE SEEN THE VIRUS!
HAVE YOU GUYS SEEN A MONSTER? LIKE THIS? GNAAAH!
EEEEEEE!
THEY WANT US TO FOLLOW THEM!
MAYBE THEY KNOW WHERE IT IS!
WAIT UP, PETS!
HEY... WHAT'S ALL THAT?
IT'S PAPER... A SEA OF PAPER!

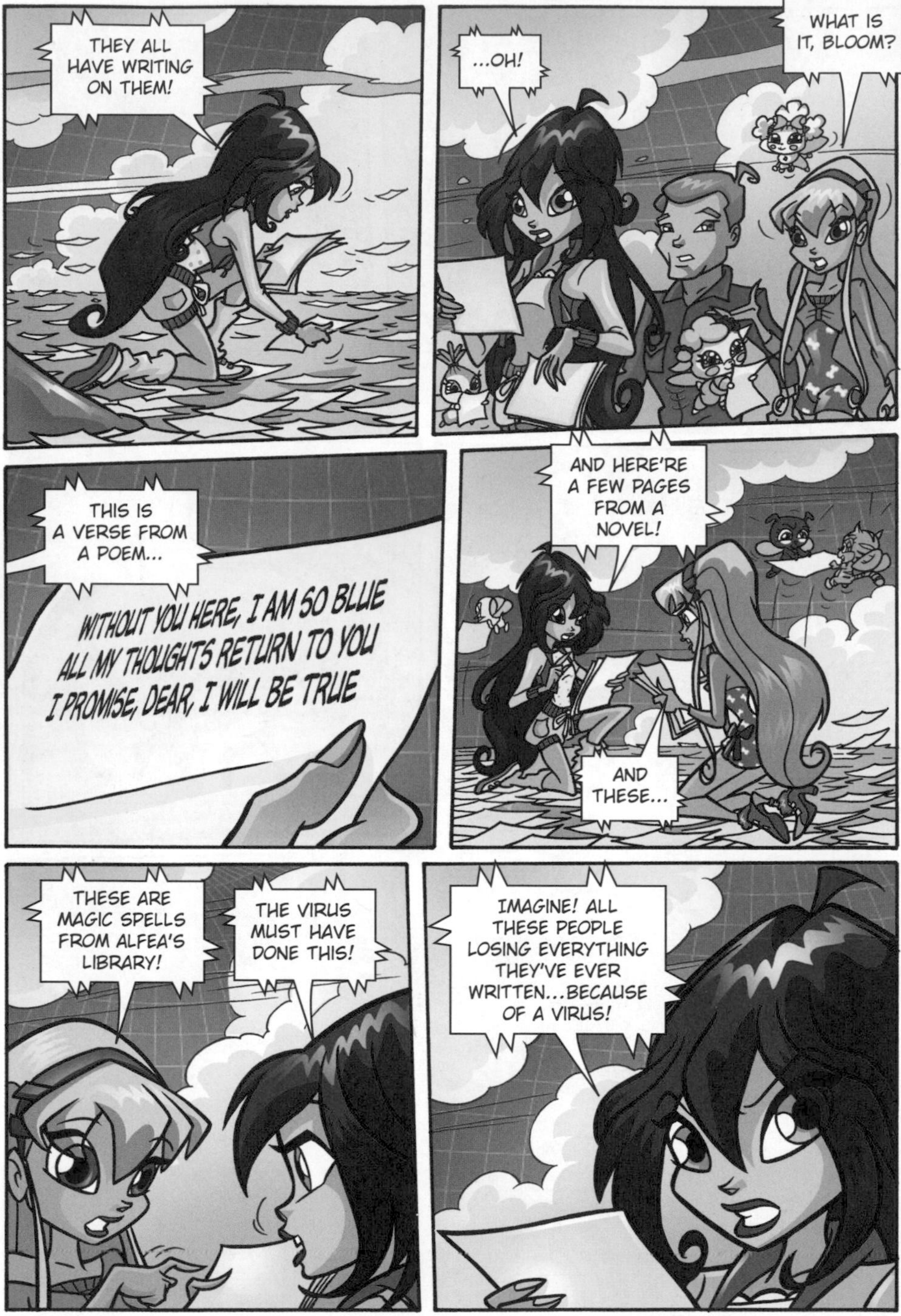
THEY ALL HAVE WRITING ON THEM!
...OH!
WHAT IS IT, BLOOM?
THIS IS A VERSE FROM A POEM...
WITHOUT YOU HERE, I AM SO BLUE
ALL MY THOUGHTS RETURN TO YOU
I PROMISE, DEAR, I WILL BE TRUE
AND HERE'RE A FEW PAGES FROM A NOVEL!
AND THESE...
THESE ARE MAGIC SPELLS FROM ALFEA'S LIBRARY!
THE VIRUS MUST HAVE DONE THIS!
IMAGINE! ALL THESE PEOPLE LOSING EVERYTHING THEY'VE EVER WRITTEN...BECAUSE OF A VIRUS!

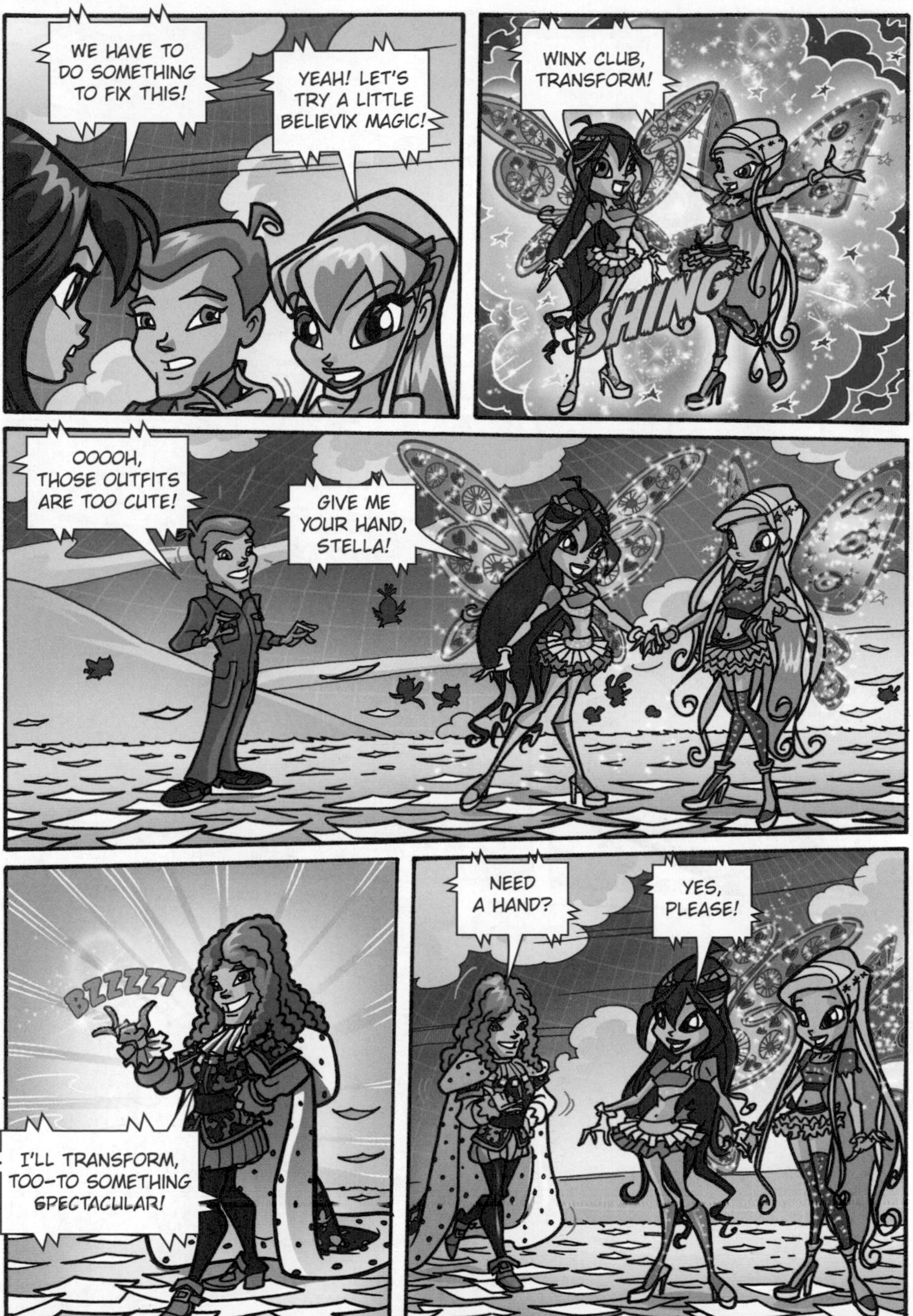
WE HAVE TO DO SOMETHING TO FIX THIS!
YEAH! LET'S TRY A LITTLE BELIEVIX MAGIC!
WINX CLUB, TRANSFORM!
SHING
OOOOH, THOSE OUTFITS ARE TOO CUTE!
GIVE ME YOUR HAND, STELLA!
BZZZZT
I'LL TRANSFORM, TOO—TO SOMETHING SPECTACULAR!
NEED A HAND?
YES, PLEASE!

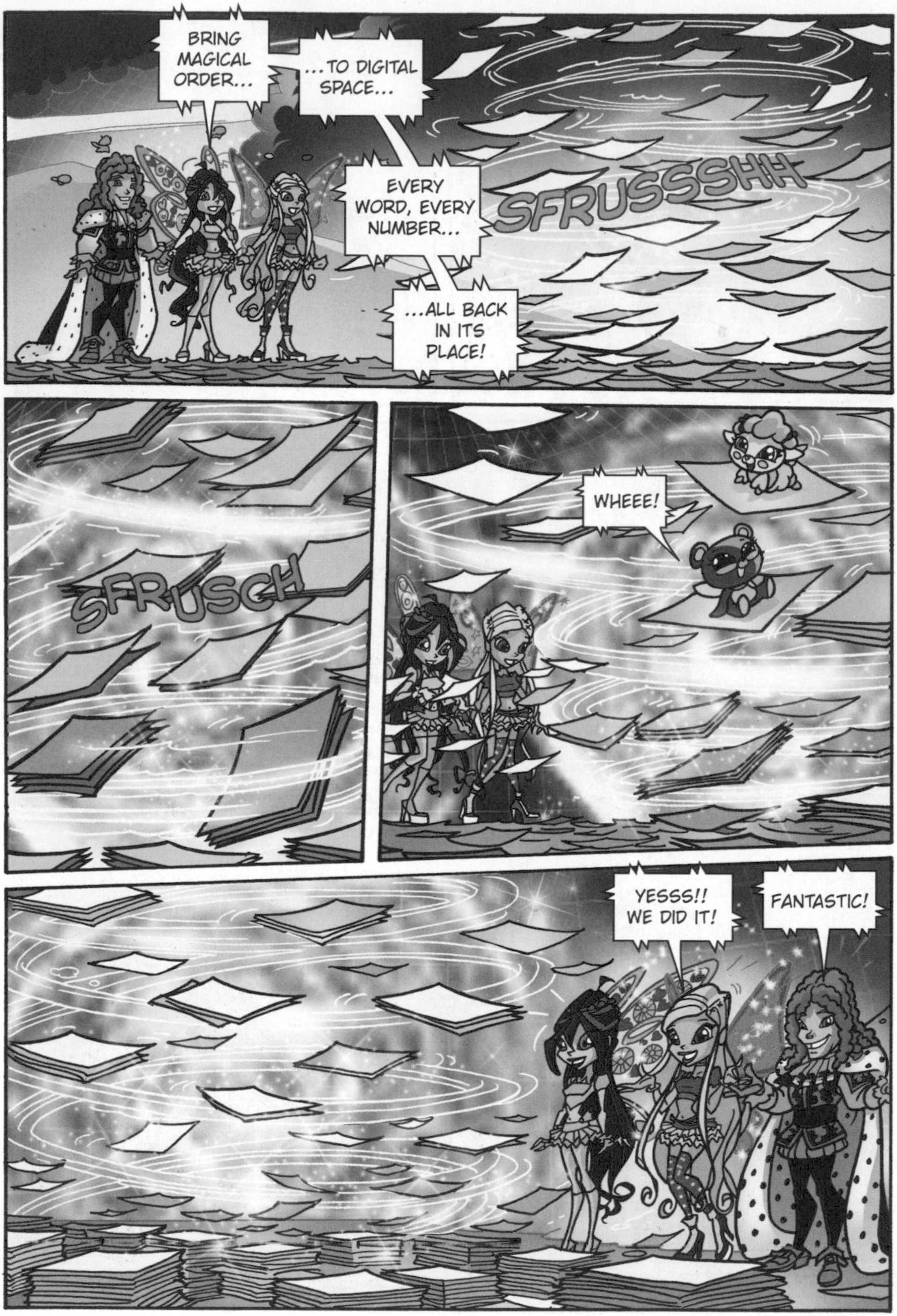
BRING MAGICAL ORDER...
...TO DIGITAL SPACE...
EVERY WORD, EVERY NUMBER...
...ALL BACK IN ITS PLACE!
SFRUSSSSHH
SFRUSCH
WHEEE!
YESSS!! WE DID IT!
FANTASTIC!

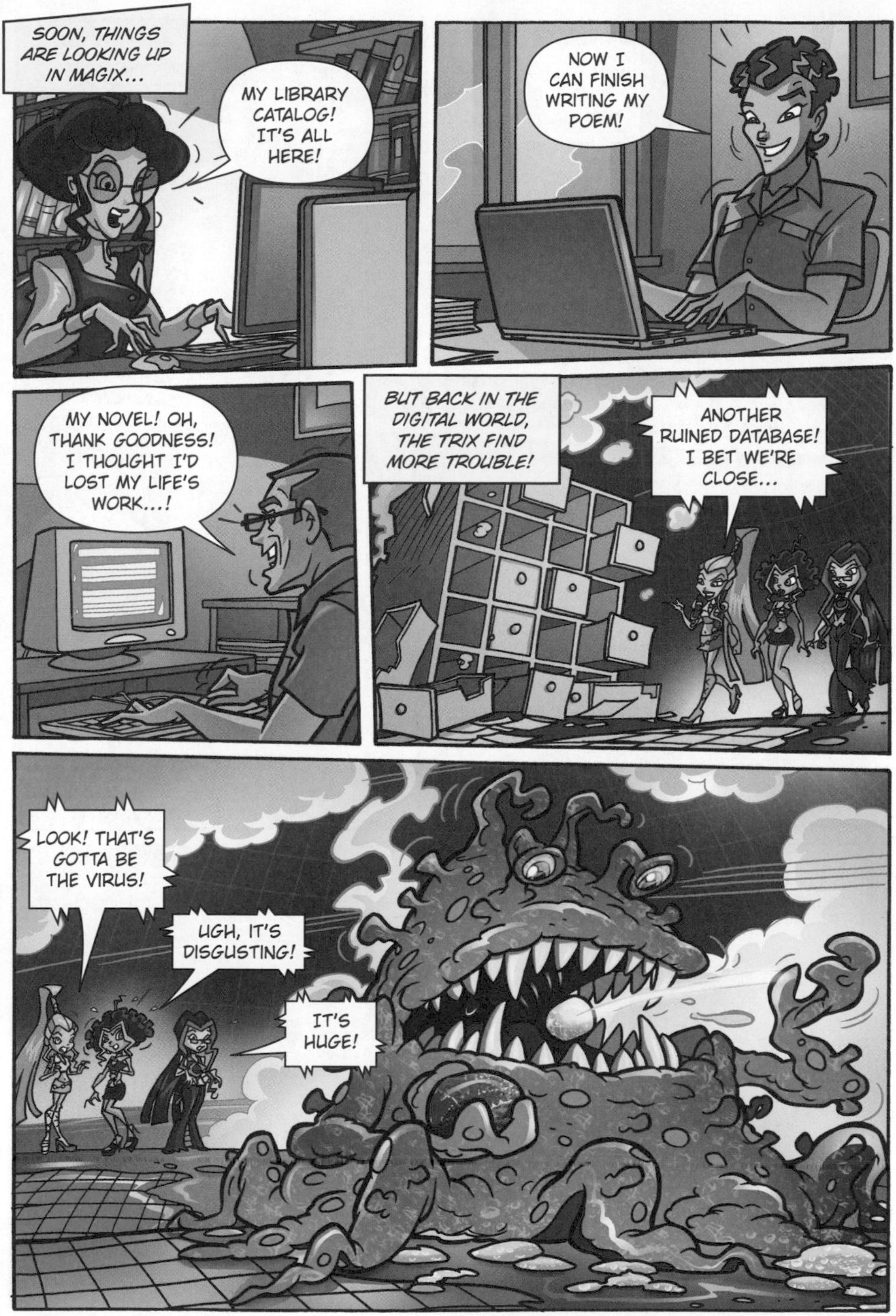
SOON, THINGS ARE LOOKING UP IN MAGIX...
MY LIBRARY CATALOG! IT'S ALL HERE!
NOW I CAN FINISH WRITING MY POEM!
MY NOVEL! OH, THANK GOODNESS! I THOUGHT I'D LOST MY LIFE'S WORK...!
BUT BACK IN THE DIGITAL WORLD, THE TRIX FIND MORE TROUBLE!
ANOTHER RUINED DATABASE! I BET WE'RE CLOSE...
LOOK! THAT'S GOTTA BE THE VIRUS!
UGH, IT'S DISGUSTING!
IT'S HUGE!

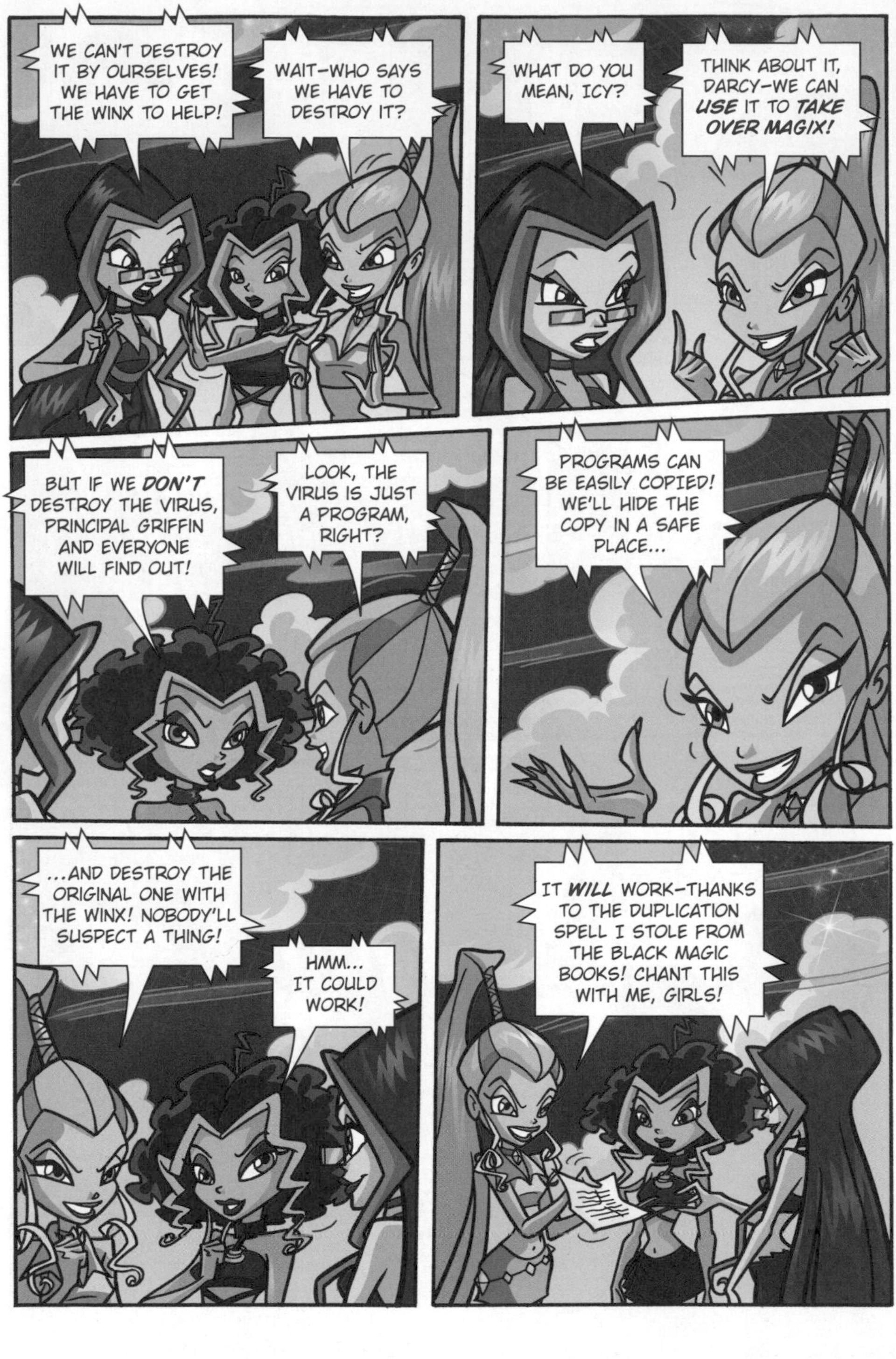
WE CAN'T DESTROY IT BY OURSELVES! WE HAVE TO GET THE WINX TO HELP!
WAIT—WHO SAYS WE HAVE TO DESTROY IT?
WHAT DO YOU MEAN, ICY?
THINK ABOUT IT, DARCY—WE CAN *USE* IT TO *TAKE OVER MAGIX!*
BUT IF WE *DON'T* DESTROY THE VIRUS, PRINCIPAL GRIFFIN AND EVERYONE WILL FIND OUT!
LOOK, THE VIRUS IS JUST A PROGRAM, RIGHT?
PROGRAMS CAN BE EASILY COPIED! WE'LL HIDE THE COPY IN A SAFE PLACE...
...AND DESTROY THE ORIGINAL ONE WITH THE WINX! NOBODY'LL SUSPECT A THING!
HMM... IT COULD WORK!
IT *WILL* WORK—THANKS TO THE DUPLICATION SPELL I STOLE FROM THE BLACK MAGIC BOOKS! CHANT THIS WITH ME, GIRLS!

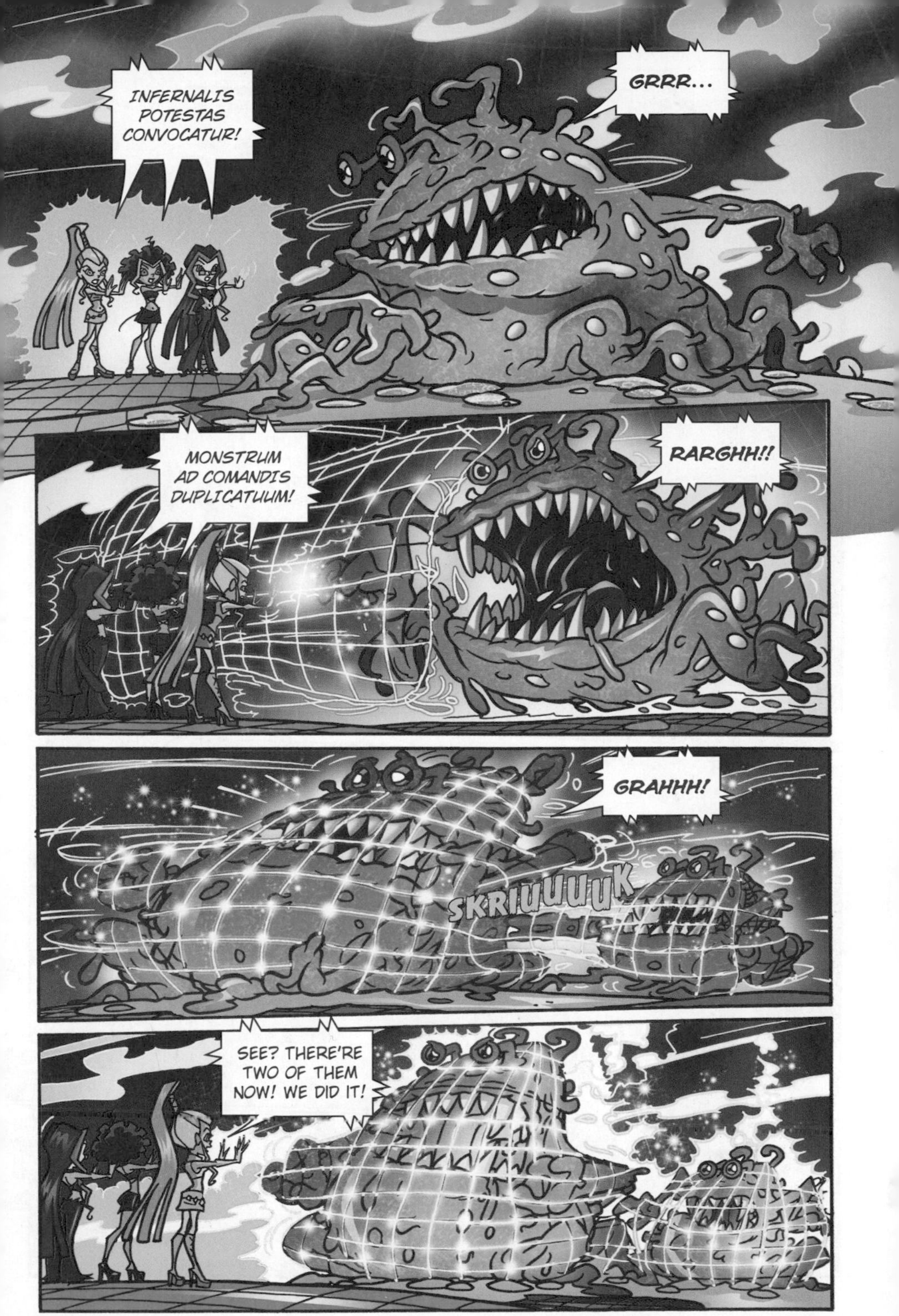
INFERNALIS POTESTAS CONVOCATUR!
GRRR...
MONSTRUM AD COMANDIS DUPLICATUUM!
RARGHH!!
GRAHHH!
SKRIUUUUUK
SEE? THERE'RE TWO OF THEM NOW! WE DID IT!

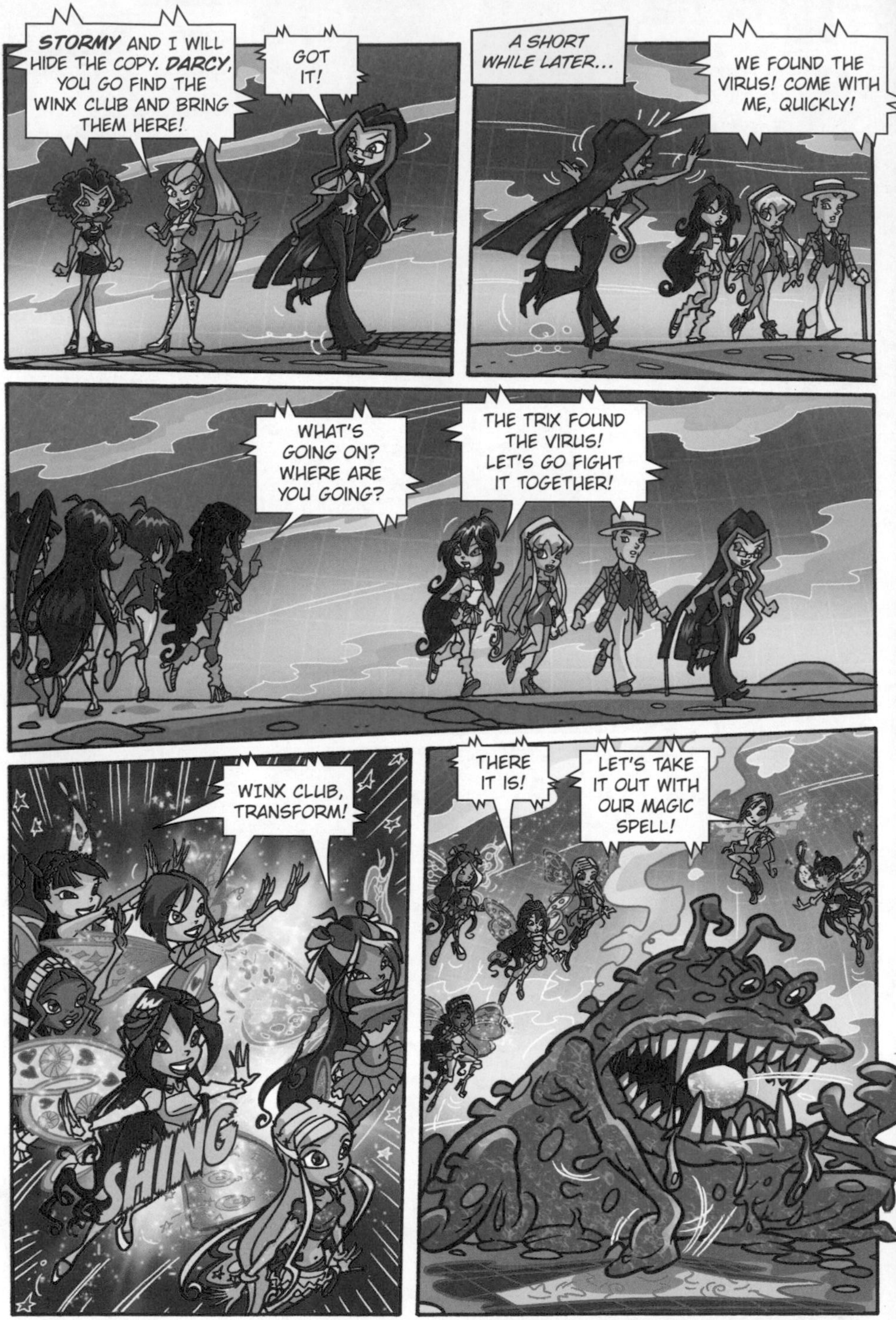
STORMY AND I WILL HIDE THE COPY. DARCY, YOU GO FIND THE WINX CLUB AND BRING THEM HERE!
GOT IT!
A SHORT WHILE LATER...
WE FOUND THE VIRUS! COME WITH ME, QUICKLY!
WHAT'S GOING ON? WHERE ARE YOU GOING?
THE TRIX FOUND THE VIRUS! LET'S GO FIGHT IT TOGETHER!
WINX CLUB, TRANSFORM!
SHING
THERE IT IS!
LET'S TAKE IT OUT WITH OUR MAGIC SPELL!

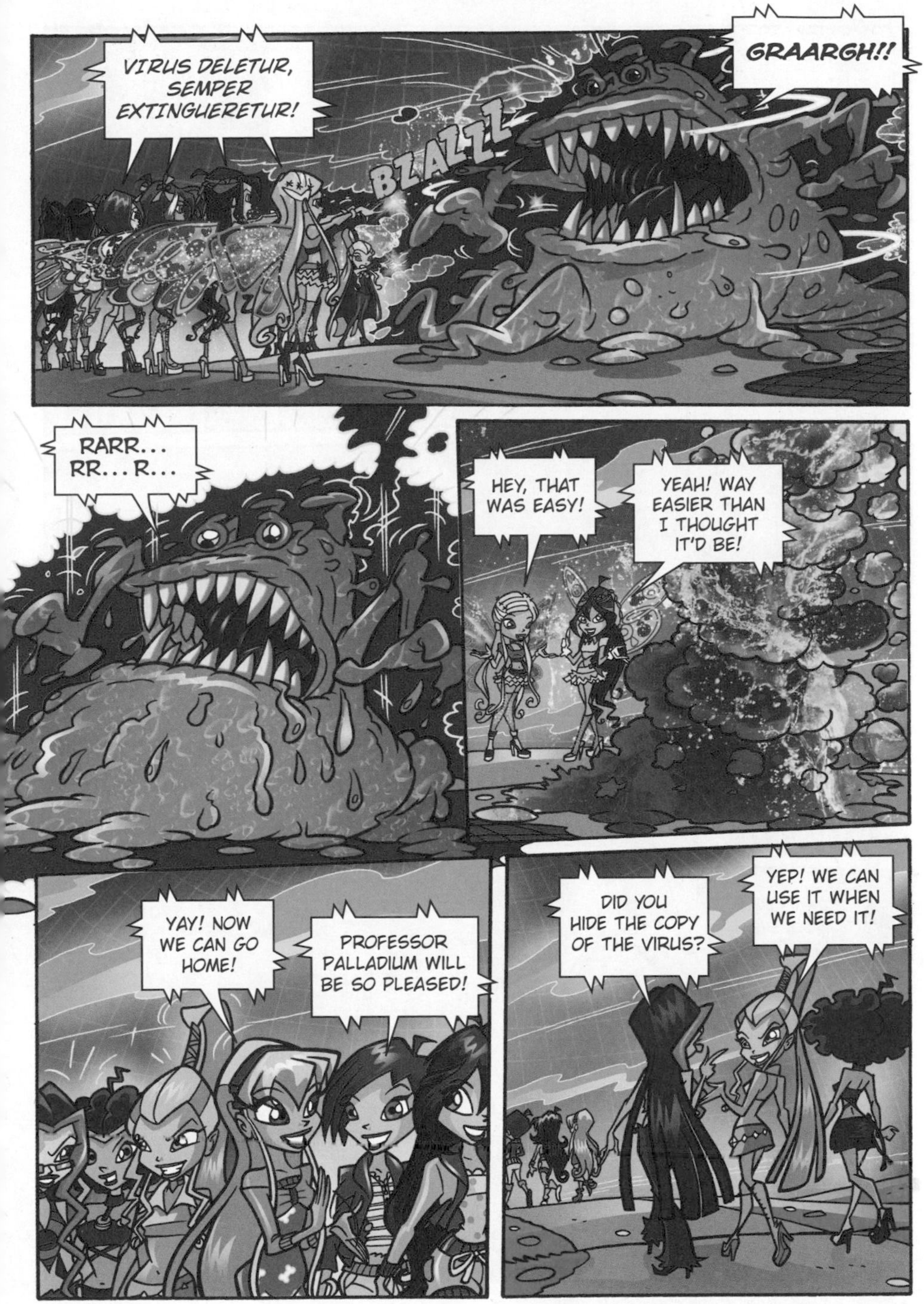
VIRUS DELETUR, SEMPER EXTINGUERETUR!
BZAZZZ
GRAARGH!!
RARR... RR... R...
HEY, THAT WAS EASY!
YEAH! WAY EASIER THAN I THOUGHT IT'D BE!
YAY! NOW WE CAN GO HOME!
PROFESSOR PALLADIUM WILL BE SO PLEASED!
DID YOU HIDE THE COPY OF THE VIRUS?
YEP! WE CAN USE IT WHEN WE NEED IT!

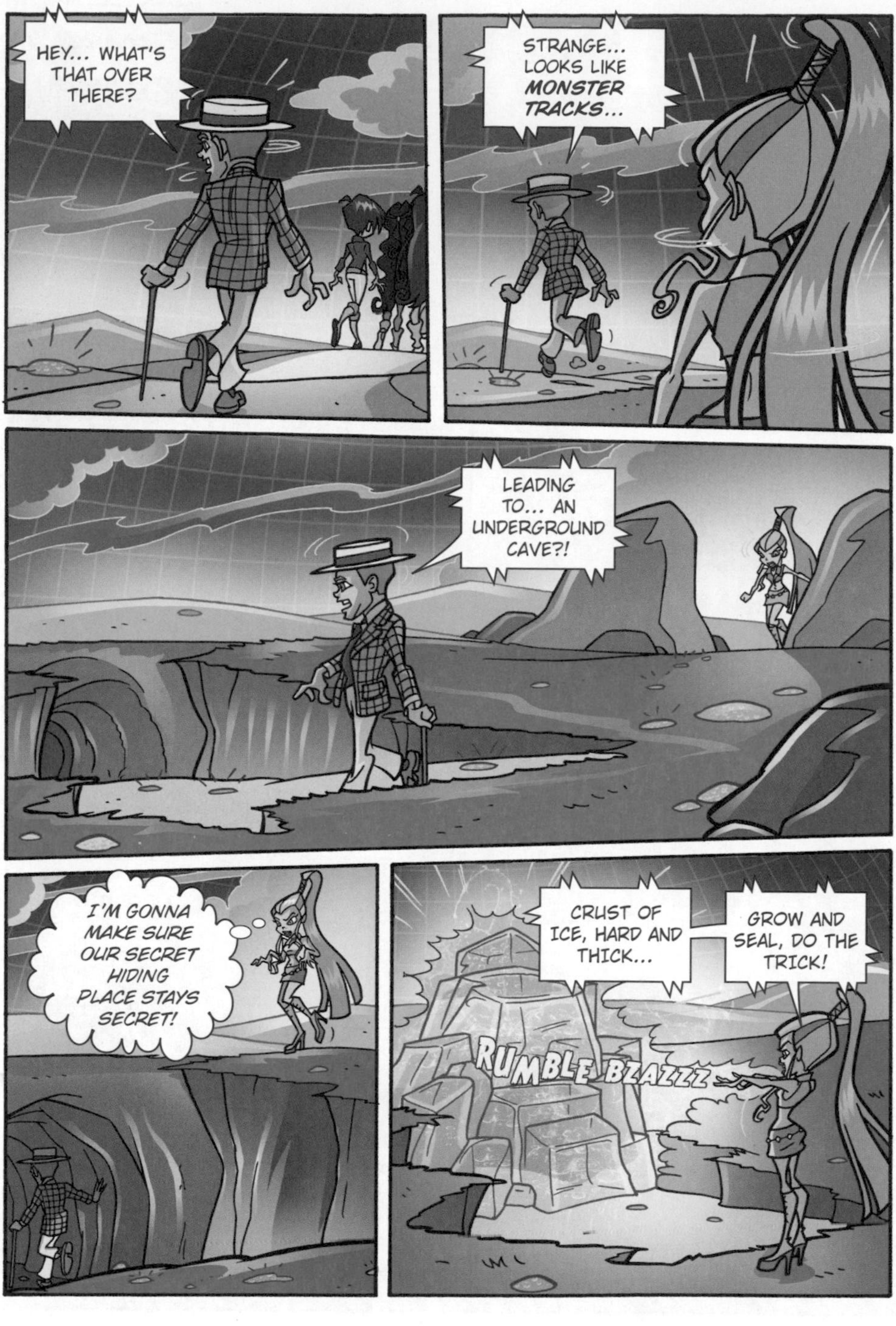
HEY... WHAT'S THAT OVER THERE?
STRANGE... LOOKS LIKE MONSTER TRACKS...
LEADING TO... AN UNDERGROUND CAVE?!
I'M GONNA MAKE SURE OUR SECRET HIDING PLACE STAYS SECRET!
CRUST OF ICE, HARD AND THICK...
GROW AND SEAL, DO THE TRICK!
RUMBLE BZAZZZ

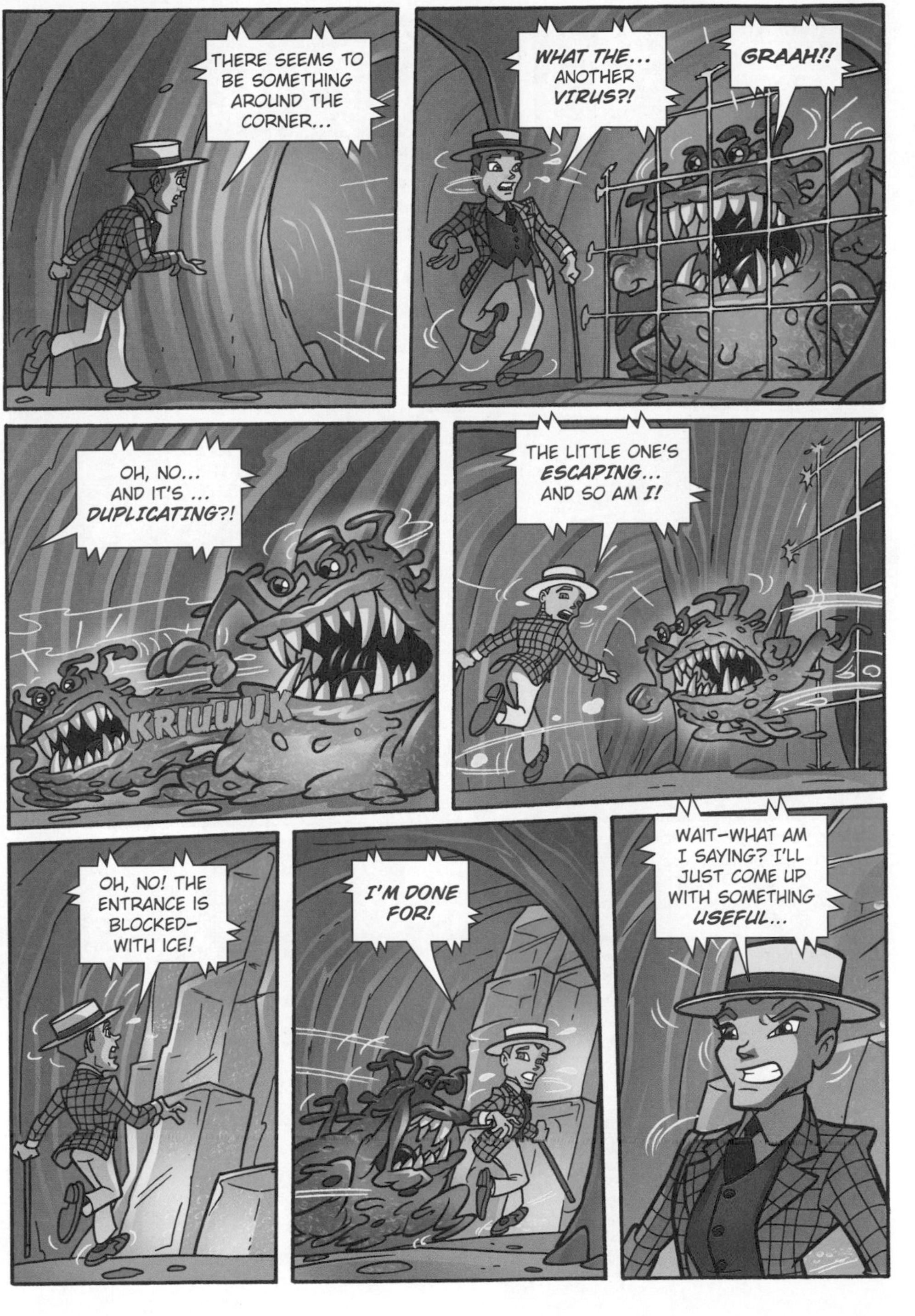
THERE SEEMS TO BE SOMETHING AROUND THE CORNER...
WHAT THE... ANOTHER VIRUS?!
GRAAH!!
OH, NO... AND IT'S ... DUPLICATING?!
KRIUUUK
THE LITTLE ONE'S ESCAPING... AND SO AM I!
OH, NO! THE ENTRANCE IS BLOCKED—WITH ICE!
I'M DONE FOR!
WAIT—WHAT AM I SAYING? I'LL JUST COME UP WITH SOMETHING USEFUL...

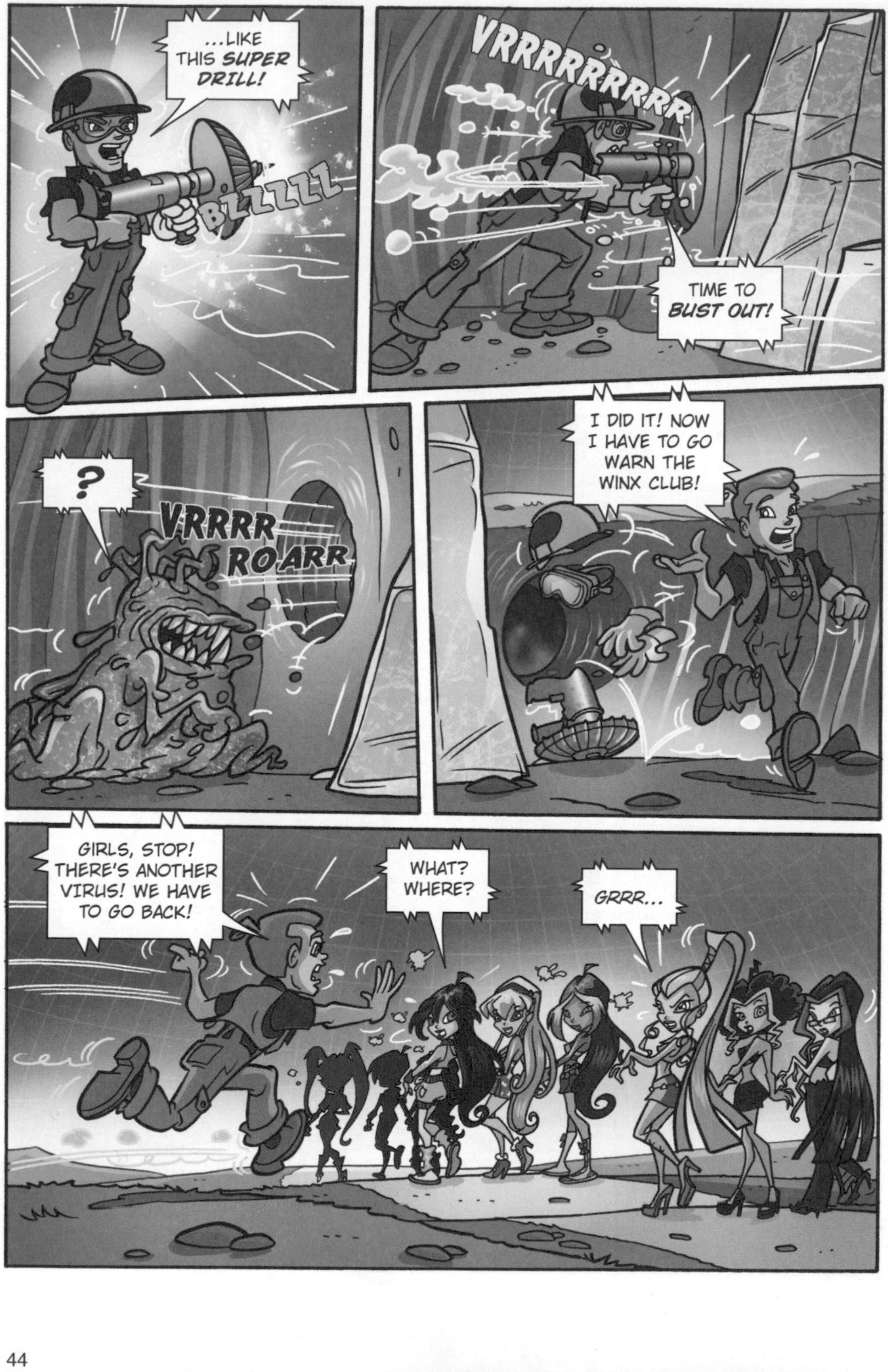
...LIKE THIS SUPER DRILL!
BZZZZZ
VRRRRRRRRRRR
TIME TO BUST OUT!
?
VRRRR ROARR
I DID IT! NOW I HAVE TO GO WARN THE WINX CLUB!
GIRLS, STOP! THERE'S ANOTHER VIRUS! WE HAVE TO GO BACK!
WHAT? WHERE?
GRRR...

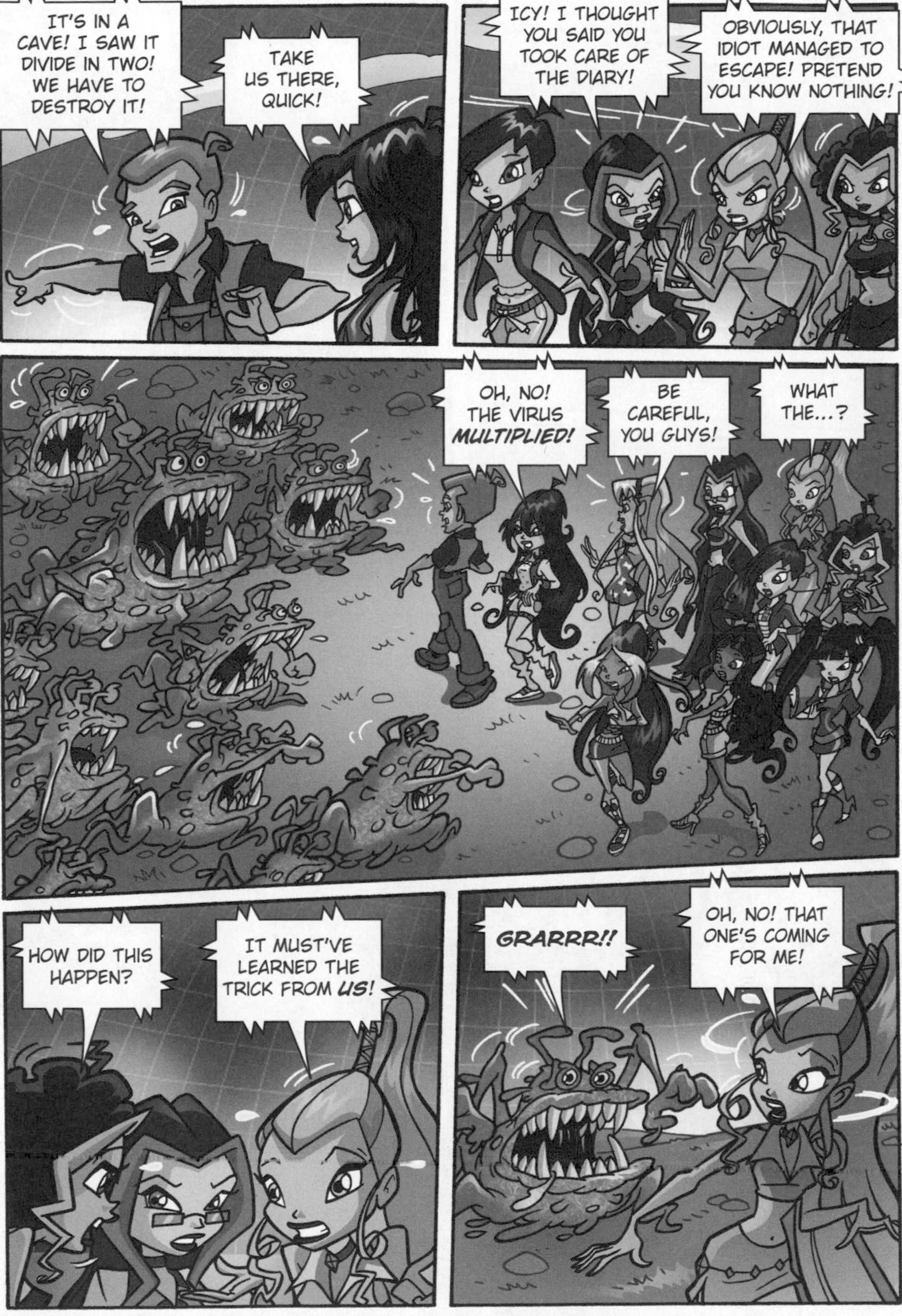
IT'S IN A CAVE! I SAW IT DIVIDE IN TWO! WE HAVE TO DESTROY IT!
TAKE US THERE, QUICK!
ICY! I THOUGHT YOU SAID YOU TOOK CARE OF THE DIARY!
OBVIOUSLY, THAT IDIOT MANAGED TO ESCAPE! PRETEND YOU KNOW NOTHING!
OH, NO! THE VIRUS MULTIPLIED!
BE CAREFUL, YOU GUYS!
WHAT THE...?
HOW DID THIS HAPPEN?
IT MUST'VE LEARNED THE TRICK FROM US!
GRARRR!!
OH, NO! THAT ONE'S COMING FOR ME!

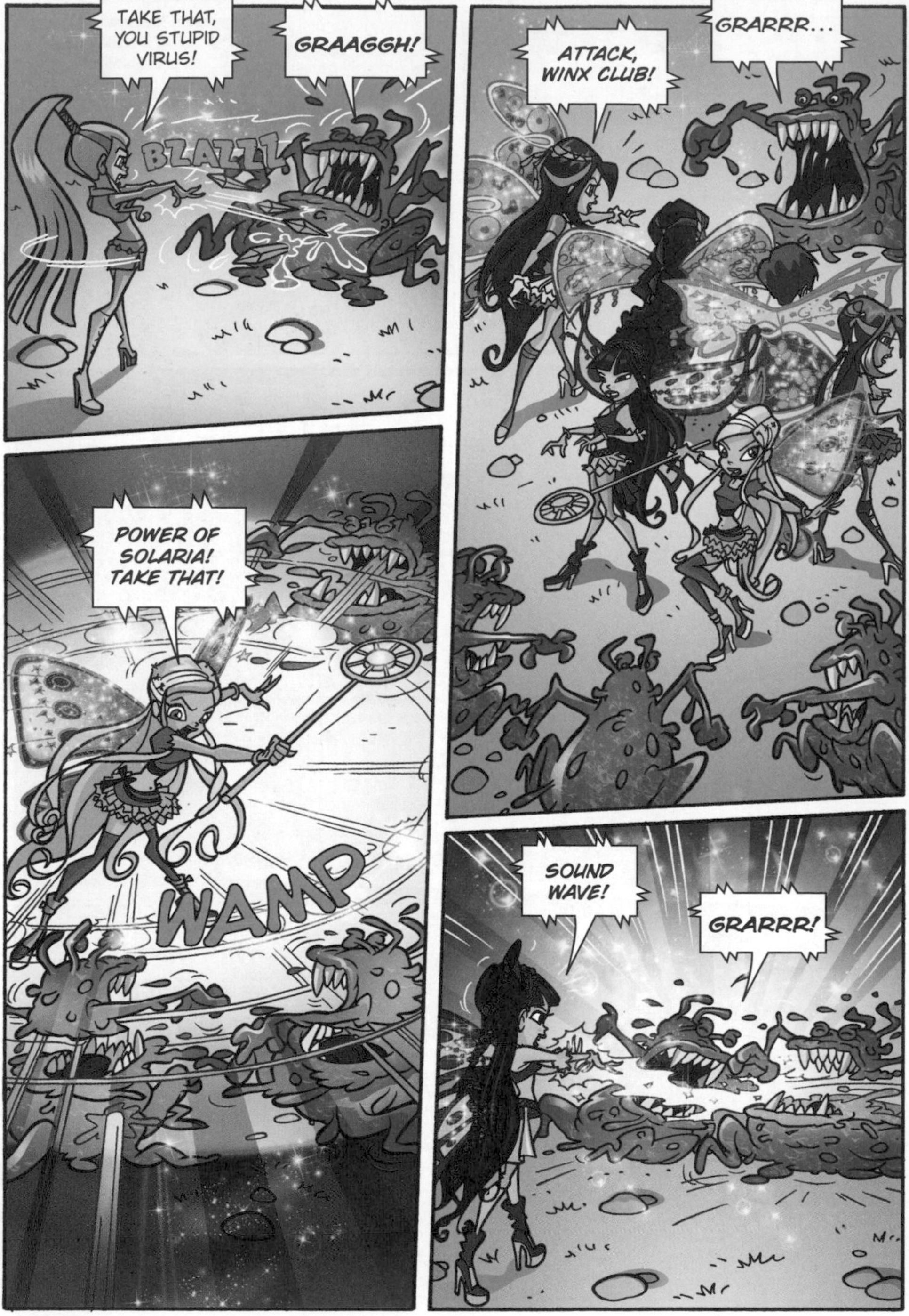
TAKE THAT, YOU STUPID VIRUS!
GRAAGGH!
BZAZZZ
ATTACK, WINX CLUB!
GRARRR...
POWER OF SOLARIA! TAKE THAT!
WAMP
SOUND WAVE!
GRARRR!

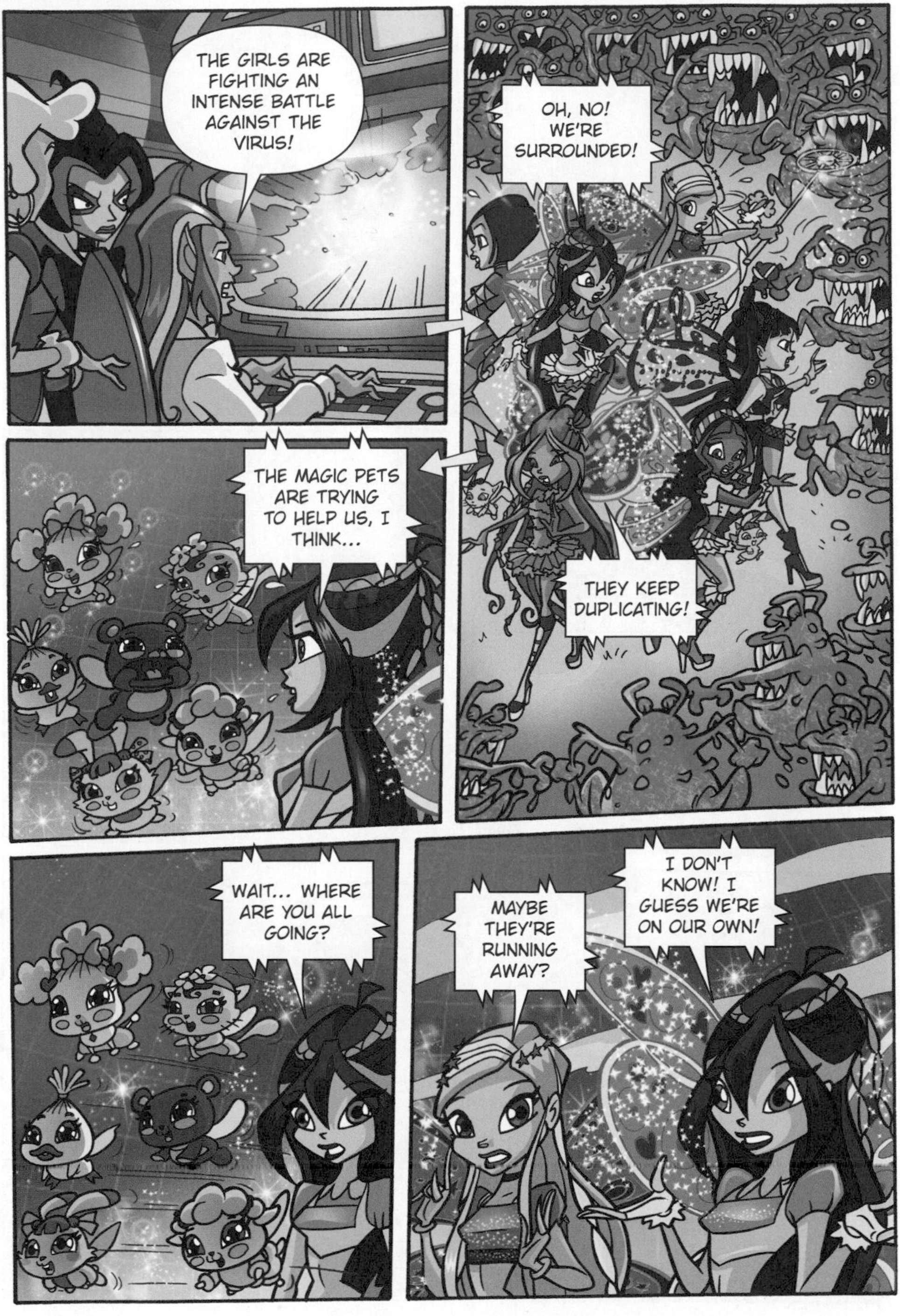
THE GIRLS ARE FIGHTING AN INTENSE BATTLE AGAINST THE VIRUS!
OH, NO! WE'RE SURROUNDED!
THE MAGIC PETS ARE TRYING TO HELP US, I THINK...
THEY KEEP DUPLICATING!
WAIT... WHERE ARE YOU ALL GOING?
MAYBE THEY'RE RUNNING AWAY?
I DON'T KNOW! I GUESS WE'RE ON OUR OWN!

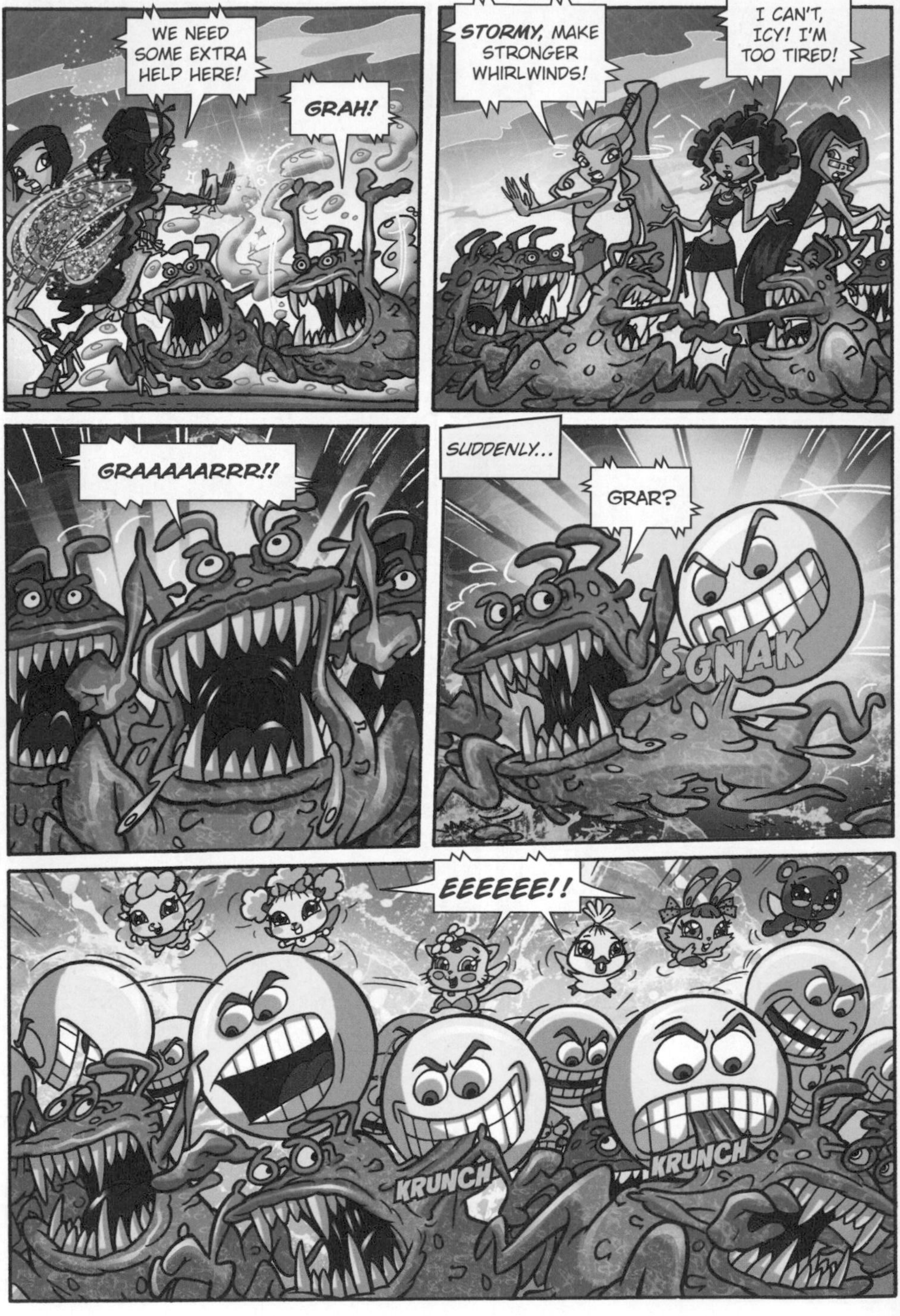
WE NEED SOME EXTRA HELP HERE!
GRAH!
STORMY, MAKE STRONGER WHIRLWINDS!
I CAN'T, ICY! I'M TOO TIRED!
GRAAAAARRR!!
SUDDENLY...
GRAR?
SGNAK
EEEEEE!!
KRUNCH
KRUNCH

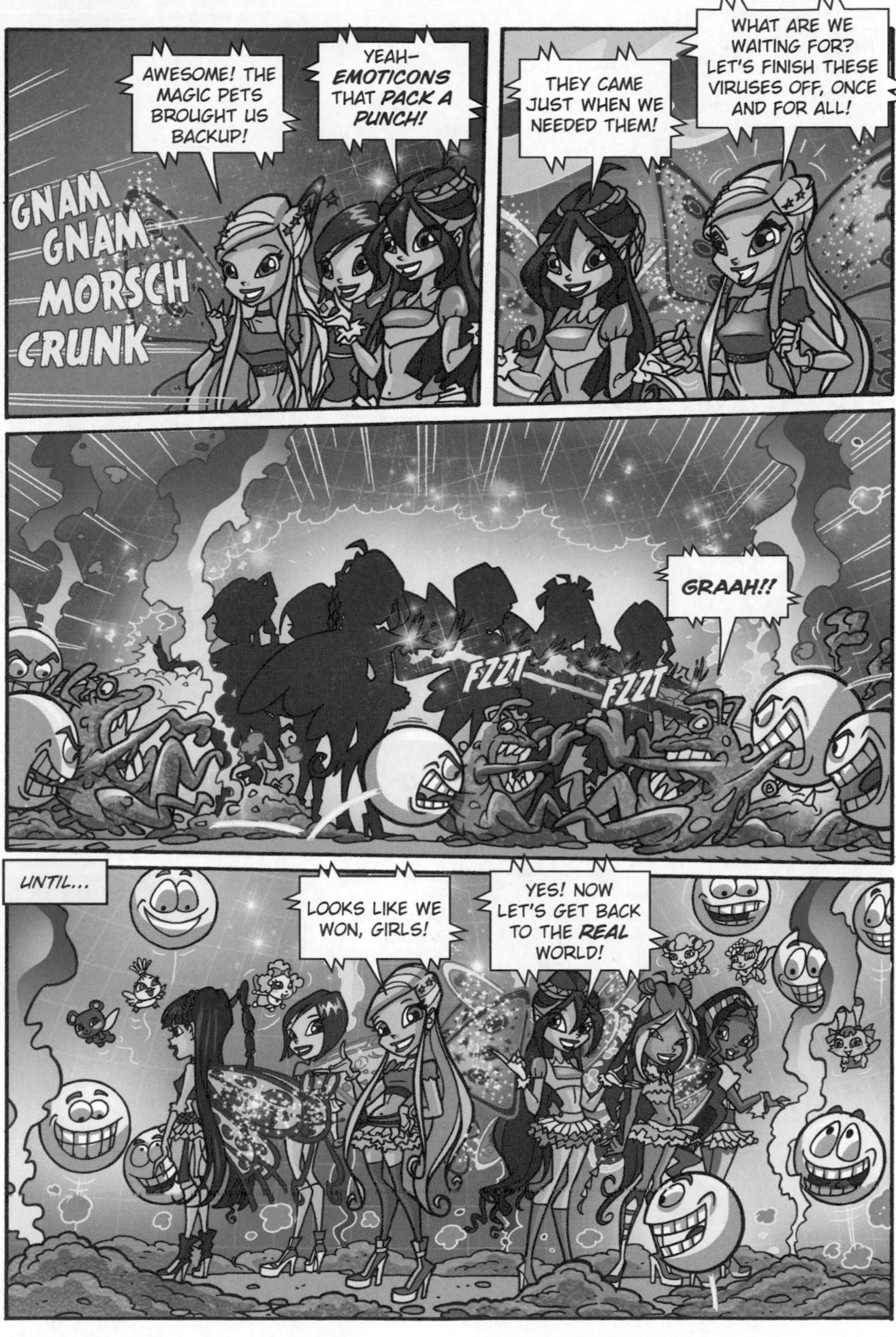
AWESOME! THE MAGIC PETS BROUGHT US BACKUP!
YEAH— EMOTICONS THAT PACK A PUNCH!
GNAM GNAM MORSCH CRUNK
THEY CAME JUST WHEN WE NEEDED THEM!
WHAT ARE WE WAITING FOR? LET'S FINISH THESE VIRUSES OFF, ONCE AND FOR ALL!
GRAAH!!
FZZT
FZZT
UNTIL...
LOOKS LIKE WE WON, GIRLS!
YES! NOW LET'S GET BACK TO THE REAL WORLD!

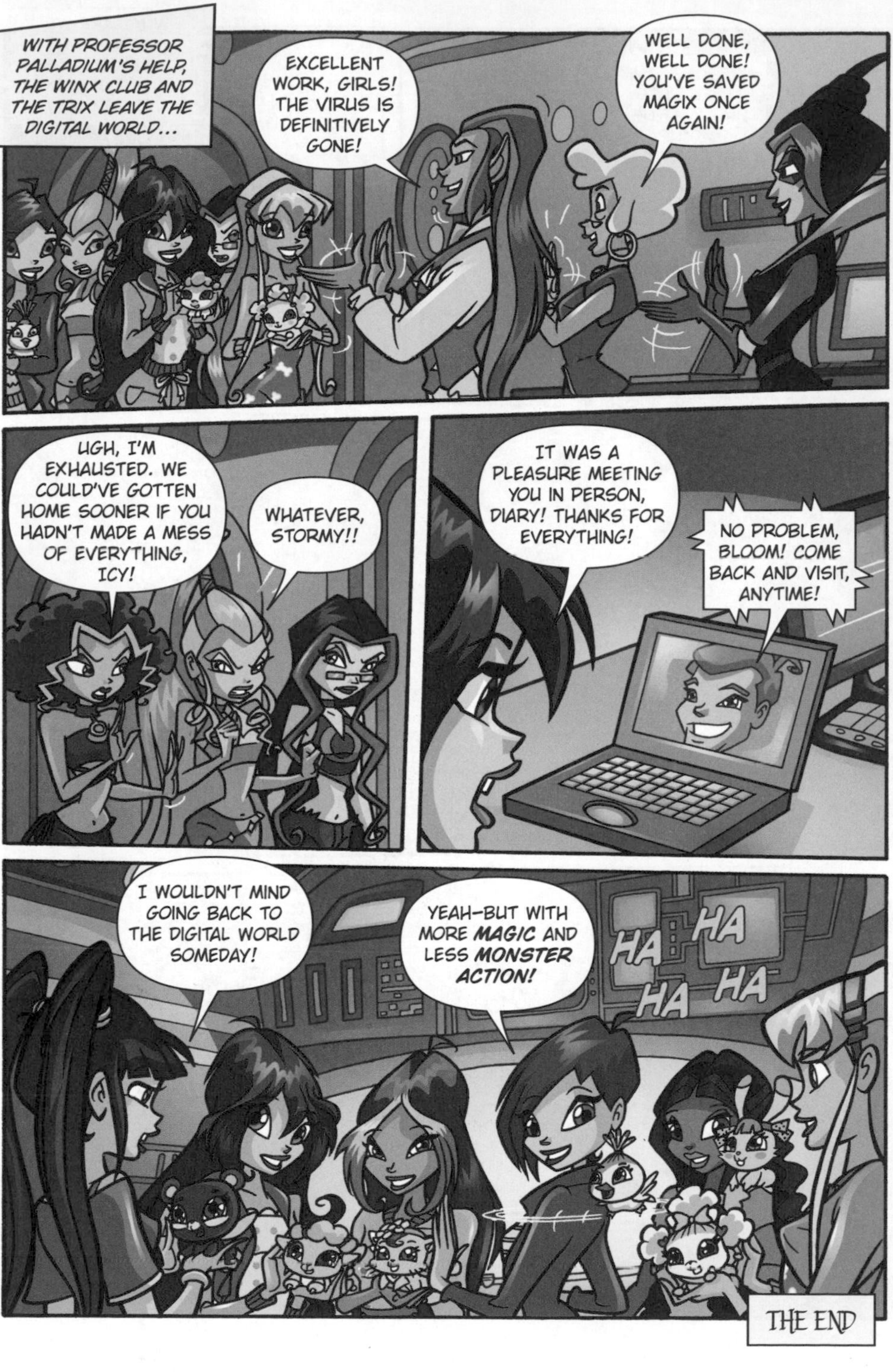
WITH PROFESSOR PALLADIUM'S HELP, THE WINX CLUB AND THE TRIX LEAVE THE DIGITAL WORLD...
EXCELLENT WORK, GIRLS! THE VIRUS IS DEFINITIVELY GONE!
WELL DONE, WELL DONE! YOU'VE SAVED MAGIX ONCE AGAIN!
UGH, I'M EXHAUSTED. WE COULD'VE GOTTEN HOME SOONER IF YOU HADN'T MADE A MESS OF EVERYTHING, ICY!
WHATEVER, STORMY!!
IT WAS A PLEASURE MEETING YOU IN PERSON, DIARY! THANKS FOR EVERYTHING!
NO PROBLEM, BLOOM! COME BACK AND VISIT, ANYTIME!
I WOULDN'T MIND GOING BACK TO THE DIGITAL WORLD SOMEDAY!
YEAH—BUT WITH MORE ***MAGIC*** AND LESS ***MONSTER ACTION!***
HA HA HA HA
THE END

Magic in the Air

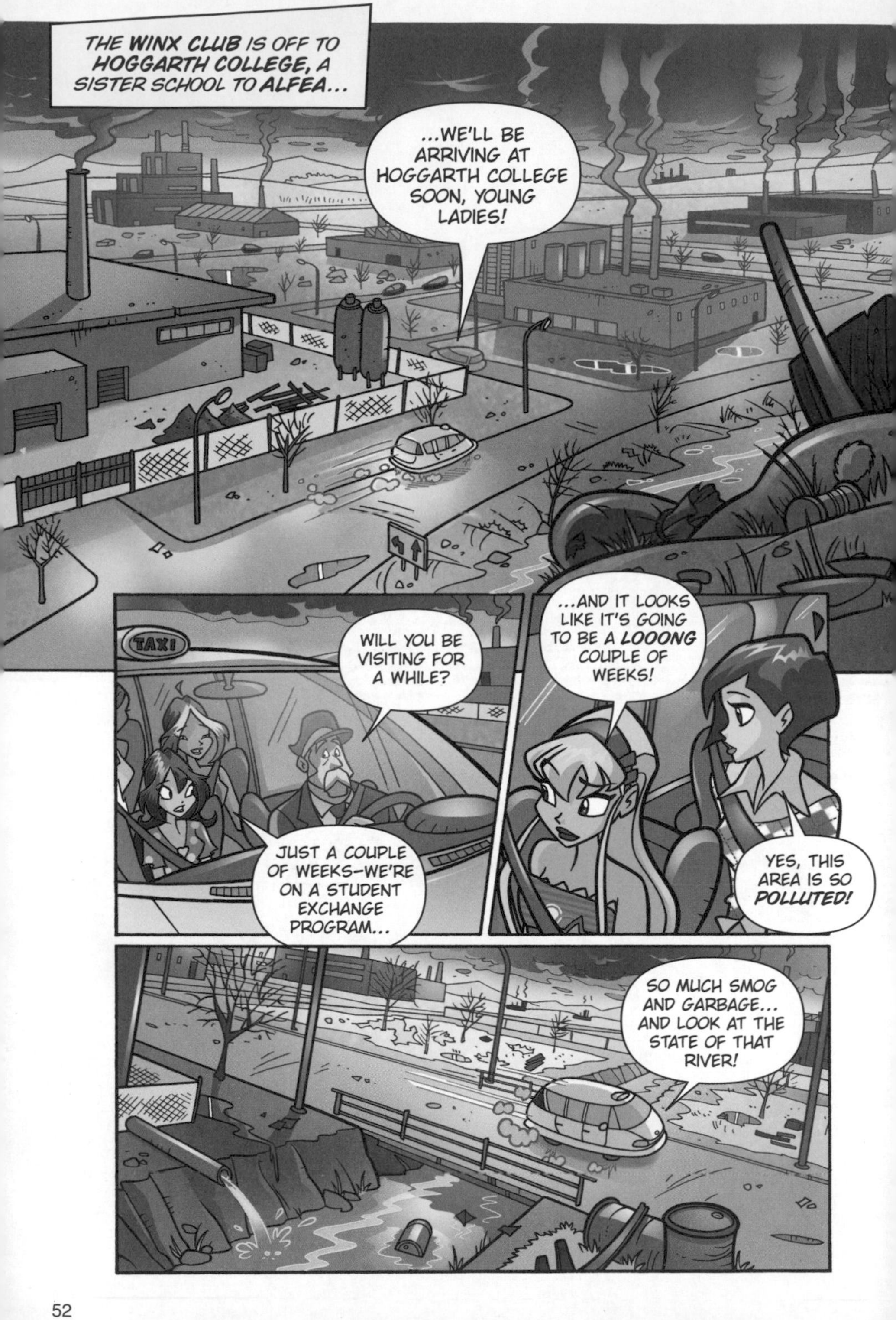
THE WINX CLUB IS OFF TO HOGGARTH COLLEGE, A SISTER SCHOOL TO ALFEA...
...WE'LL BE ARRIVING AT HOGGARTH COLLEGE SOON, YOUNG LADIES!
TAXI
WILL YOU BE VISITING FOR A WHILE?
JUST A COUPLE OF WEEKS–WE'RE ON A STUDENT EXCHANGE PROGRAM...
...AND IT LOOKS LIKE IT'S GOING TO BE A LOOONG COUPLE OF WEEKS!
YES, THIS AREA IS SO POLLUTED!
SO MUCH SMOG AND GARBAGE... AND LOOK AT THE STATE OF THAT RIVER!

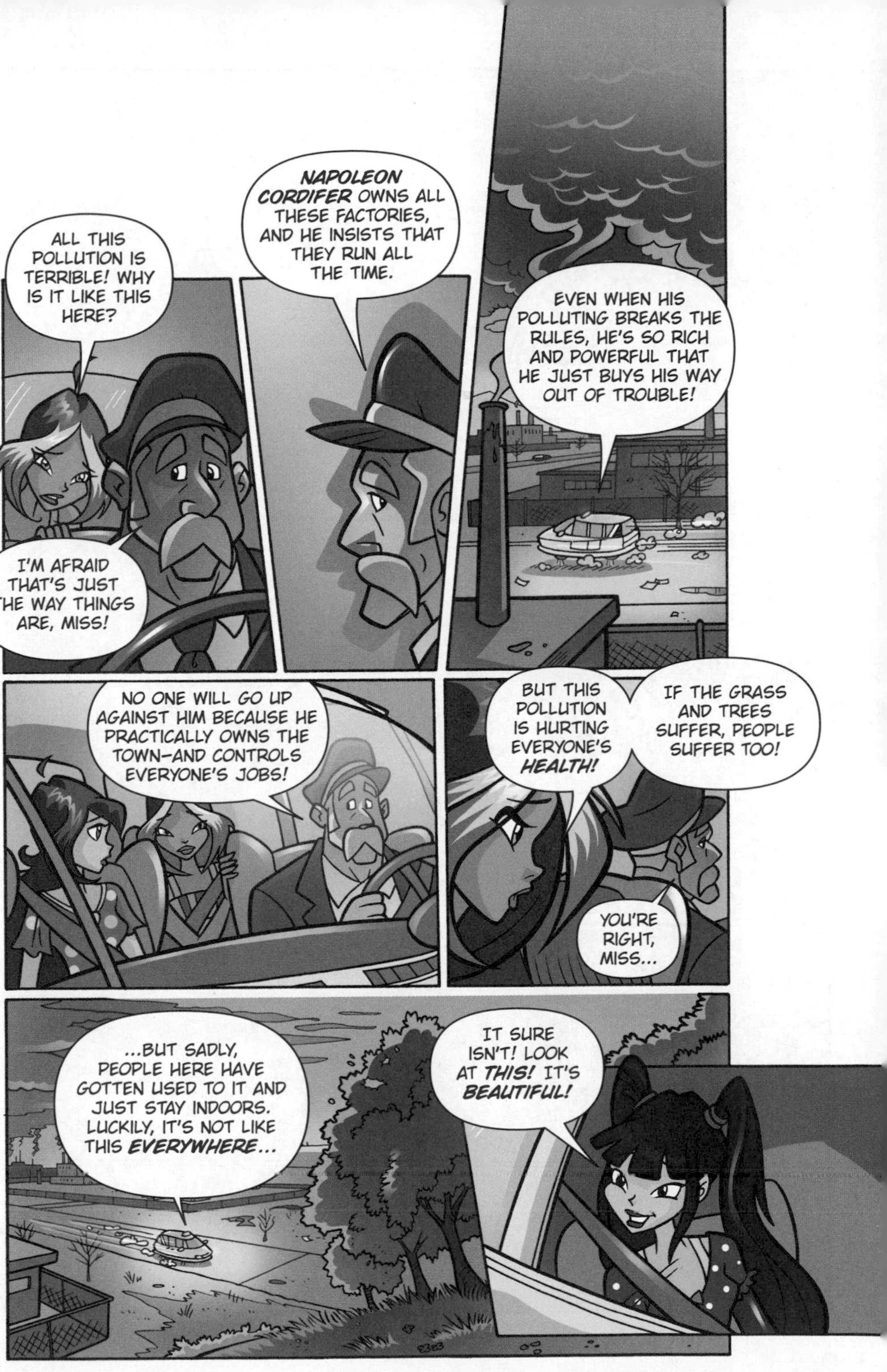
ALL THIS POLLUTION IS TERRIBLE! WHY IS IT LIKE THIS HERE?
I'M AFRAID THAT'S JUST THE WAY THINGS ARE, MISS!
NAPOLEON CORDIFER OWNS ALL THESE FACTORIES, AND HE INSISTS THAT THEY RUN ALL THE TIME.
EVEN WHEN HIS POLLUTING BREAKS THE RULES, HE'S SO RICH AND POWERFUL THAT HE JUST BUYS HIS WAY OUT OF TROUBLE!
NO ONE WILL GO UP AGAINST HIM BECAUSE HE PRACTICALLY OWNS THE TOWN—AND CONTROLS EVERYONE'S JOBS!
BUT THIS POLLUTION IS HURTING EVERYONE'S HEALTH!
IF THE GRASS AND TREES SUFFER, PEOPLE SUFFER TOO!
YOU'RE RIGHT, MISS...
...BUT SADLY, PEOPLE HERE HAVE GOTTEN USED TO IT AND JUST STAY INDOORS. LUCKILY, IT'S NOT LIKE THIS EVERYWHERE...
IT SURE ISN'T! LOOK AT THIS! IT'S BEAUTIFUL!

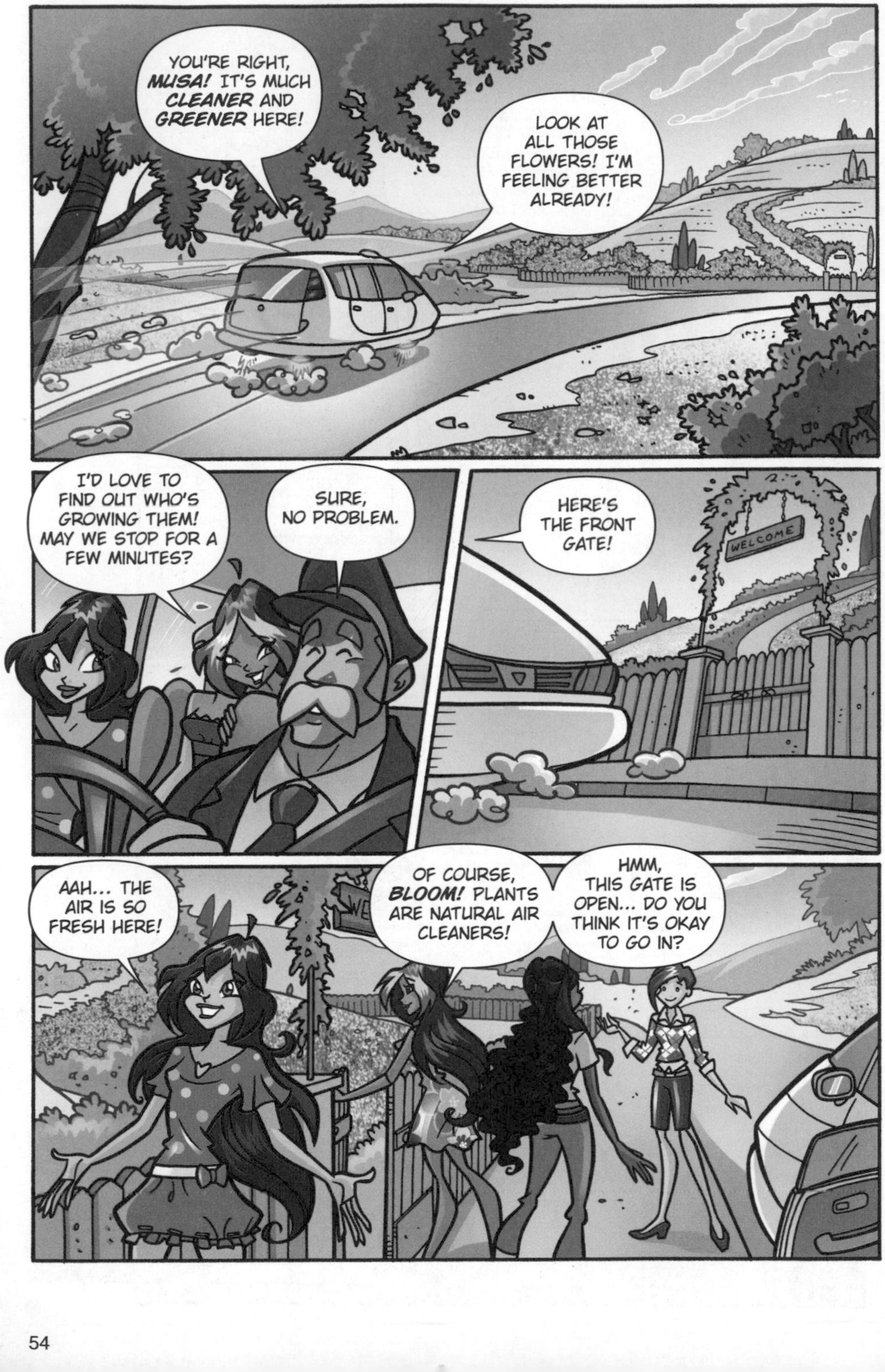
YOU'RE RIGHT, MUSA! IT'S MUCH CLEANER AND GREENER HERE!
LOOK AT ALL THOSE FLOWERS! I'M FEELING BETTER ALREADY!
I'D LOVE TO FIND OUT WHO'S GROWING THEM! MAY WE STOP FOR A FEW MINUTES?
SURE, NO PROBLEM.
HERE'S THE FRONT GATE!
WELCOME
AAH... THE AIR IS SO FRESH HERE!
OF COURSE, BLOOM! PLANTS ARE NATURAL AIR CLEANERS!
HMM, THIS GATE IS OPEN... DO YOU THINK IT'S OKAY TO GO IN?

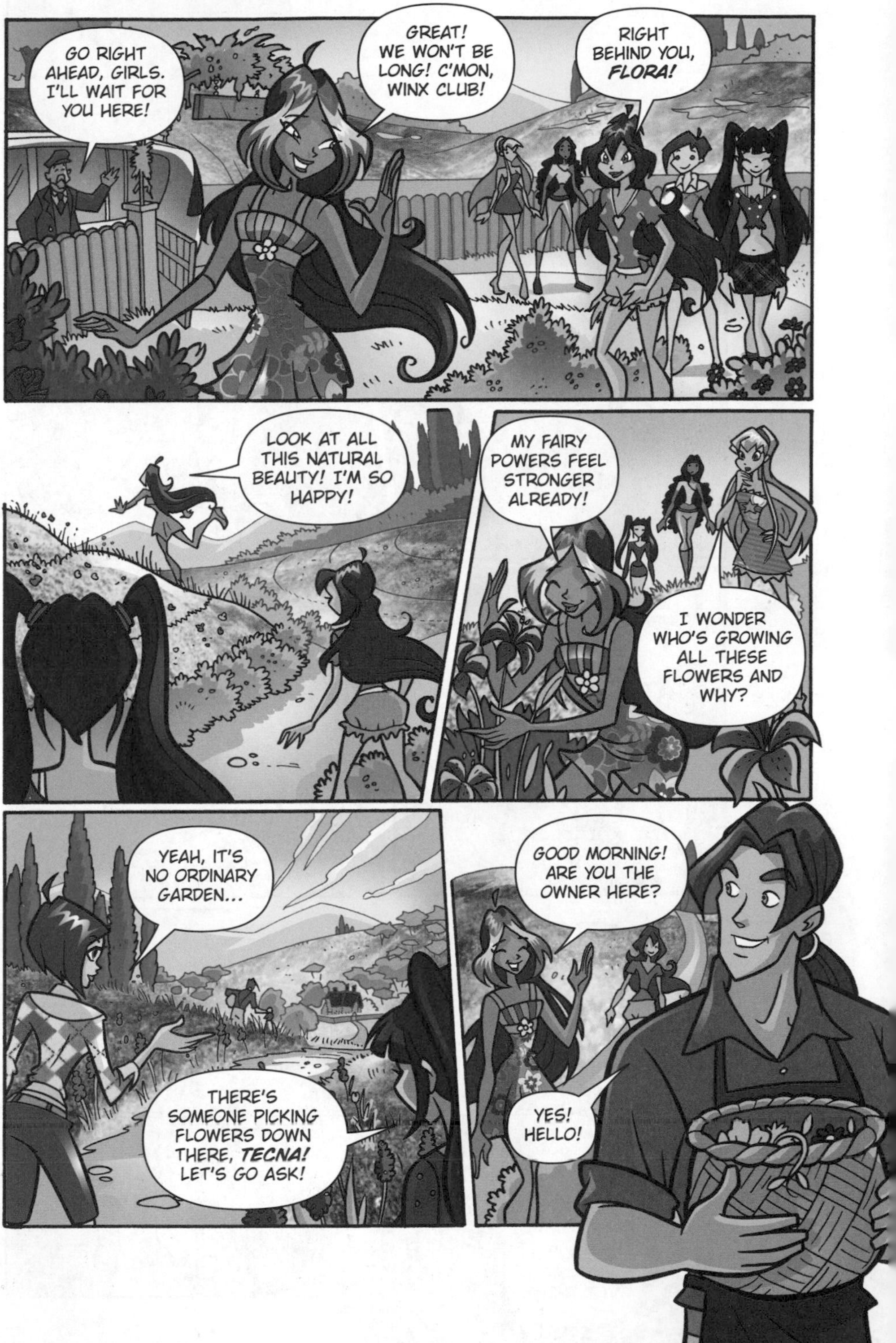
GO RIGHT AHEAD, GIRLS. I'LL WAIT FOR YOU HERE!
GREAT! WE WON'T BE LONG! C'MON, WINX CLUB!
RIGHT BEHIND YOU, ***FLORA!***
LOOK AT ALL THIS NATURAL BEAUTY! I'M SO HAPPY!
MY FAIRY POWERS FEEL STRONGER ALREADY!
I WONDER WHO'S GROWING ALL THESE FLOWERS AND WHY?
YEAH, IT'S NO ORDINARY GARDEN...
THERE'S SOMEONE PICKING FLOWERS DOWN THERE, ***TECNA!*** LET'S GO ASK!
GOOD MORNING! ARE YOU THE OWNER HERE?
YES! HELLO!

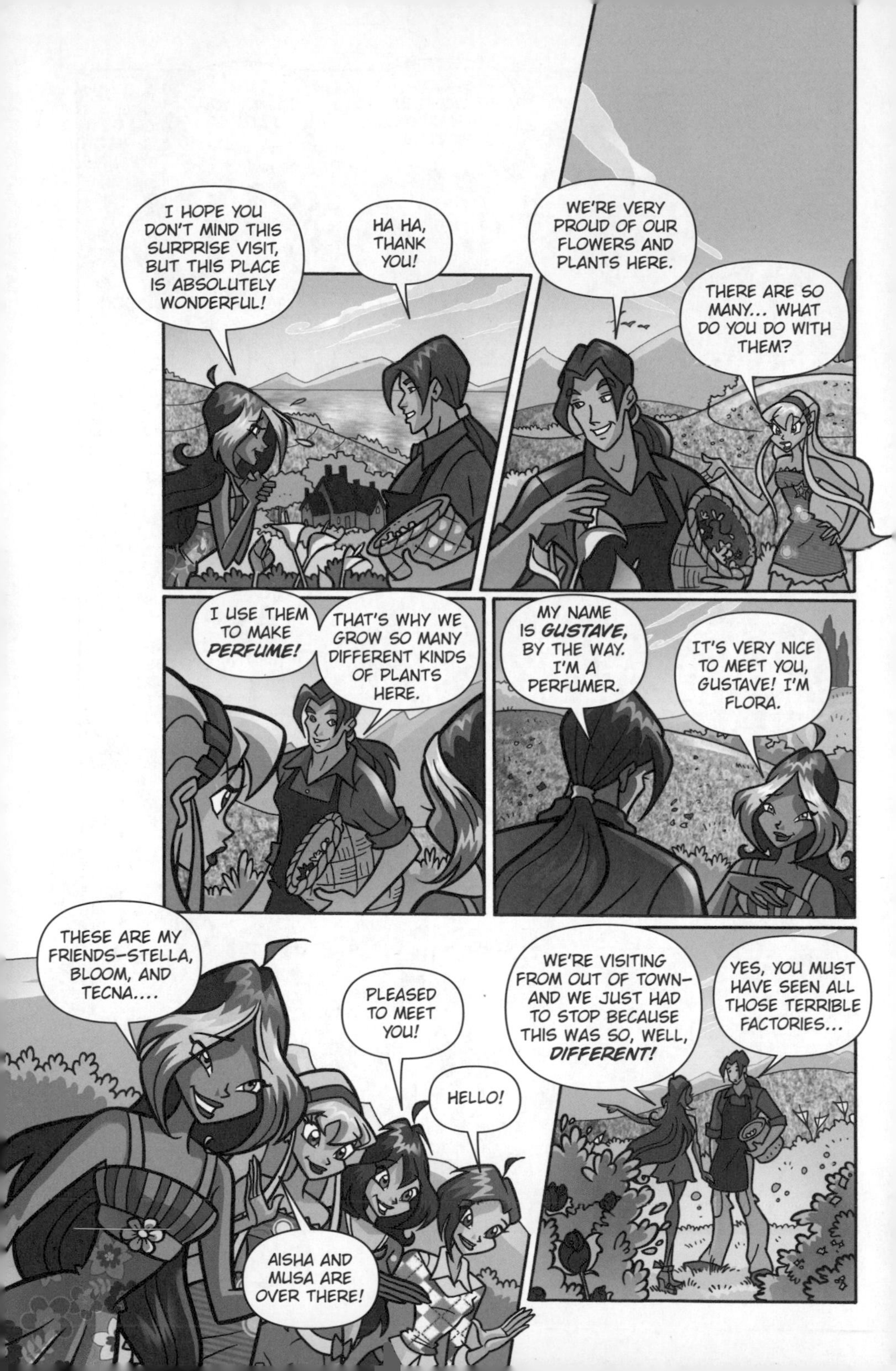
I HOPE YOU DON'T MIND THIS SURPRISE VISIT, BUT THIS PLACE IS ABSOLUTELY WONDERFUL!
HA HA, THANK YOU!
WE'RE VERY PROUD OF OUR FLOWERS AND PLANTS HERE.
THERE ARE SO MANY... WHAT DO YOU DO WITH THEM?
I USE THEM TO MAKE PERFUME!
THAT'S WHY WE GROW SO MANY DIFFERENT KINDS OF PLANTS HERE.
MY NAME IS GUSTAVE, BY THE WAY. I'M A PERFUMER.
IT'S VERY NICE TO MEET YOU, GUSTAVE! I'M FLORA.
THESE ARE MY FRIENDS—STELLA, BLOOM, AND TECNA....
PLEASED TO MEET YOU!
HELLO!
AISHA AND MUSA ARE OVER THERE!
WE'RE VISITING FROM OUT OF TOWN—AND WE JUST HAD TO STOP BECAUSE THIS WAS SO, WELL, DIFFERENT!
YES, YOU MUST HAVE SEEN ALL THOSE TERRIBLE FACTORIES...

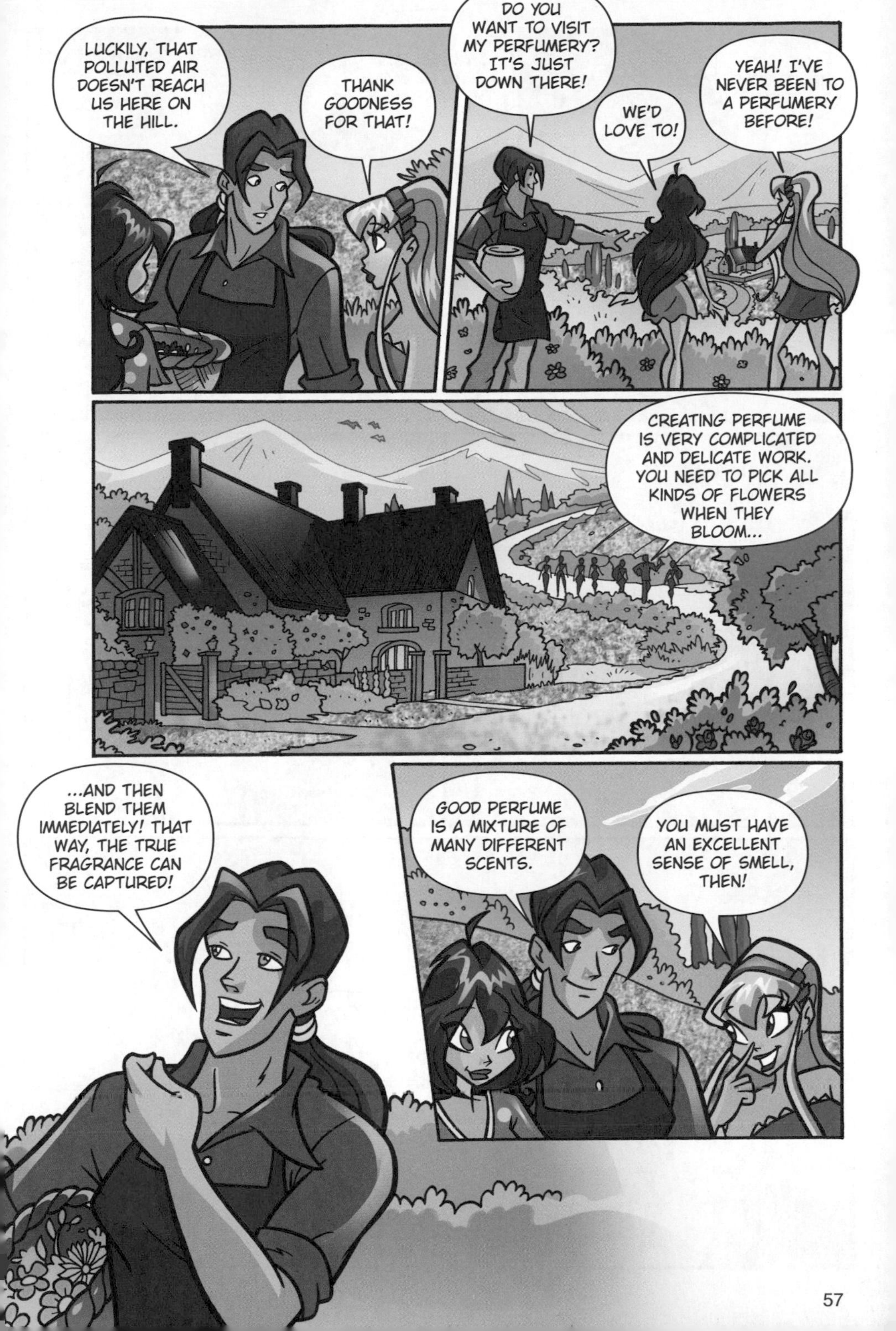
LUCKILY, THAT POLLUTED AIR DOESN'T REACH US HERE ON THE HILL.
THANK GOODNESS FOR THAT!
DO YOU WANT TO VISIT MY PERFUMERY? IT'S JUST DOWN THERE!
WE'D LOVE TO!
YEAH! I'VE NEVER BEEN TO A PERFUMERY BEFORE!
CREATING PERFUME IS VERY COMPLICATED AND DELICATE WORK. YOU NEED TO PICK ALL KINDS OF FLOWERS WHEN THEY BLOOM...
...AND THEN BLEND THEM IMMEDIATELY! THAT WAY, THE TRUE FRAGRANCE CAN BE CAPTURED!
GOOD PERFUME IS A MIXTURE OF MANY DIFFERENT SCENTS.
YOU MUST HAVE AN EXCELLENT SENSE OF SMELL, THEN!

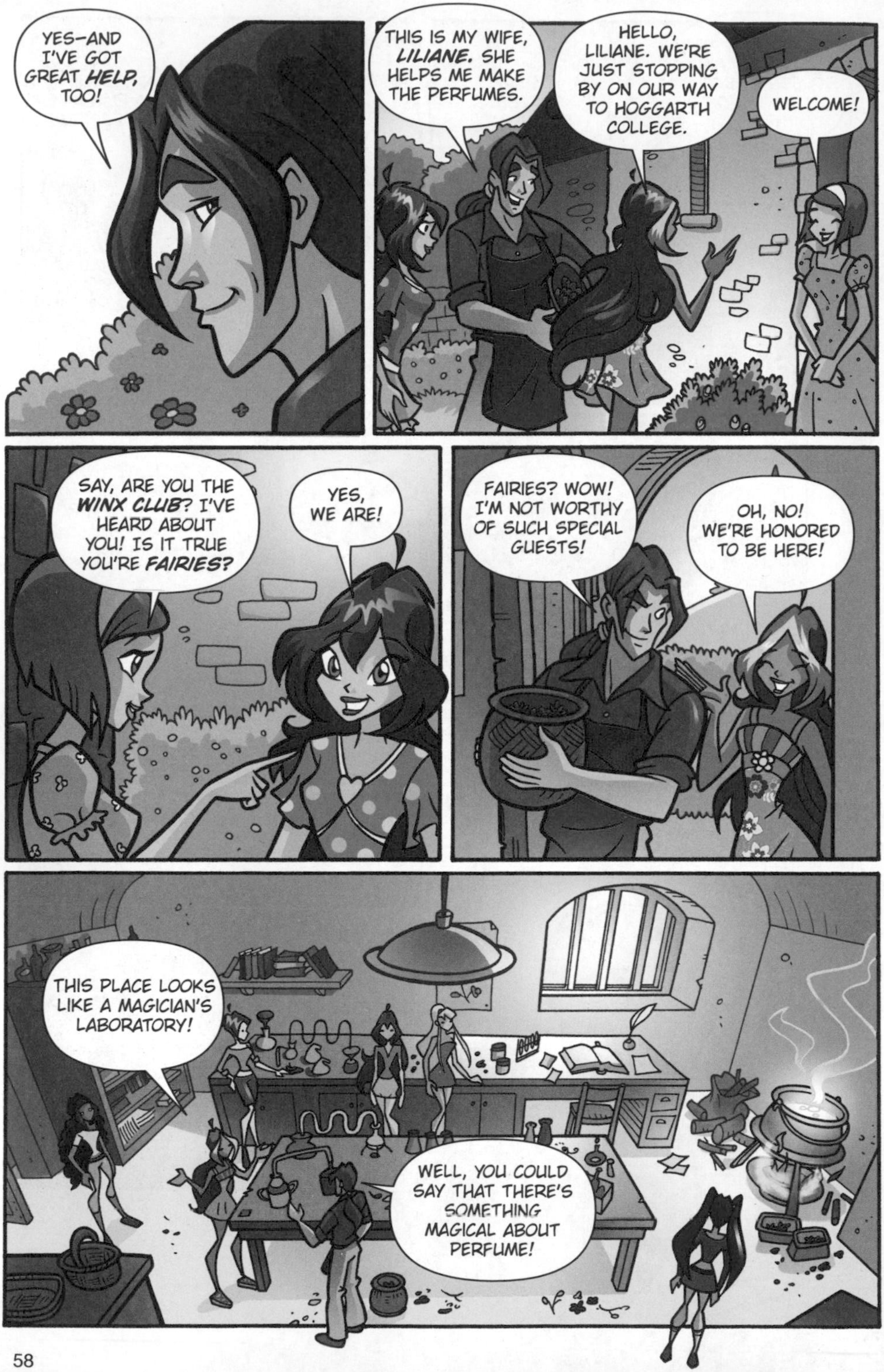
YES—AND I'VE GOT GREAT HELP, TOO!
THIS IS MY WIFE, LILIANE. SHE HELPS ME MAKE THE PERFUMES.
HELLO, LILIANE. WE'RE JUST STOPPING BY ON OUR WAY TO HOGGARTH COLLEGE.
WELCOME!
SAY, ARE YOU THE WINX CLUB? I'VE HEARD ABOUT YOU! IS IT TRUE YOU'RE FAIRIES?
YES, WE ARE!
FAIRIES? WOW! I'M NOT WORTHY OF SUCH SPECIAL GUESTS!
OH, NO! WE'RE HONORED TO BE HERE!
THIS PLACE LOOKS LIKE A MAGICIAN'S LABORATORY!
WELL, YOU COULD SAY THAT THERE'S SOMETHING MAGICAL ABOUT PERFUME!

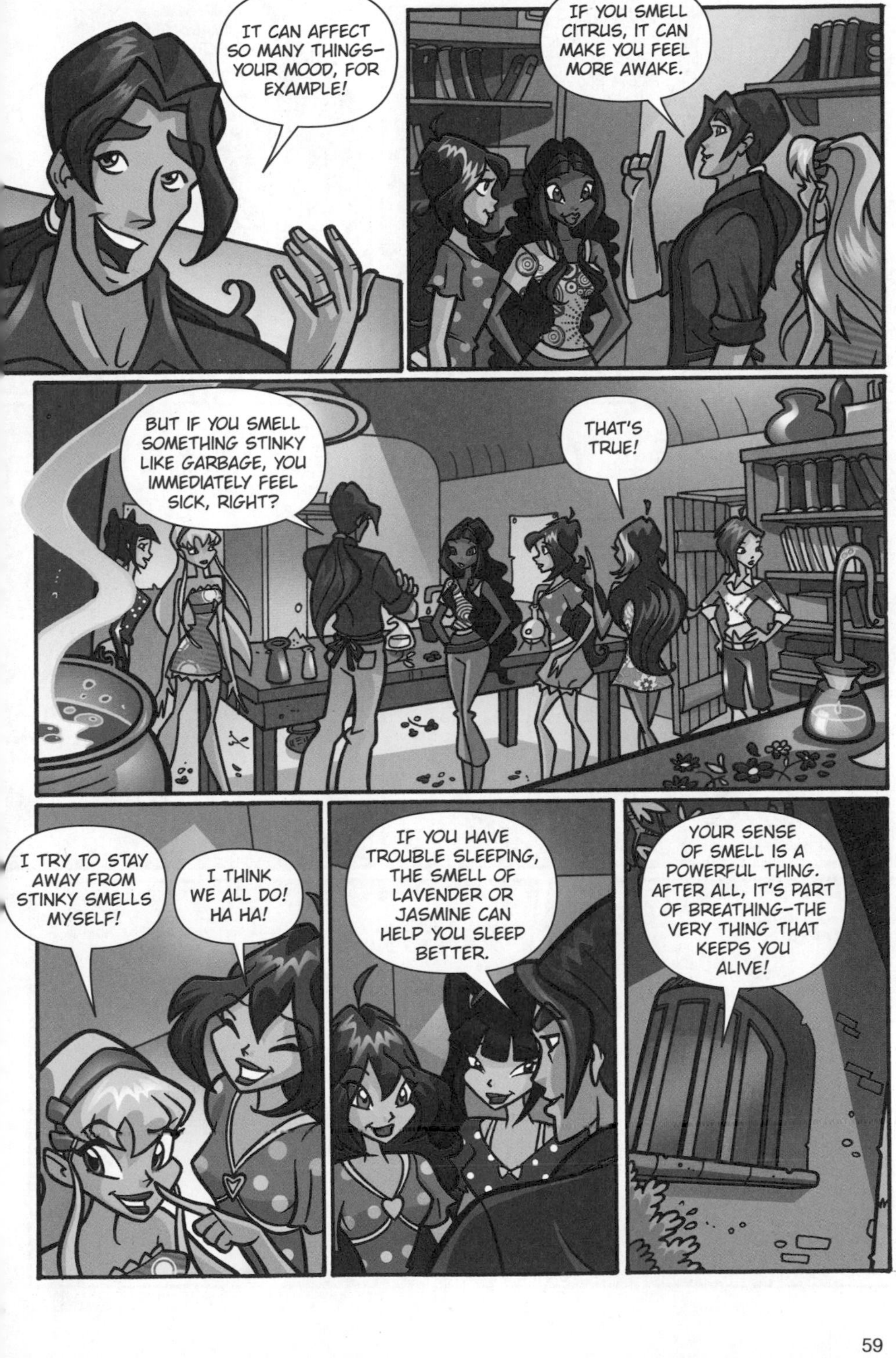
IT CAN AFFECT SO MANY THINGS– YOUR MOOD, FOR EXAMPLE!
IF YOU SMELL CITRUS, IT CAN MAKE YOU FEEL MORE AWAKE.
BUT IF YOU SMELL SOMETHING STINKY LIKE GARBAGE, YOU IMMEDIATELY FEEL SICK, RIGHT?
THAT'S TRUE!
I TRY TO STAY AWAY FROM STINKY SMELLS MYSELF!
I THINK WE ALL DO! HA HA!
IF YOU HAVE TROUBLE SLEEPING, THE SMELL OF LAVENDER OR JASMINE CAN HELP YOU SLEEP BETTER.
YOUR SENSE OF SMELL IS A POWERFUL THING. AFTER ALL, IT'S PART OF BREATHING–THE VERY THING THAT KEEPS YOU ALIVE!

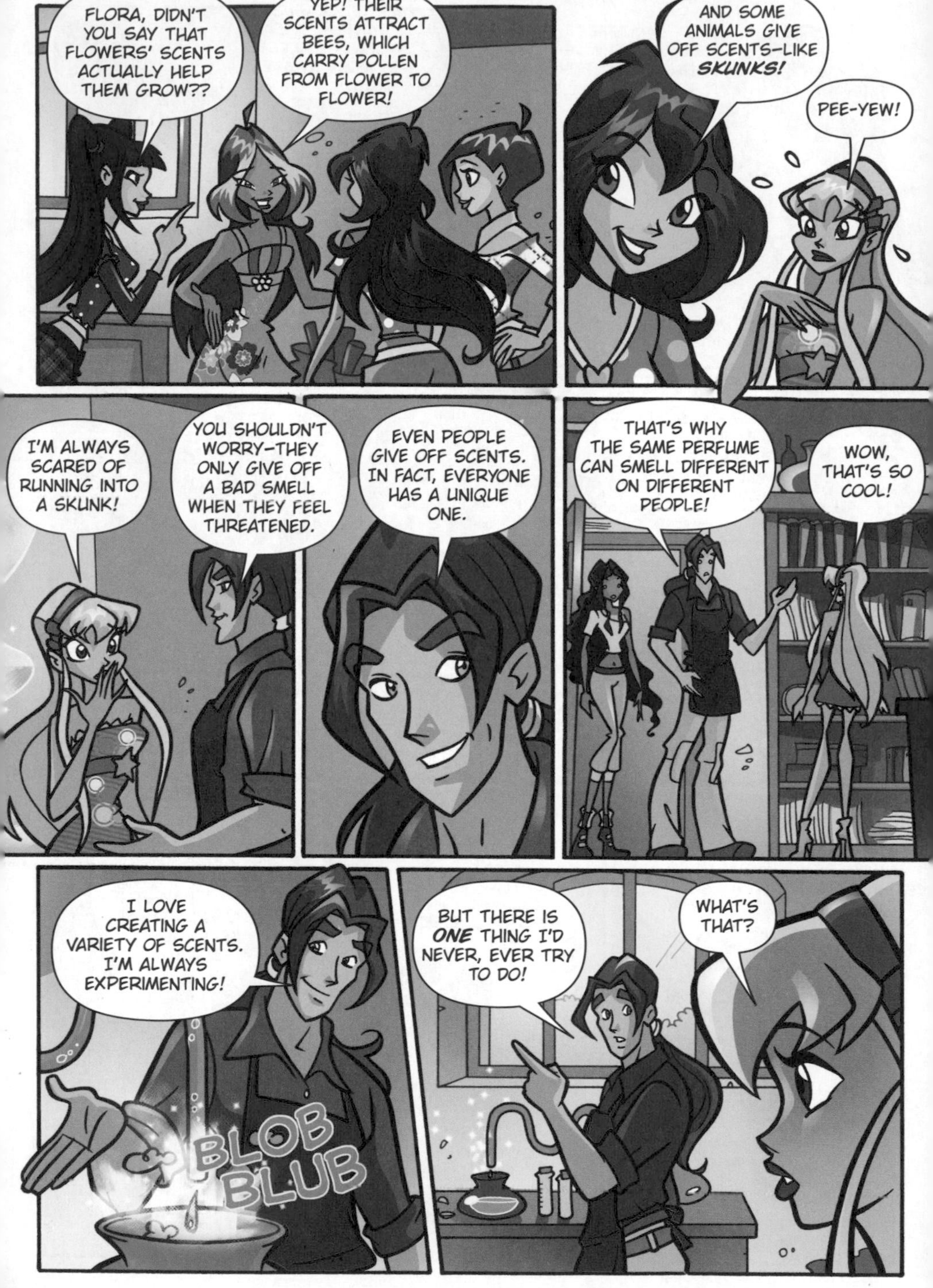
FLORA, DIDN'T YOU SAY THAT FLOWERS' SCENTS ACTUALLY HELP THEM GROW??
YEP! THEIR SCENTS ATTRACT BEES, WHICH CARRY POLLEN FROM FLOWER TO FLOWER!
AND SOME ANIMALS GIVE OFF SCENTS—LIKE **SKUNKS!**
PEE-YEW!
I'M ALWAYS SCARED OF RUNNING INTO A SKUNK!
YOU SHOULDN'T WORRY—THEY ONLY GIVE OFF A BAD SMELL WHEN THEY FEEL THREATENED.
EVEN PEOPLE GIVE OFF SCENTS. IN FACT, EVERYONE HAS A UNIQUE ONE.
THAT'S WHY THE SAME PERFUME CAN SMELL DIFFERENT ON DIFFERENT PEOPLE!
WOW, THAT'S SO COOL!
I LOVE CREATING A VARIETY OF SCENTS. I'M ALWAYS EXPERIMENTING!
BLOB BLUB
BUT THERE IS ***ONE*** THING I'D NEVER, EVER TRY TO DO!
WHAT'S THAT?

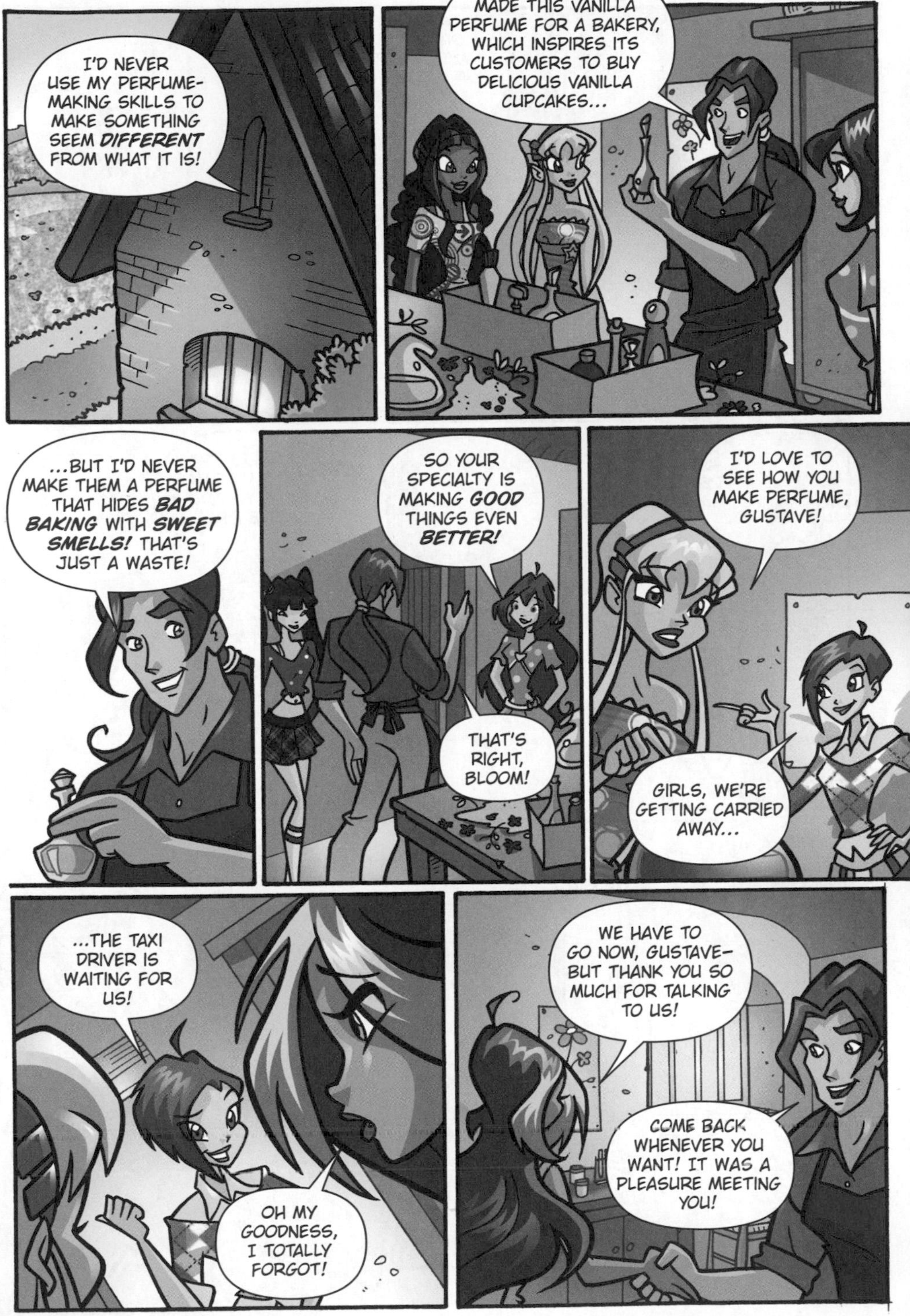
I'D NEVER USE MY PERFUME-MAKING SKILLS TO MAKE SOMETHING SEEM DIFFERENT FROM WHAT IT IS!
FOR INSTANCE, I MADE THIS VANILLA PERFUME FOR A BAKERY, WHICH INSPIRES ITS CUSTOMERS TO BUY DELICIOUS VANILLA CUPCAKES...
...BUT I'D NEVER MAKE THEM A PERFUME THAT HIDES BAD BAKING WITH SWEET SMELLS! THAT'S JUST A WASTE!
SO YOUR SPECIALTY IS MAKING GOOD THINGS EVEN BETTER!
THAT'S RIGHT, BLOOM!
I'D LOVE TO SEE HOW YOU MAKE PERFUME, GUSTAVE!
GIRLS, WE'RE GETTING CARRIED AWAY...
...THE TAXI DRIVER IS WAITING FOR US!
OH MY GOODNESS, I TOTALLY FORGOT!
WE HAVE TO GO NOW, GUSTAVE-BUT THANK YOU SO MUCH FOR TALKING TO US!
COME BACK WHENEVER YOU WANT! IT WAS A PLEASURE MEETING YOU!

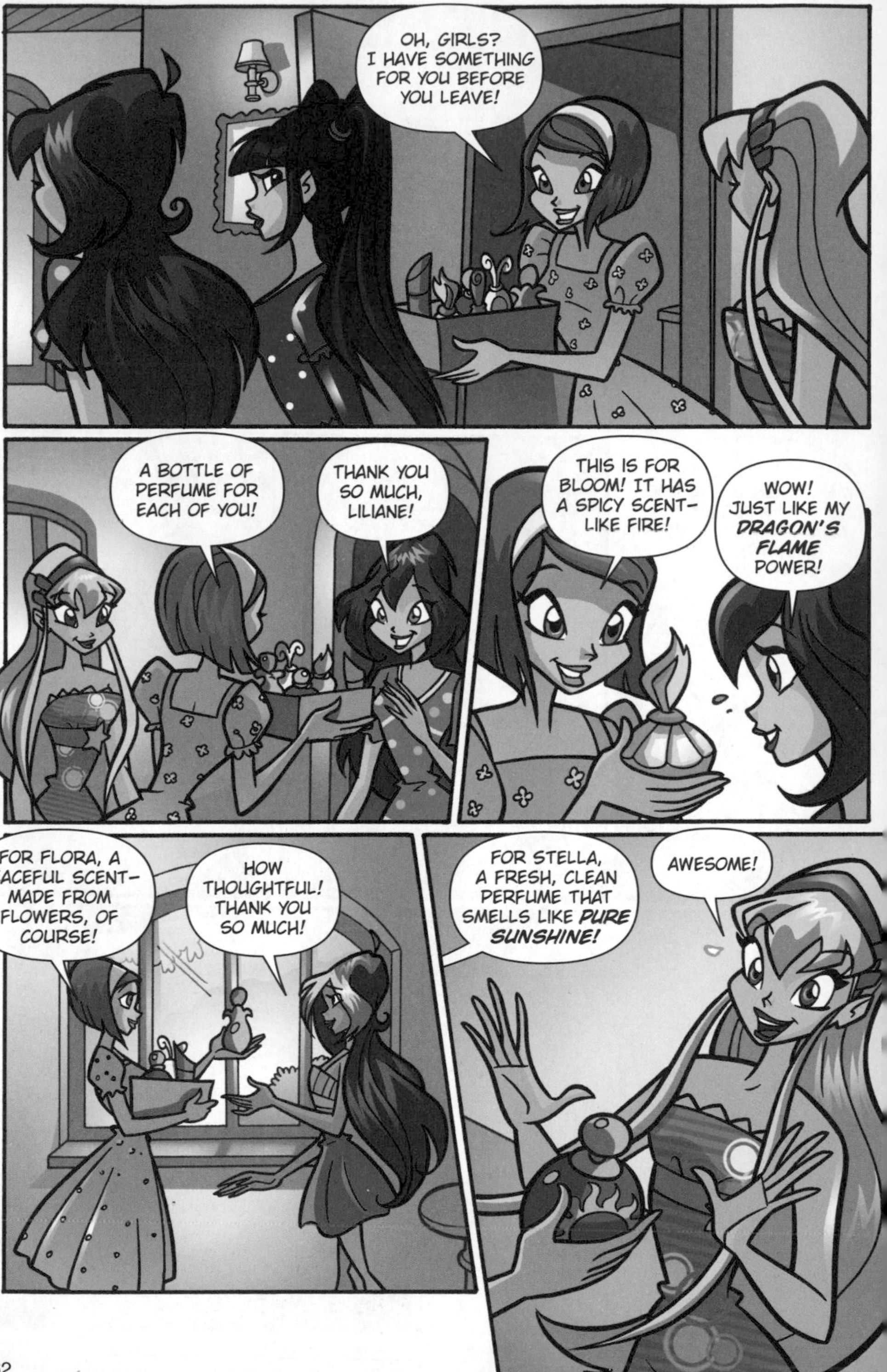
OH, GIRLS? I HAVE SOMETHING FOR YOU BEFORE YOU LEAVE!
A BOTTLE OF PERFUME FOR EACH OF YOU!
THANK YOU SO MUCH, LILIANE!
THIS IS FOR BLOOM! IT HAS A SPICY SCENT- LIKE FIRE!
WOW! JUST LIKE MY DRAGON'S FLAME POWER!
FOR FLORA, A PEACEFUL SCENT- MADE FROM FLOWERS, OF COURSE!
HOW THOUGHTFUL! THANK YOU SO MUCH!
FOR STELLA, A FRESH, CLEAN PERFUME THAT SMELLS LIKE PURE SUNSHINE!
AWESOME!

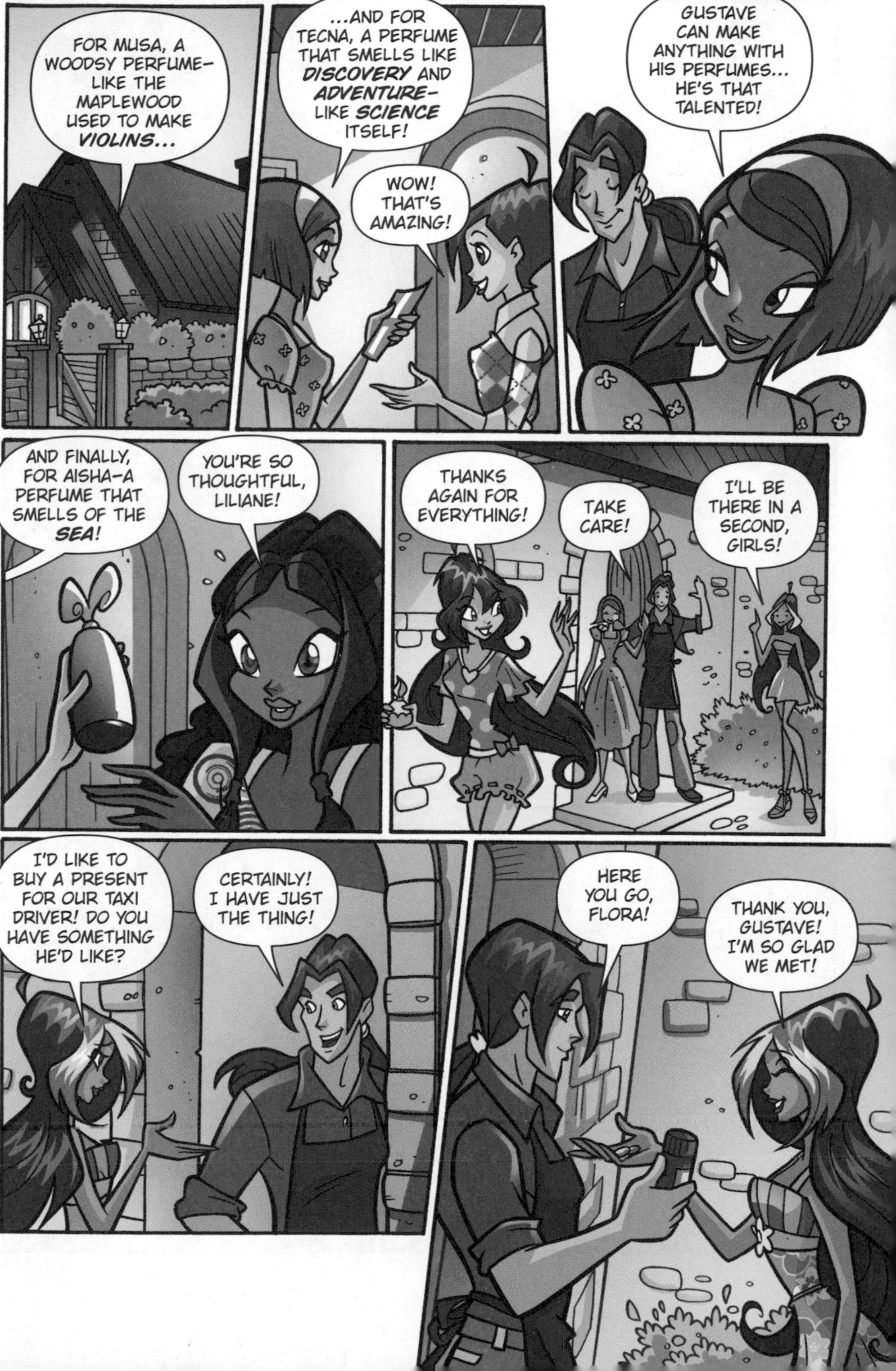
FOR MUSA, A WOODSY PERFUME—LIKE THE MAPLEWOOD USED TO MAKE VIOLINS...
...AND FOR TECNA, A PERFUME THAT SMELLS LIKE DISCOVERY AND ADVENTURE—LIKE SCIENCE ITSELF!
WOW! THAT'S AMAZING!
GUSTAVE CAN MAKE ANYTHING WITH HIS PERFUMES... HE'S THAT TALENTED!
AND FINALLY, FOR AISHA—A PERFUME THAT SMELLS OF THE SEA!
YOU'RE SO THOUGHTFUL, LILIANE!
THANKS AGAIN FOR EVERYTHING!
TAKE CARE!
I'LL BE THERE IN A SECOND, GIRLS!
I'D LIKE TO BUY A PRESENT FOR OUR TAXI DRIVER! DO YOU HAVE SOMETHING HE'D LIKE?
CERTAINLY! I HAVE JUST THE THING!
HERE YOU GO, FLORA!
THANK YOU, GUSTAVE! I'M SO GLAD WE MET!

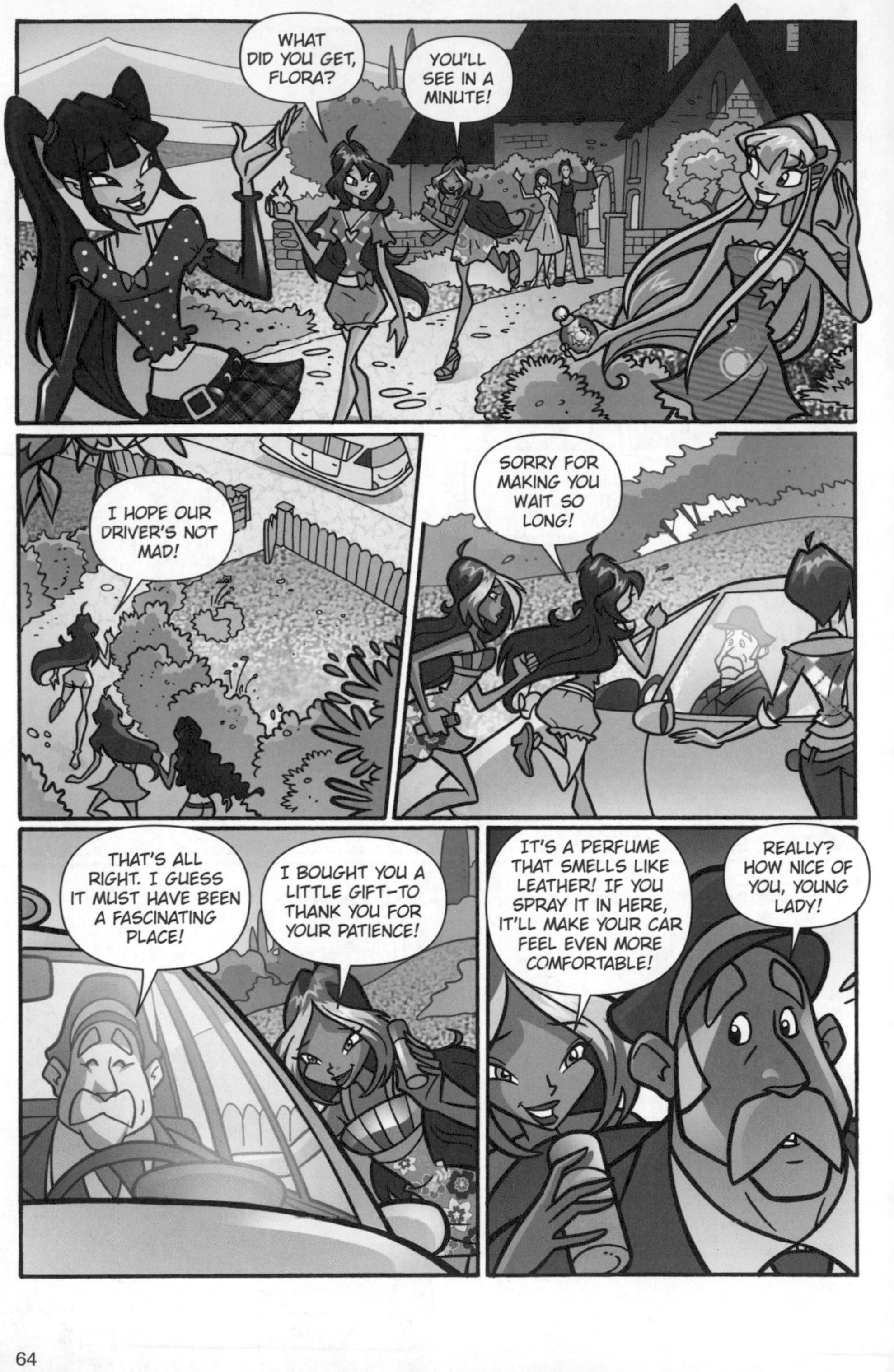
WHAT DID YOU GET, FLORA?
YOU'LL SEE IN A MINUTE!
I HOPE OUR DRIVER'S NOT MAD!
SORRY FOR MAKING YOU WAIT SO LONG!
THAT'S ALL RIGHT. I GUESS IT MUST HAVE BEEN A FASCINATING PLACE!
I BOUGHT YOU A LITTLE GIFT—TO THANK YOU FOR YOUR PATIENCE!
IT'S A PERFUME THAT SMELLS LIKE LEATHER! IF YOU SPRAY IT IN HERE, IT'LL MAKE YOUR CAR FEEL EVEN MORE COMFORTABLE!
REALLY? HOW NICE OF YOU, YOUNG LADY!

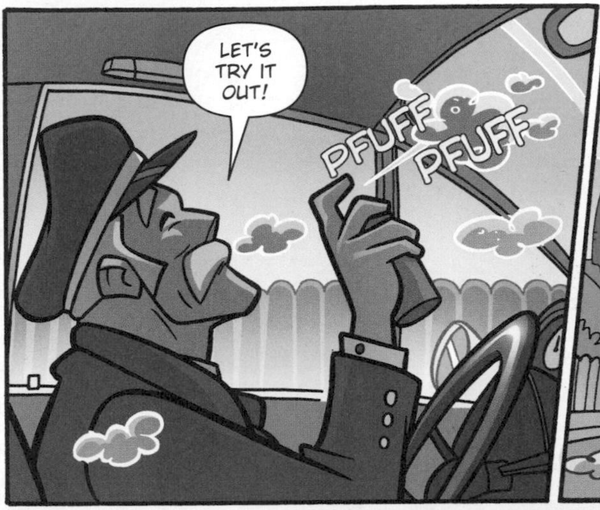
LET'S TRY IT OUT!
PFUFF PFUFF

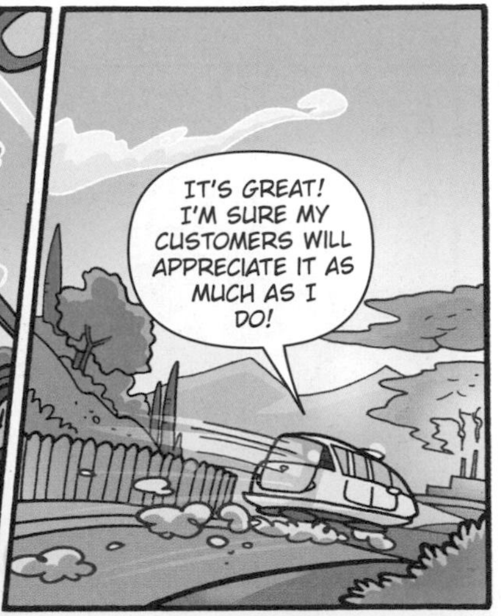
IT'S GREAT! I'M SURE MY CUSTOMERS WILL APPRECIATE IT AS MUCH AS I DO!

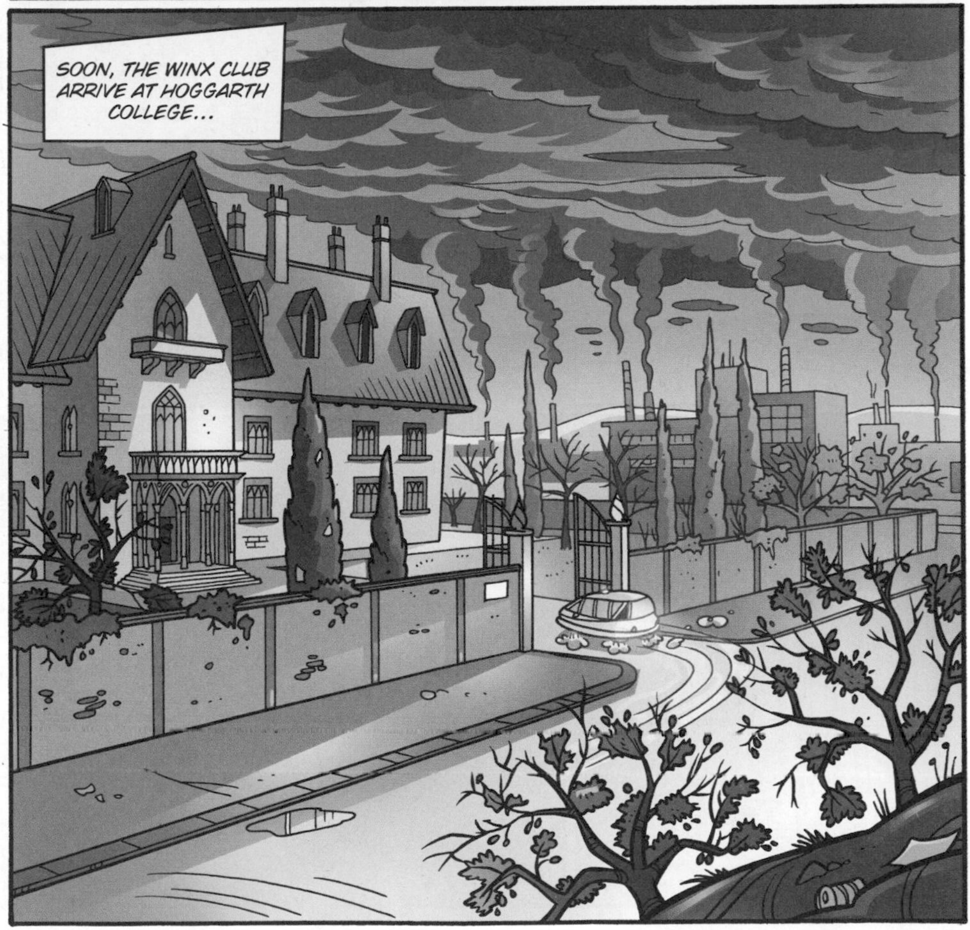
SOON, THE WINX CLUB ARRIVE AT HOGGARTH COLLEGE...

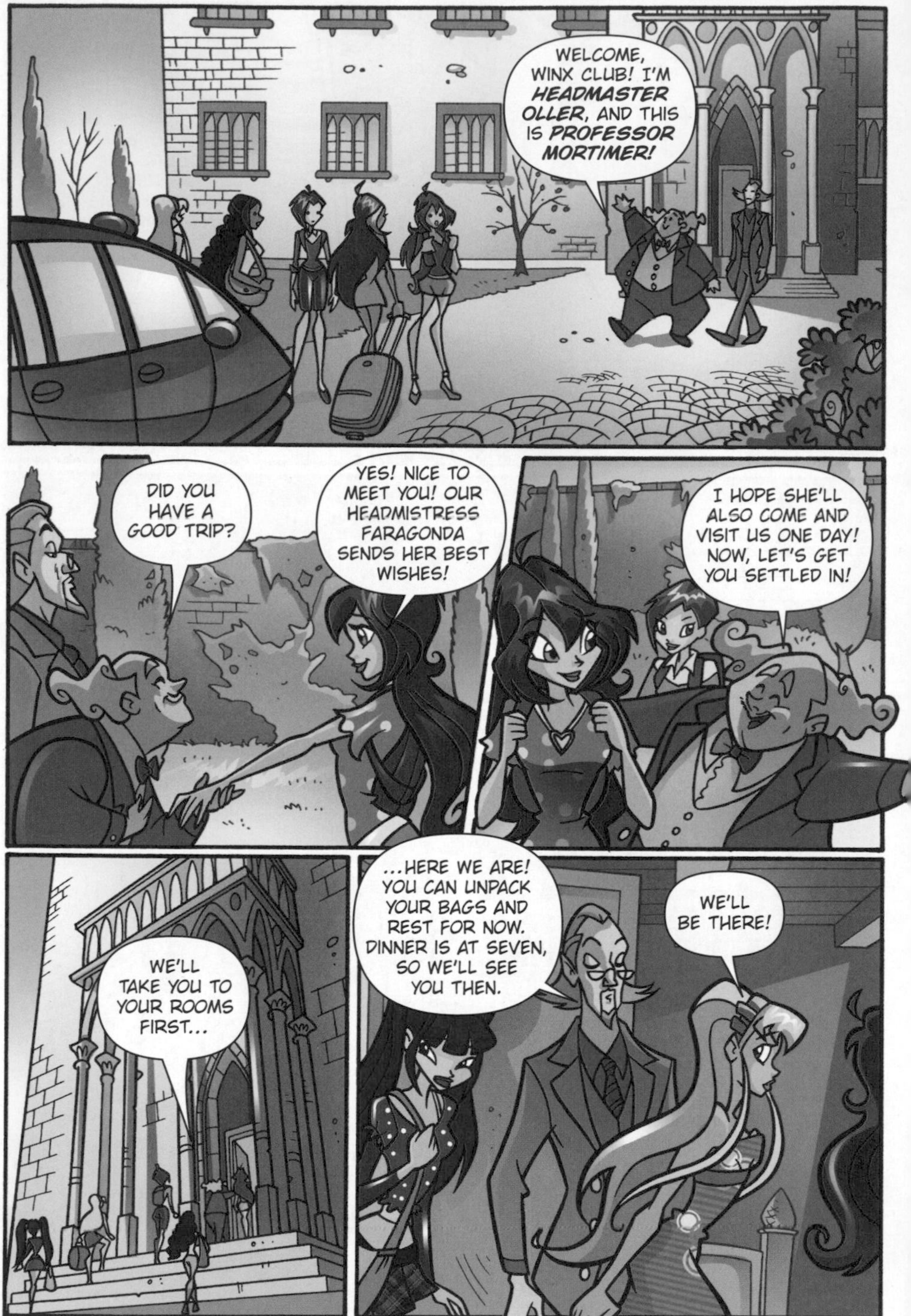
WELCOME, WINX CLUB! I'M HEADMASTER OLLER, AND THIS IS PROFESSOR MORTIMER!
DID YOU HAVE A GOOD TRIP?
YES! NICE TO MEET YOU! OUR HEADMISTRESS FARAGONDA SENDS HER BEST WISHES!
I HOPE SHE'LL ALSO COME AND VISIT US ONE DAY! NOW, LET'S GET YOU SETTLED IN!
WE'LL TAKE YOU TO YOUR ROOMS FIRST...
...HERE WE ARE! YOU CAN UNPACK YOUR BAGS AND REST FOR NOW. DINNER IS AT SEVEN, SO WE'LL SEE YOU THEN.
WE'LL BE THERE!

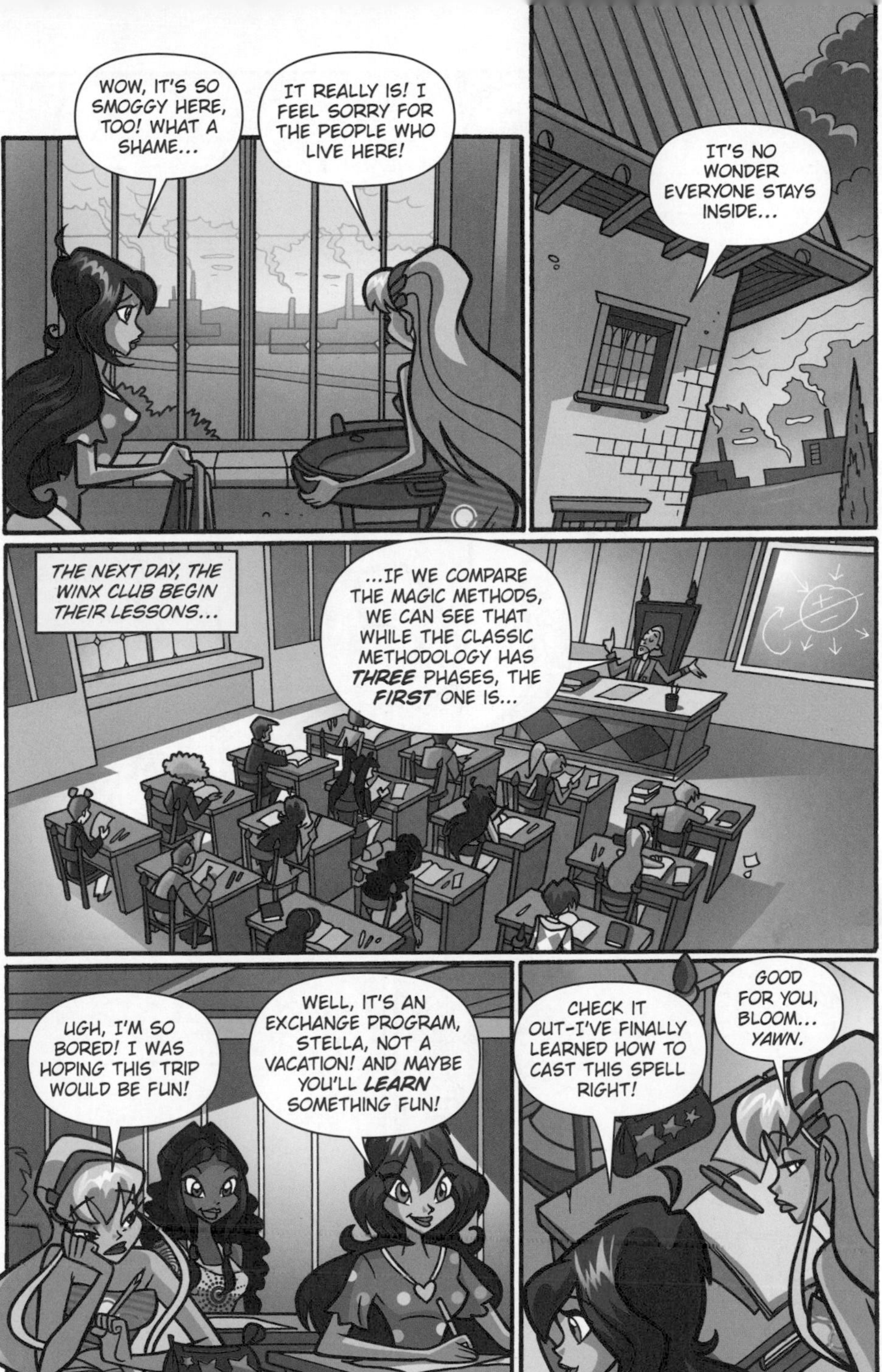
WOW, IT'S SO SMOGGY HERE, TOO! WHAT A SHAME...
IT REALLY IS! I FEEL SORRY FOR THE PEOPLE WHO LIVE HERE!
IT'S NO WONDER EVERYONE STAYS INSIDE...
THE NEXT DAY, THE WINX CLUB BEGIN THEIR LESSONS...
...IF WE COMPARE THE MAGIC METHODS, WE CAN SEE THAT WHILE THE CLASSIC METHODOLOGY HAS THREE PHASES, THE FIRST ONE IS...
UGH, I'M SO BORED! I WAS HOPING THIS TRIP WOULD BE FUN!
WELL, IT'S AN EXCHANGE PROGRAM, STELLA, NOT A VACATION! AND MAYBE YOU'LL LEARN SOMETHING FUN!
CHECK IT OUT-I'VE FINALLY LEARNED HOW TO CAST THIS SPELL RIGHT!
GOOD FOR YOU, BLOOM... YAWN.

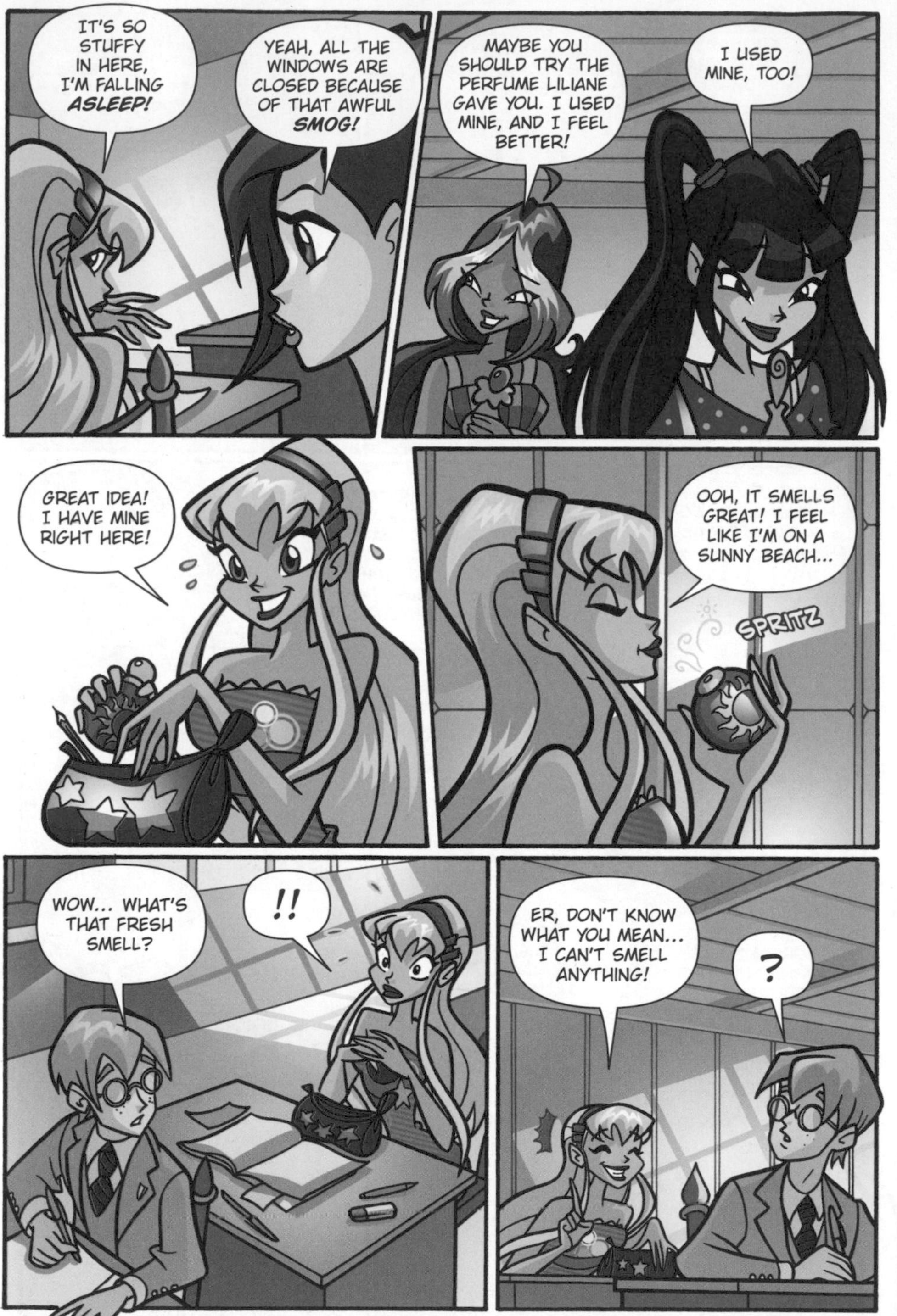
IT'S SO STUFFY IN HERE, I'M FALLING ASLEEP!
YEAH, ALL THE WINDOWS ARE CLOSED BECAUSE OF THAT AWFUL SMOG!
MAYBE YOU SHOULD TRY THE PERFUME LILIANE GAVE YOU. I USED MINE, AND I FEEL BETTER!
I USED MINE, TOO!
GREAT IDEA! I HAVE MINE RIGHT HERE!
OOH, IT SMELLS GREAT! I FEEL LIKE I'M ON A SUNNY BEACH...
SPRITZ
WOW... WHAT'S THAT FRESH SMELL?
!!
ER, DON'T KNOW WHAT YOU MEAN... I CAN'T SMELL ANYTHING!
?

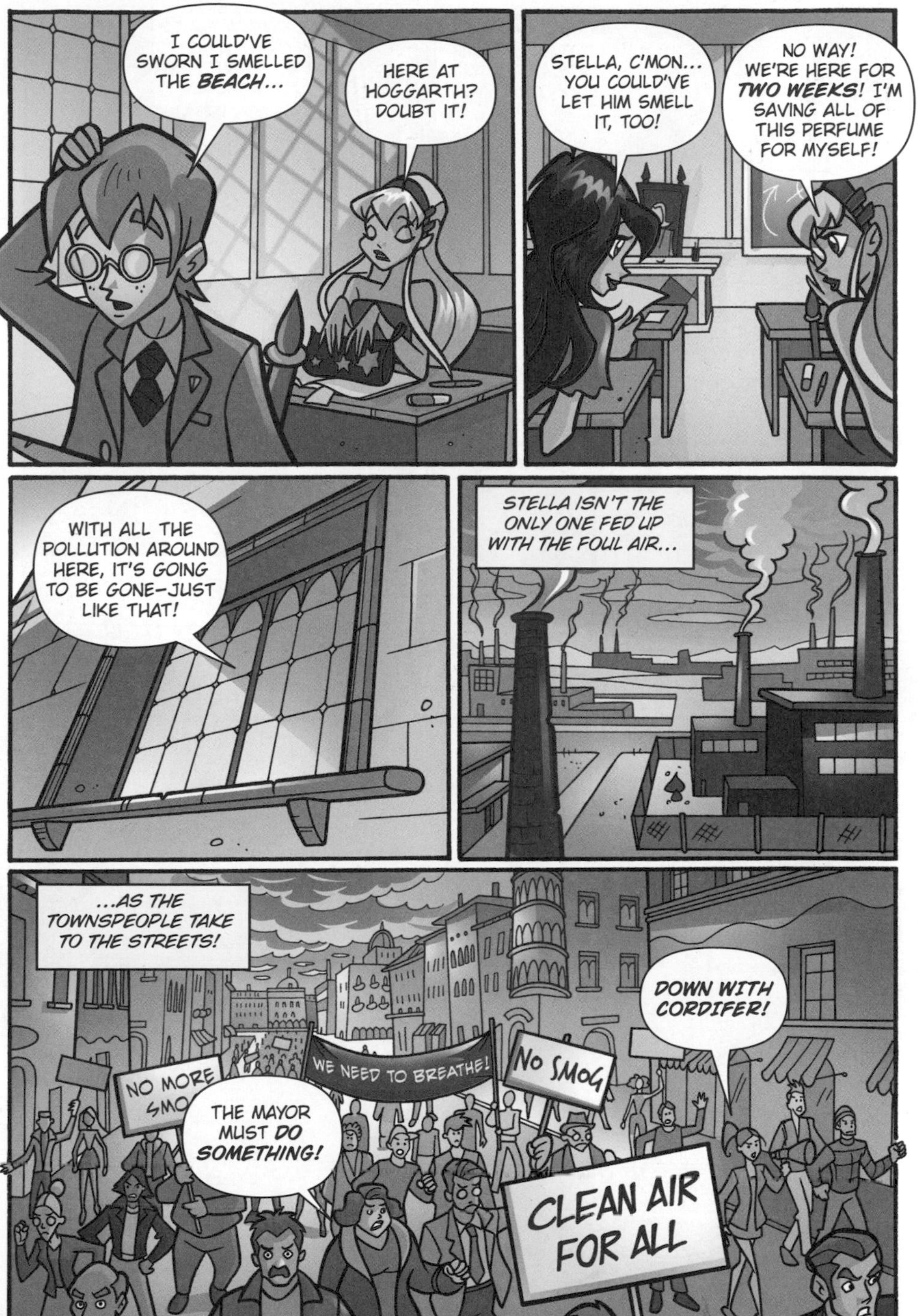
I COULD'VE SWORN I SMELLED THE BEACH...
HERE AT HOGGARTH? DOUBT IT!
STELLA, C'MON... YOU COULD'VE LET HIM SMELL IT, TOO!
NO WAY! WE'RE HERE FOR TWO WEEKS! I'M SAVING ALL OF THIS PERFUME FOR MYSELF!
WITH ALL THE POLLUTION AROUND HERE, IT'S GOING TO BE GONE—JUST LIKE THAT!
STELLA ISN'T THE ONLY ONE FED UP WITH THE FOUL AIR...
...AS THE TOWNSPEOPLE TAKE TO THE STREETS!
DOWN WITH CORDIFER!
WE NEED TO BREATHE!
NO SMOG
NO MORE SMO
THE MAYOR MUST DO SOMETHING!
CLEAN AIR FOR ALL

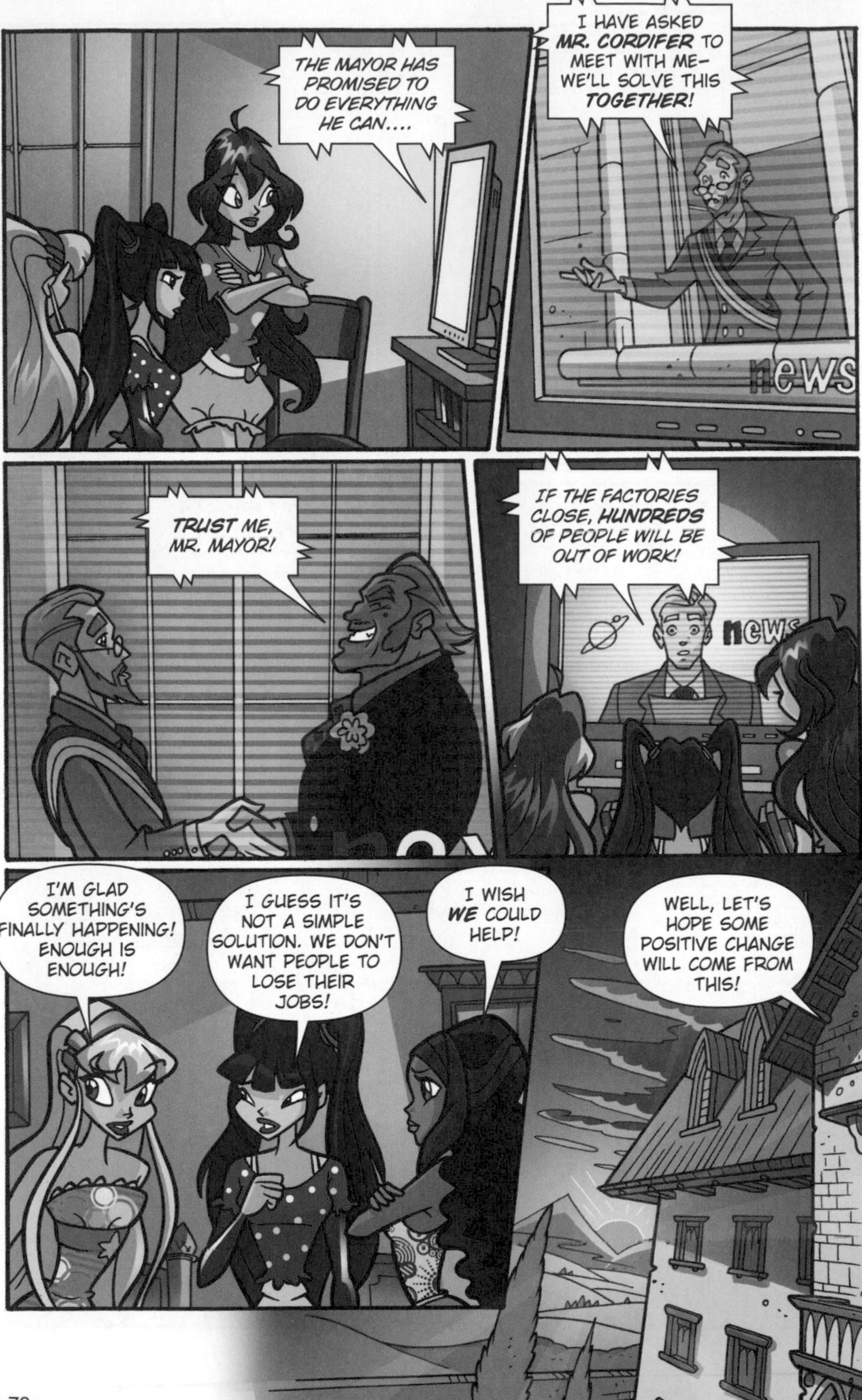
THE MAYOR HAS PROMISED TO DO EVERYTHING HE CAN....
I HAVE ASKED MR. CORDIFER TO MEET WITH ME–WE'LL SOLVE THIS TOGETHER!
news
TRUST ME, MR. MAYOR!
IF THE FACTORIES CLOSE, HUNDREDS OF PEOPLE WILL BE OUT OF WORK!
news
I'M GLAD SOMETHING'S FINALLY HAPPENING! ENOUGH IS ENOUGH!
I GUESS IT'S NOT A SIMPLE SOLUTION. WE DON'T WANT PEOPLE TO LOSE THEIR JOBS!
I WISH WE COULD HELP!
WELL, LET'S HOPE SOME POSITIVE CHANGE WILL COME FROM THIS!

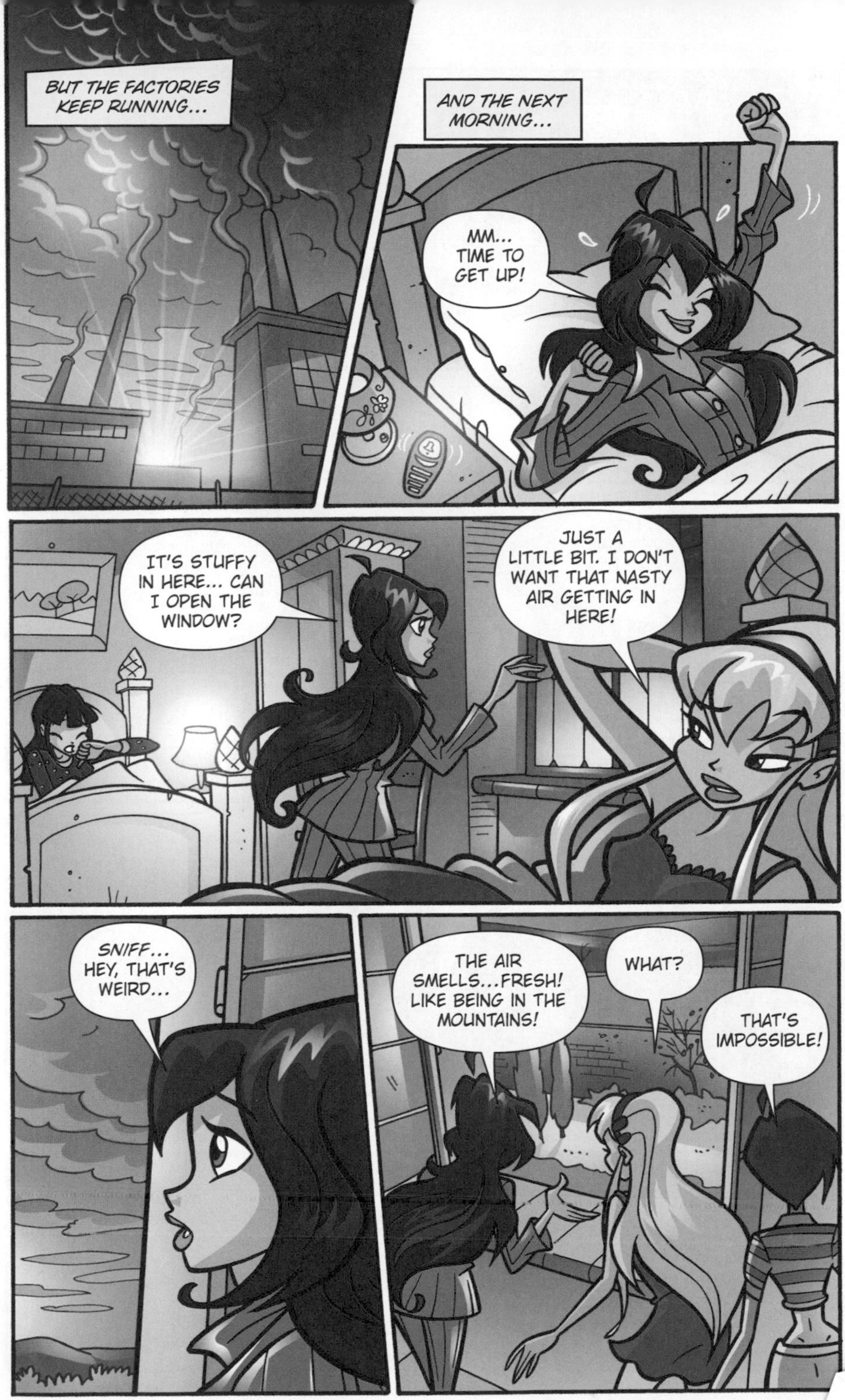
BUT THE FACTORIES KEEP RUNNING...
AND THE NEXT MORNING...
MM... TIME TO GET UP!
IT'S STUFFY IN HERE... CAN I OPEN THE WINDOW?
JUST A LITTLE BIT. I DON'T WANT THAT NASTY AIR GETTING IN HERE!
SNIFF... HEY, THAT'S WEIRD...
THE AIR SMELLS...FRESH! LIKE BEING IN THE MOUNTAINS!
WHAT?
THAT'S IMPOSSIBLE!

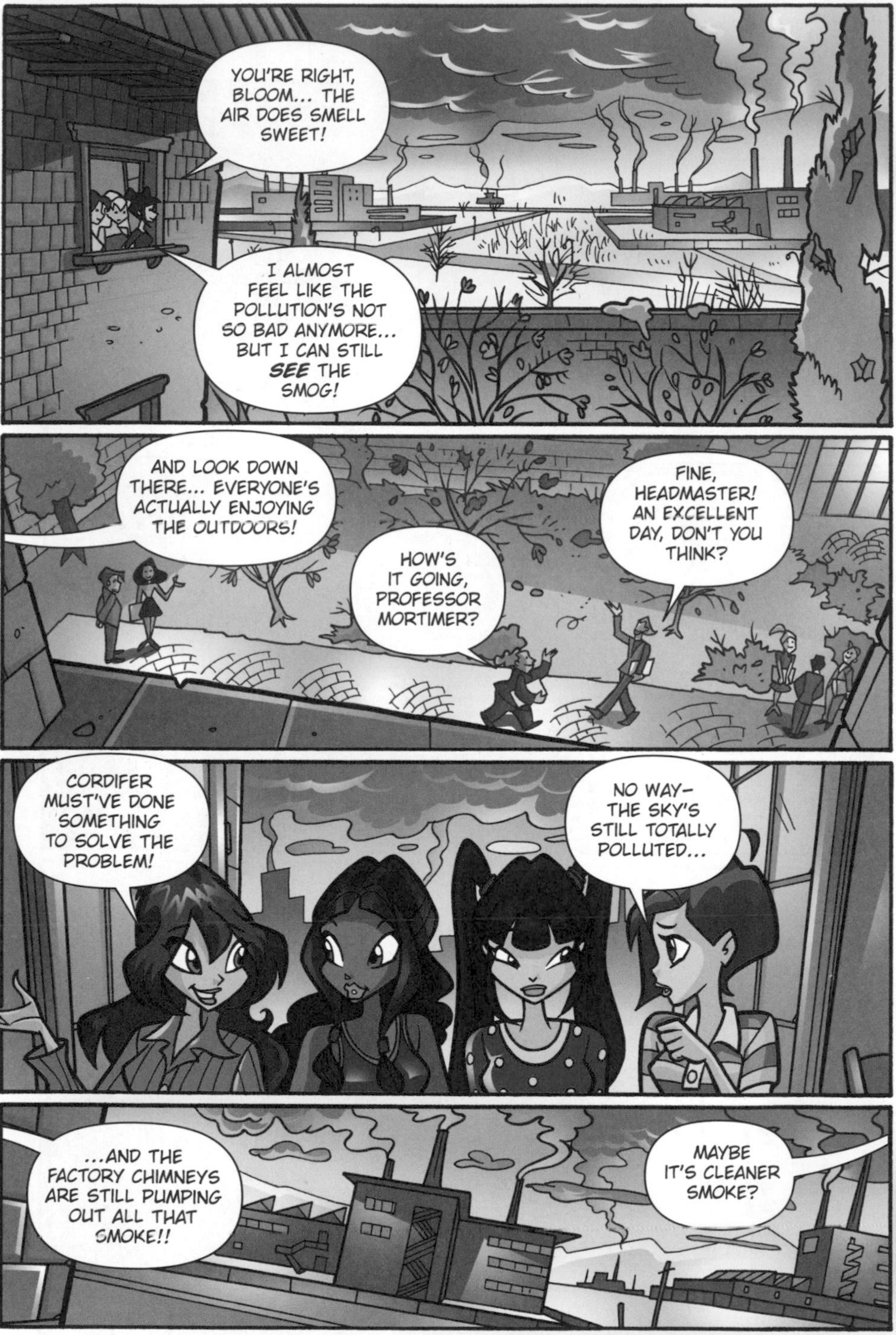
YOU'RE RIGHT, BLOOM... THE AIR DOES SMELL SWEET!
I ALMOST FEEL LIKE THE POLLUTION'S NOT SO BAD ANYMORE... BUT I CAN STILL SEE THE SMOG!
AND LOOK DOWN THERE... EVERYONE'S ACTUALLY ENJOYING THE OUTDOORS!
HOW'S IT GOING, PROFESSOR MORTIMER?
FINE, HEADMASTER! AN EXCELLENT DAY, DON'T YOU THINK?
CORDIFER MUST'VE DONE SOMETHING TO SOLVE THE PROBLEM!
NO WAY— THE SKY'S STILL TOTALLY POLLUTED...
...AND THE FACTORY CHIMNEYS ARE STILL PUMPING OUT ALL THAT SMOKE!!
MAYBE IT'S CLEANER SMOKE?

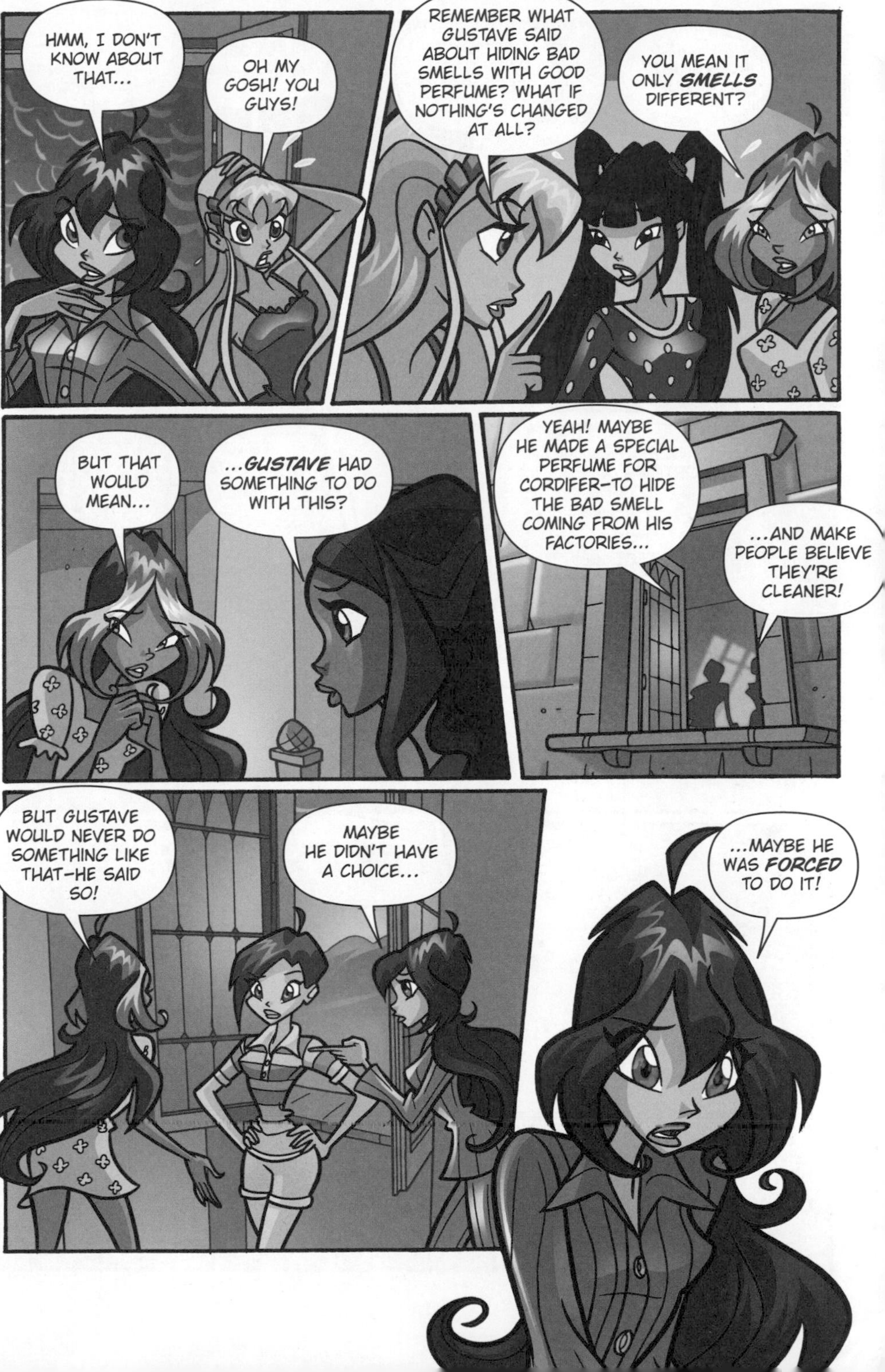
HMM, I DON'T KNOW ABOUT THAT...
OH MY GOSH! YOU GUYS!
REMEMBER WHAT GUSTAVE SAID ABOUT HIDING BAD SMELLS WITH GOOD PERFUME? WHAT IF NOTHING'S CHANGED AT ALL?
YOU MEAN IT ONLY ***SMELLS*** DIFFERENT?
BUT THAT WOULD MEAN...
...***GUSTAVE*** HAD SOMETHING TO DO WITH THIS?
YEAH! MAYBE HE MADE A SPECIAL PERFUME FOR CORDIFER—TO HIDE THE BAD SMELL COMING FROM HIS FACTORIES...
...AND MAKE PEOPLE BELIEVE THEY'RE CLEANER!
BUT GUSTAVE WOULD NEVER DO SOMETHING LIKE THAT—HE SAID SO!
MAYBE HE DIDN'T HAVE A CHOICE...
...MAYBE HE WAS ***FORCED*** TO DO IT!

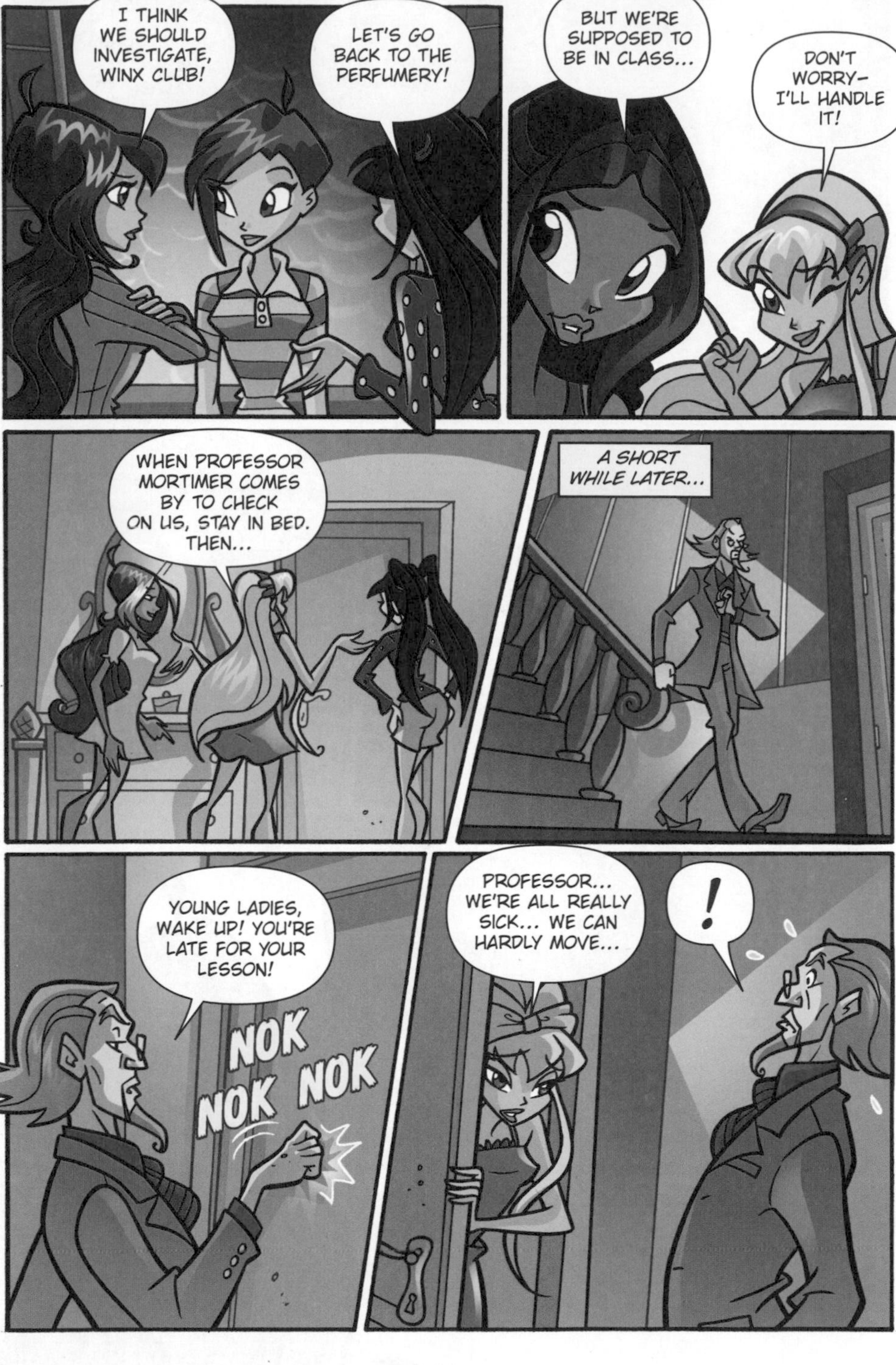
I THINK WE SHOULD INVESTIGATE, WINX CLUB!
LET'S GO BACK TO THE PERFUMERY!
BUT WE'RE SUPPOSED TO BE IN CLASS...
DON'T WORRY— I'LL HANDLE IT!
WHEN PROFESSOR MORTIMER COMES BY TO CHECK ON US, STAY IN BED. THEN...
A SHORT WHILE LATER...
YOUNG LADIES, WAKE UP! YOU'RE LATE FOR YOUR LESSON!
NOK NOK NOK
PROFESSOR... WE'RE ALL REALLY SICK... WE CAN HARDLY MOVE...
!

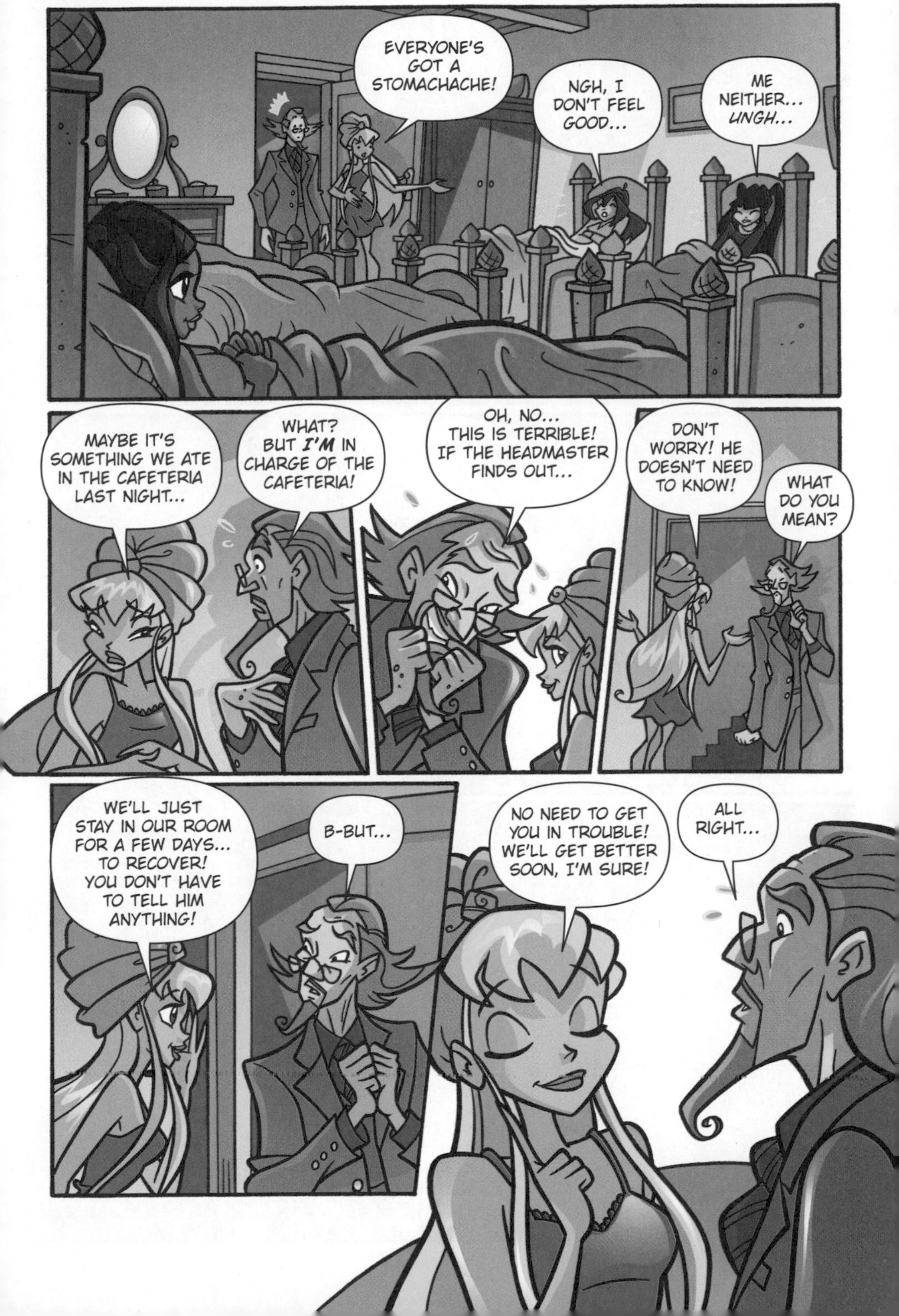
EVERYONE'S GOT A STOMACHACHE!
NGH, I DON'T FEEL GOOD...
ME NEITHER... *UNGH...*
MAYBE IT'S SOMETHING WE ATE IN THE CAFETERIA LAST NIGHT...
WHAT? BUT ***I'M*** IN CHARGE OF THE CAFETERIA!
OH, NO... THIS IS TERRIBLE! IF THE HEADMASTER FINDS OUT...
DON'T WORRY! HE DOESN'T NEED TO KNOW!
WHAT DO YOU MEAN?
WE'LL JUST STAY IN OUR ROOM FOR A FEW DAYS... TO RECOVER! YOU DON'T HAVE TO TELL HIM ANYTHING!
B-BUT...
NO NEED TO GET YOU IN TROUBLE! WE'LL GET BETTER SOON, I'M SURE!
ALL RIGHT...

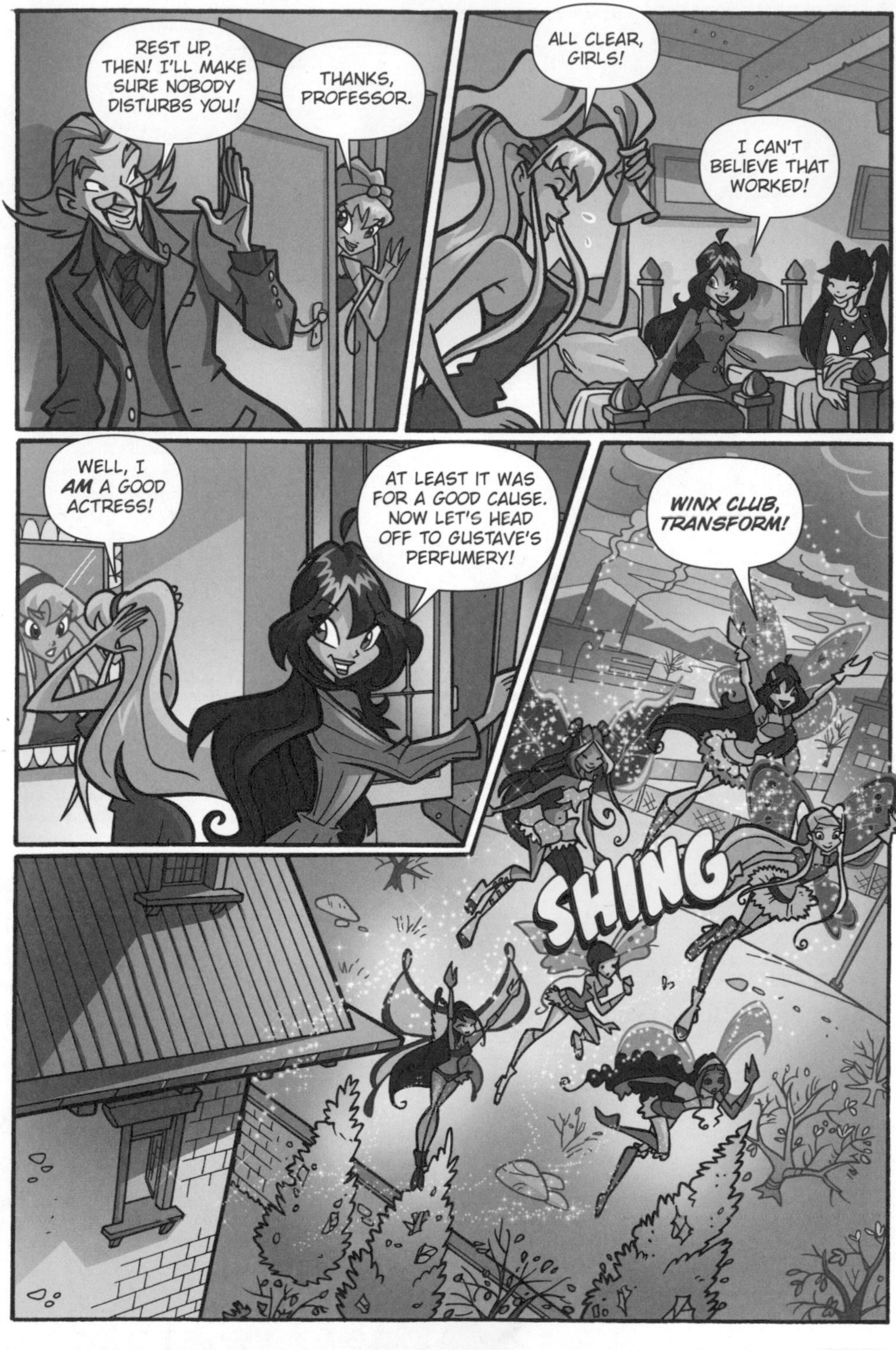
REST UP, THEN! I'LL MAKE SURE NOBODY DISTURBS YOU!
THANKS, PROFESSOR.
ALL CLEAR, GIRLS!
I CAN'T BELIEVE THAT WORKED!
WELL, I AM A GOOD ACTRESS!
AT LEAST IT WAS FOR A GOOD CAUSE. NOW LET'S HEAD OFF TO GUSTAVE'S PERFUMERY!
WINX CLUB, TRANSFORM!
SHING

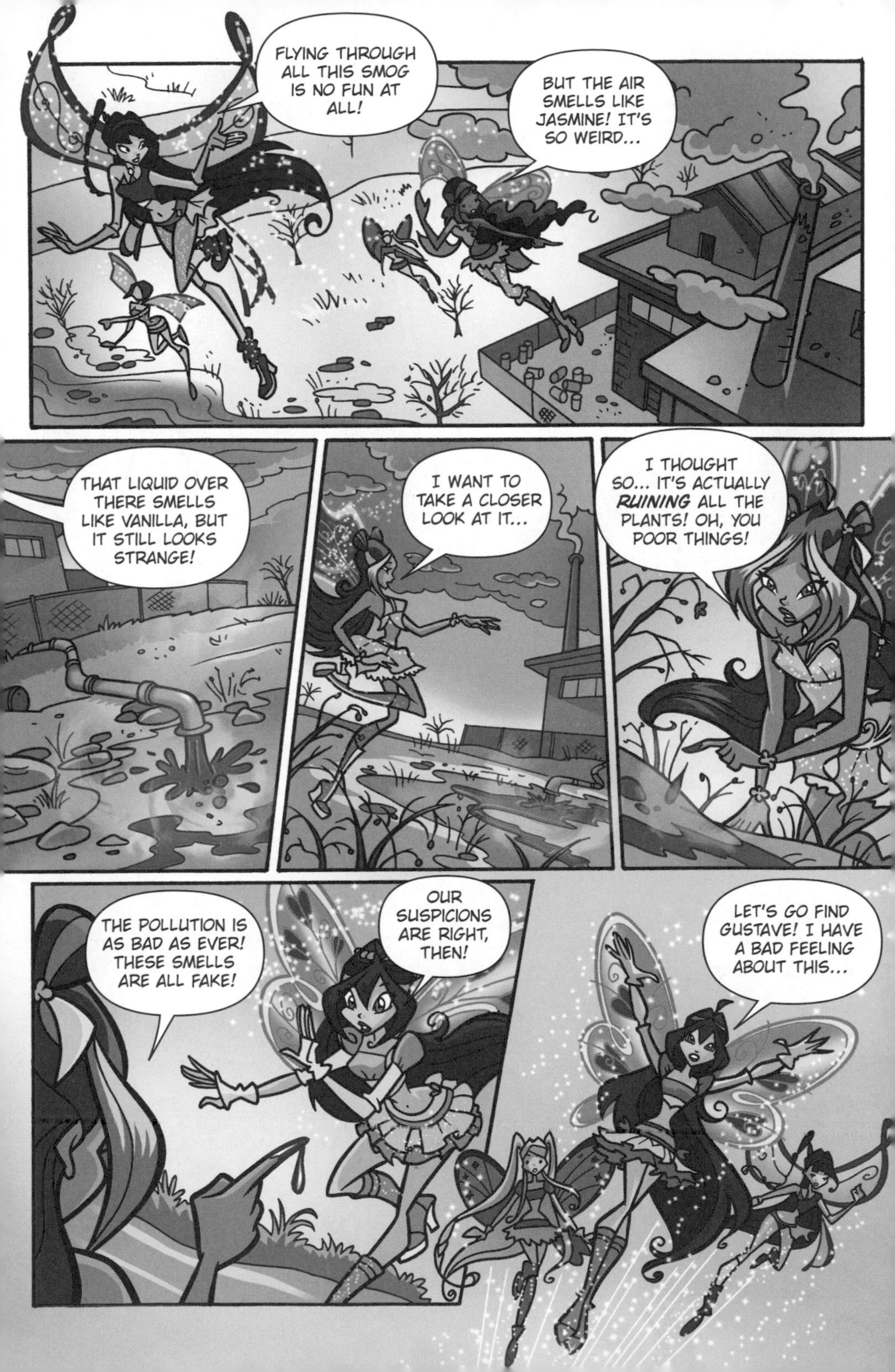
FLYING THROUGH ALL THIS SMOG IS NO FUN AT ALL!
BUT THE AIR SMELLS LIKE JASMINE! IT'S SO WEIRD...
THAT LIQUID OVER THERE SMELLS LIKE VANILLA, BUT IT STILL LOOKS STRANGE!
I WANT TO TAKE A CLOSER LOOK AT IT...
I THOUGHT SO... IT'S ACTUALLY RUINING ALL THE PLANTS! OH, YOU POOR THINGS!
THE POLLUTION IS AS BAD AS EVER! THESE SMELLS ARE ALL FAKE!
OUR SUSPICIONS ARE RIGHT, THEN!
LET'S GO FIND GUSTAVE! I HAVE A BAD FEELING ABOUT THIS...

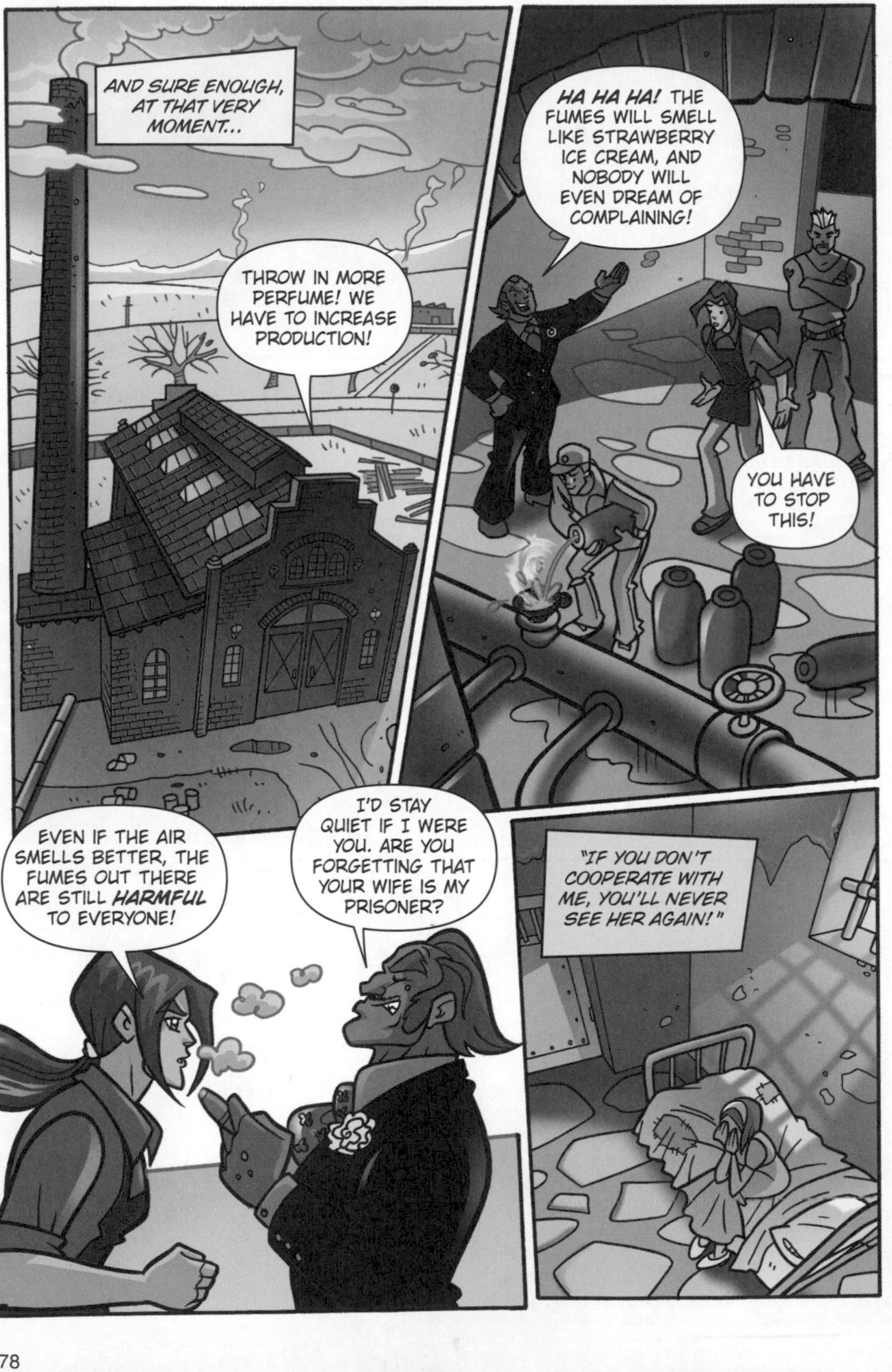
AND SURE ENOUGH, AT THAT VERY MOMENT...
THROW IN MORE PERFUME! WE HAVE TO INCREASE PRODUCTION!
HA HA HA! THE FUMES WILL SMELL LIKE STRAWBERRY ICE CREAM, AND NOBODY WILL EVEN DREAM OF COMPLAINING!
YOU HAVE TO STOP THIS!
EVEN IF THE AIR SMELLS BETTER, THE FUMES OUT THERE ARE STILL HARMFUL TO EVERYONE!
I'D STAY QUIET IF I WERE YOU. ARE YOU FORGETTING THAT YOUR WIFE IS MY PRISONER?
"IF YOU DON'T COOPERATE WITH ME, YOU'LL NEVER SEE HER AGAIN!"

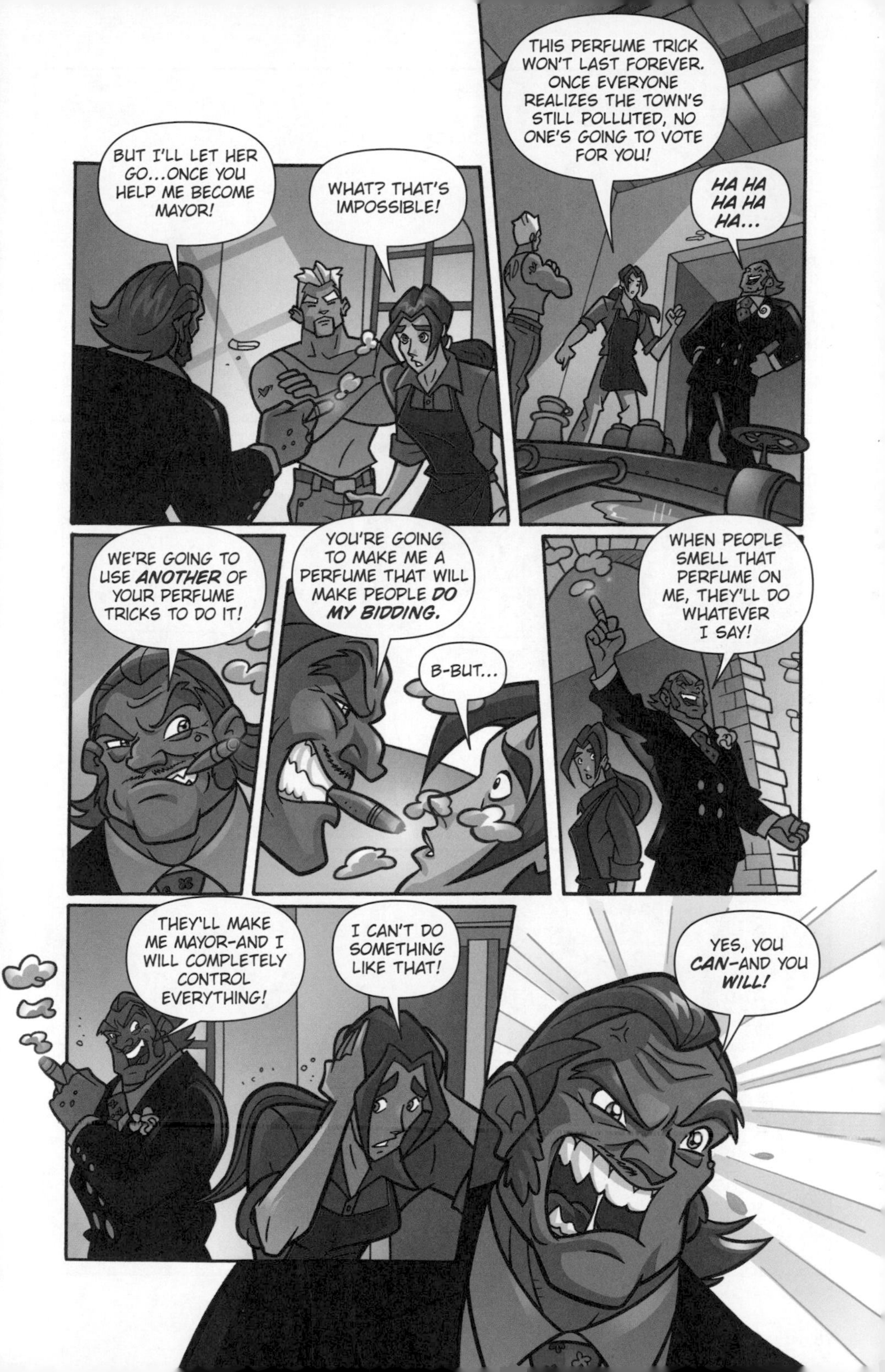
BUT I'LL LET HER GO...ONCE YOU HELP ME BECOME MAYOR!
WHAT? THAT'S IMPOSSIBLE!
THIS PERFUME TRICK WON'T LAST FOREVER. ONCE EVERYONE REALIZES THE TOWN'S STILL POLLUTED, NO ONE'S GOING TO VOTE FOR YOU!
HA HA HA HA HA...
WE'RE GOING TO USE ANOTHER OF YOUR PERFUME TRICKS TO DO IT!
YOU'RE GOING TO MAKE ME A PERFUME THAT WILL MAKE PEOPLE DO MY BIDDING.
B-BUT...
WHEN PEOPLE SMELL THAT PERFUME ON ME, THEY'LL DO WHATEVER I SAY!
THEY'LL MAKE ME MAYOR-AND I WILL COMPLETELY CONTROL EVERYTHING!
I CAN'T DO SOMETHING LIKE THAT!
YES, YOU CAN-AND YOU WILL!

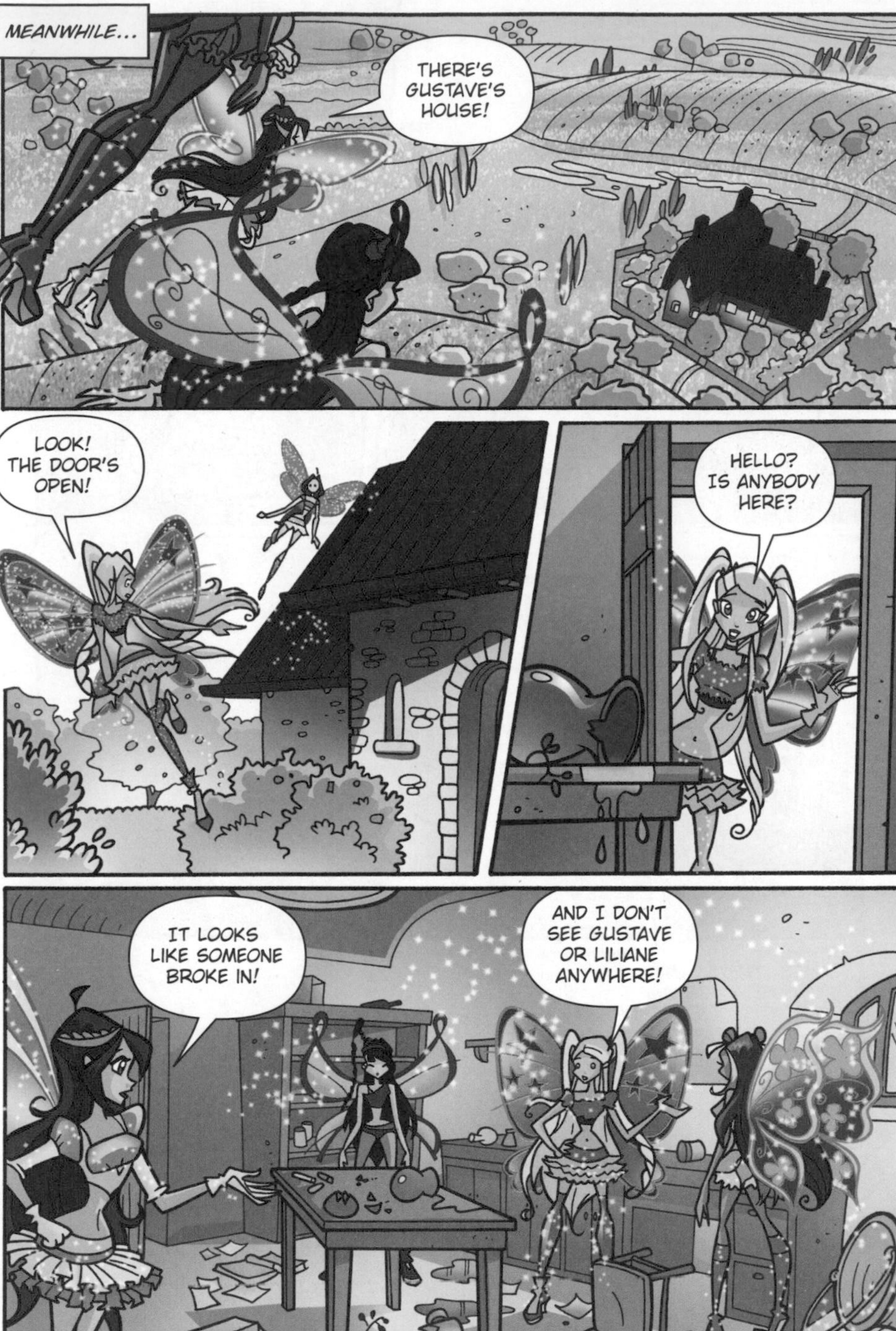
MEANWHILE...
THERE'S GUSTAVE'S HOUSE!
LOOK! THE DOOR'S OPEN!
HELLO? IS ANYBODY HERE?
IT LOOKS LIKE SOMEONE BROKE IN!
AND I DON'T SEE GUSTAVE OR LILIANE ANYWHERE!

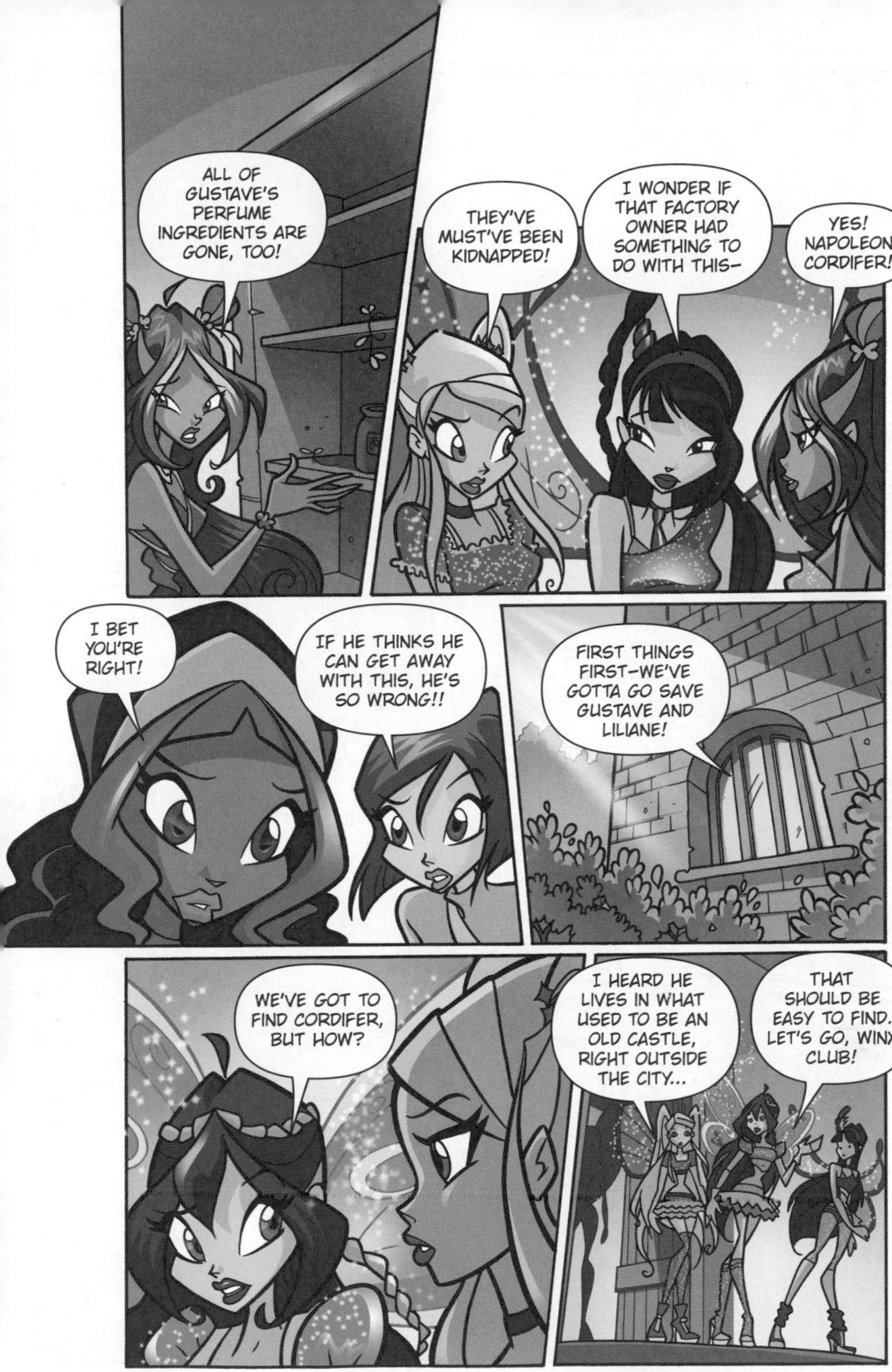
ALL OF GUSTAVE'S PERFUME INGREDIENTS ARE GONE, TOO!
THEY'VE MUST'VE BEEN KIDNAPPED!
I WONDER IF THAT FACTORY OWNER HAD SOMETHING TO DO WITH THIS-
YES! NAPOLEON CORDIFER!
I BET YOU'RE RIGHT!
IF HE THINKS HE CAN GET AWAY WITH THIS, HE'S SO WRONG!!
FIRST THINGS FIRST-WE'VE GOTTA GO SAVE GUSTAVE AND LILIANE!
WE'VE GOT TO FIND CORDIFER, BUT HOW?
I HEARD HE LIVES IN WHAT USED TO BE AN OLD CASTLE, RIGHT OUTSIDE THE CITY...
THAT SHOULD BE EASY TO FIND. LET'S GO, WINX CLUB!

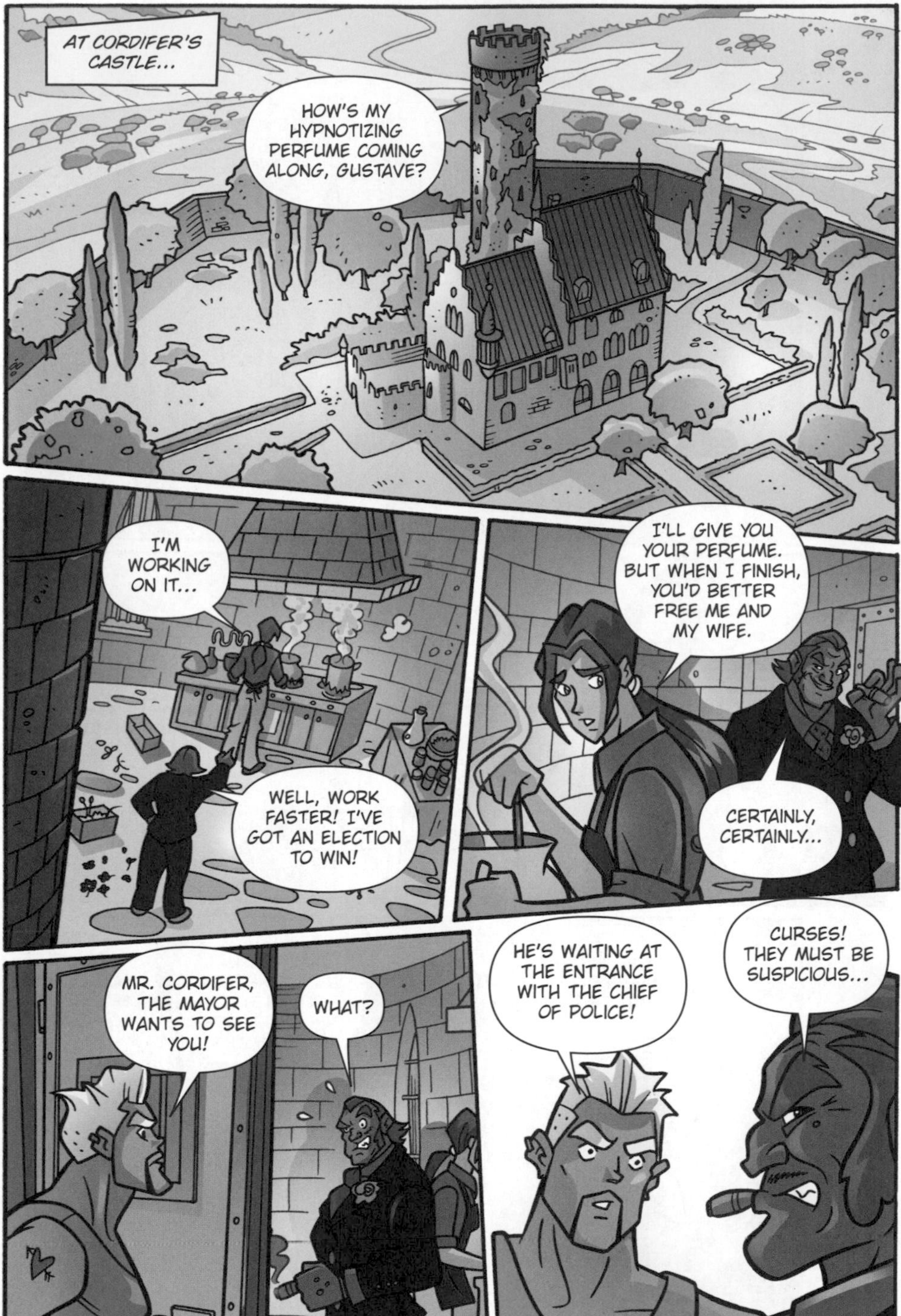
AT CORDIFER'S CASTLE...
HOW'S MY HYPNOTIZING PERFUME COMING ALONG, GUSTAVE?
I'M WORKING ON IT...
WELL, WORK FASTER! I'VE GOT AN ELECTION TO WIN!
I'LL GIVE YOU YOUR PERFUME. BUT WHEN I FINISH, YOU'D BETTER FREE ME AND MY WIFE.
CERTAINLY, CERTAINLY...
MR. CORDIFER, THE MAYOR WANTS TO SEE YOU!
WHAT?
HE'S WAITING AT THE ENTRANCE WITH THE CHIEF OF POLICE!
CURSES! THEY MUST BE SUSPICIOUS...

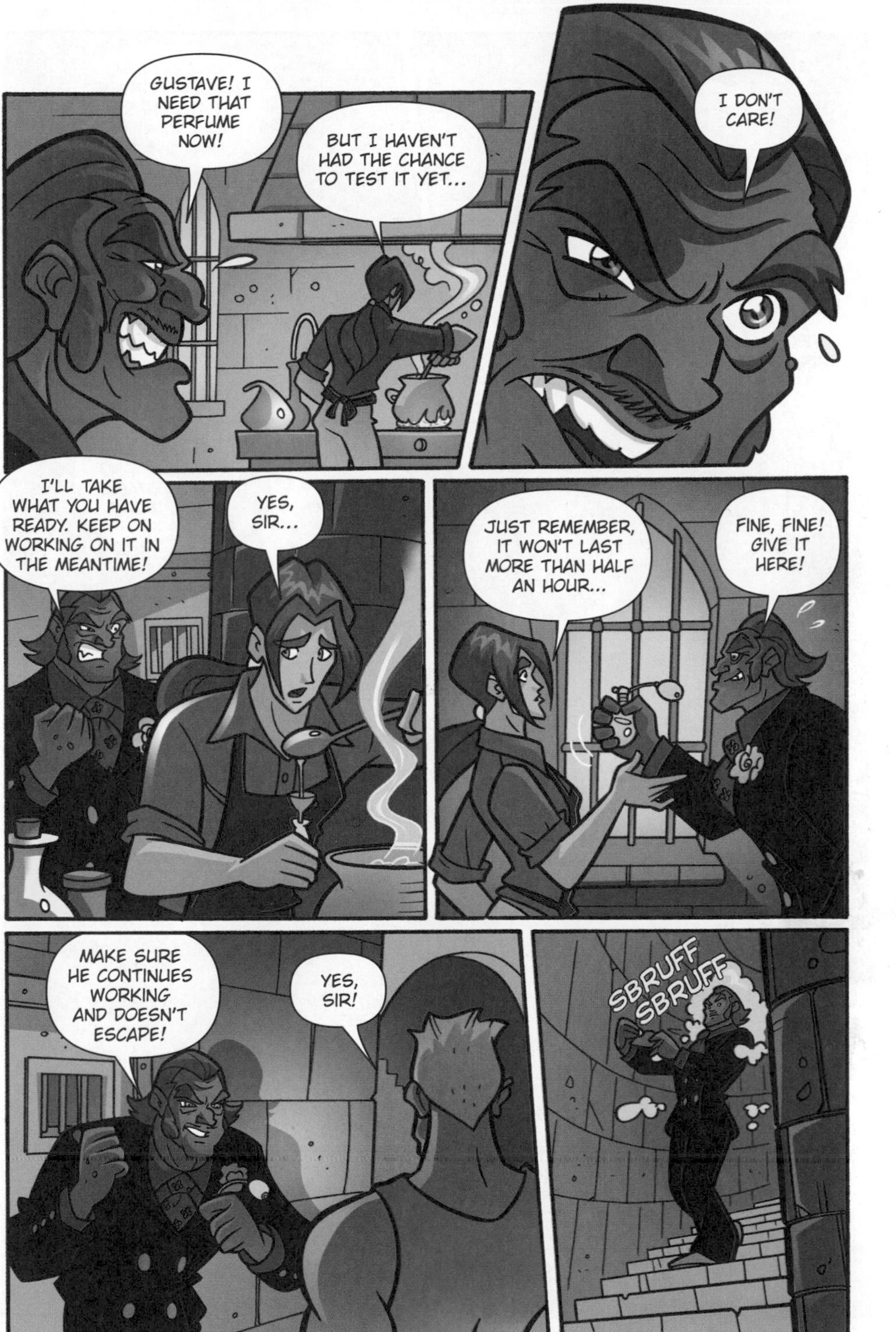
GUSTAVE! I NEED THAT PERFUME NOW!
BUT I HAVEN'T HAD THE CHANCE TO TEST IT YET...
I DON'T CARE!
I'LL TAKE WHAT YOU HAVE READY. KEEP ON WORKING ON IT IN THE MEANTIME!
YES, SIR...
JUST REMEMBER, IT WON'T LAST MORE THAN HALF AN HOUR...
FINE, FINE! GIVE IT HERE!
MAKE SURE HE CONTINUES WORKING AND DOESN'T ESCAPE!
YES, SIR!
SBRUFF SBRUFF

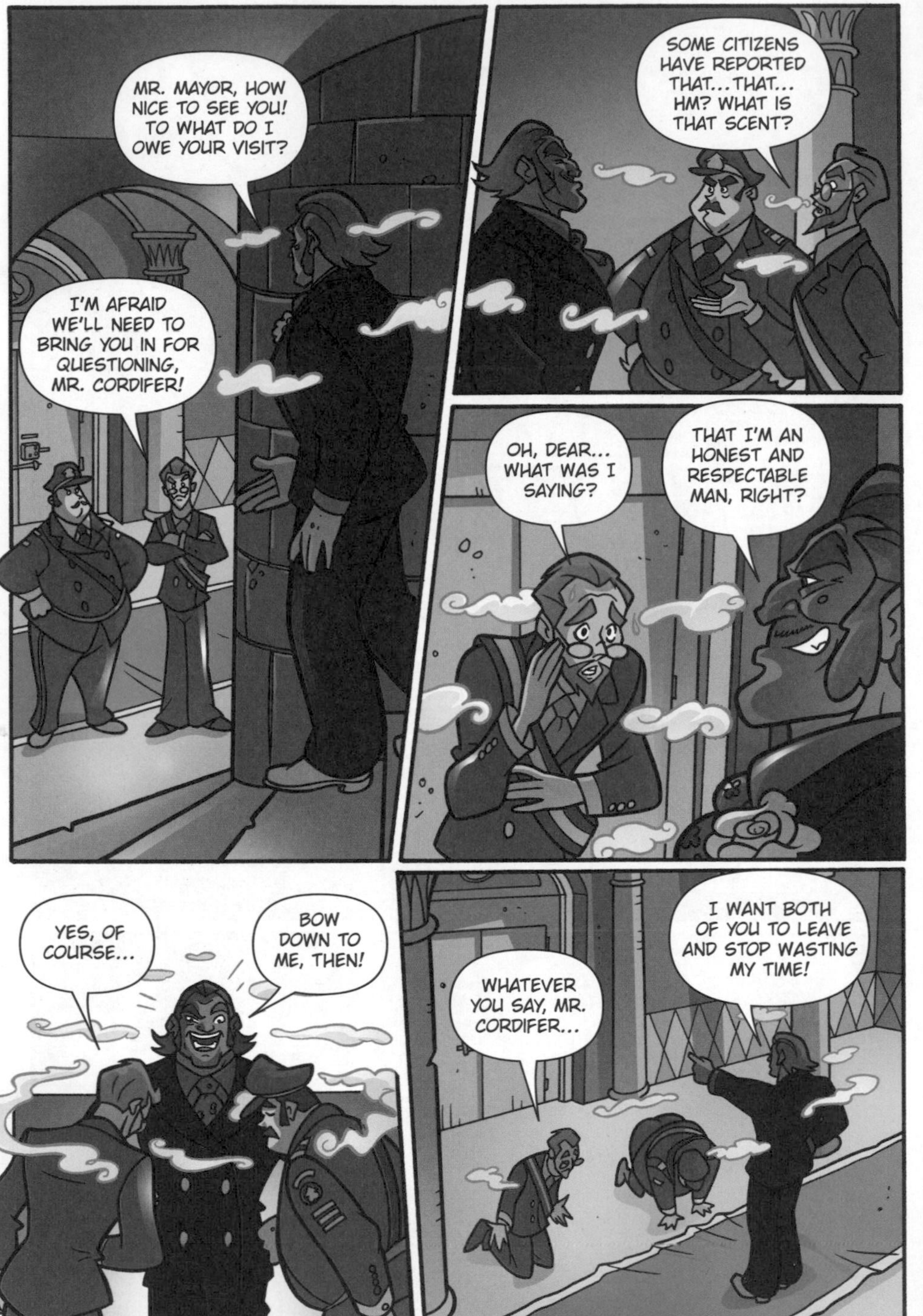
MR. MAYOR, HOW NICE TO SEE YOU! TO WHAT DO I OWE YOUR VISIT?
I'M AFRAID WE'LL NEED TO BRING YOU IN FOR QUESTIONING, MR. CORDIFER!
SOME CITIZENS HAVE REPORTED THAT...THAT... HM? WHAT IS THAT SCENT?
OH, DEAR... WHAT WAS I SAYING?
THAT I'M AN HONEST AND RESPECTABLE MAN, RIGHT?
YES, OF COURSE...
BOW DOWN TO ME, THEN!
I WANT BOTH OF YOU TO LEAVE AND STOP WASTING MY TIME!
WHATEVER YOU SAY, MR. CORDIFER...

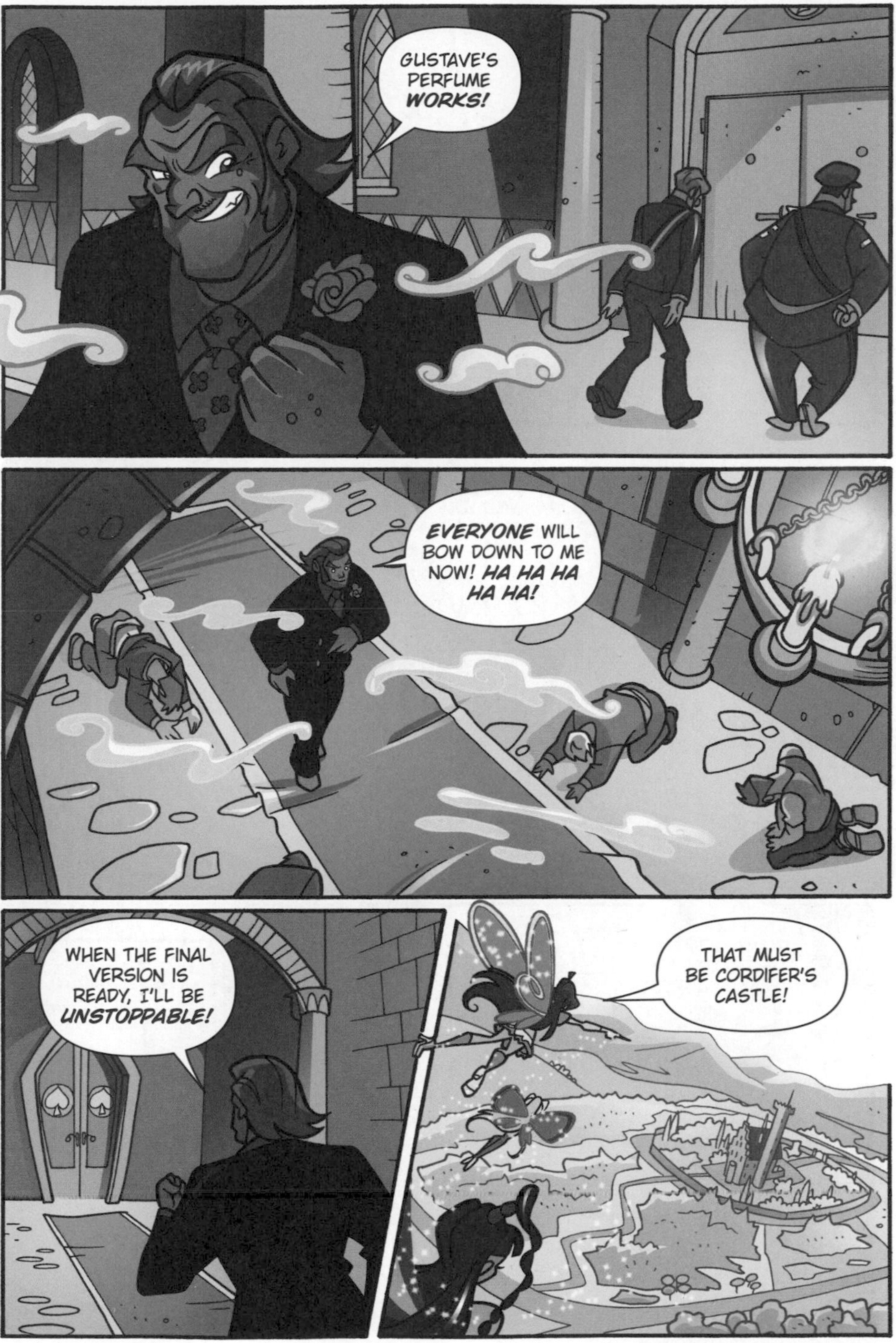
GUSTAVE'S PERFUME WORKS!
EVERYONE WILL BOW DOWN TO ME NOW! HA HA HA HA HA!
WHEN THE FINAL VERSION IS READY, I'LL BE UNSTOPPABLE!
THAT MUST BE CORDIFER'S CASTLE!

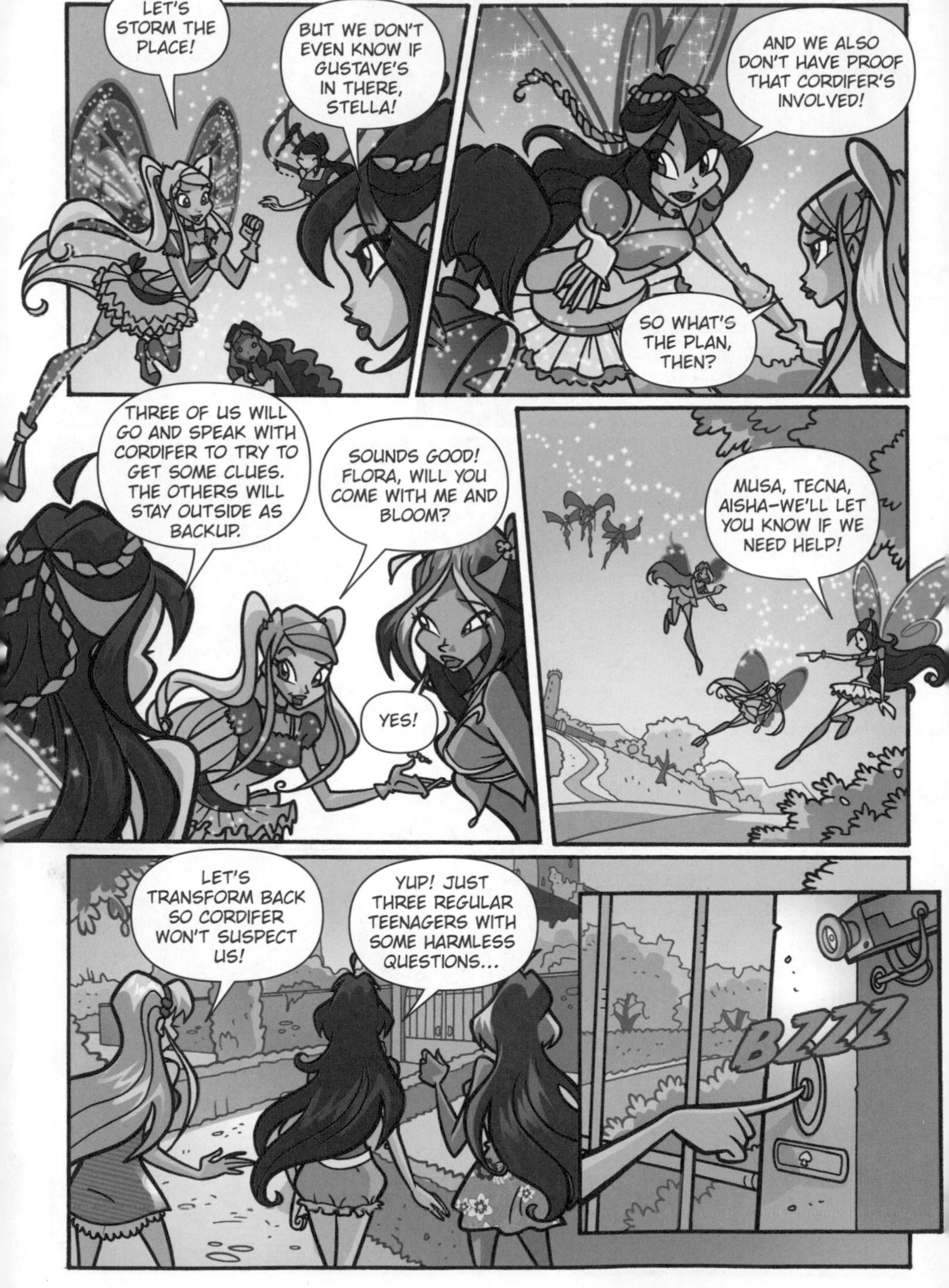
LET'S STORM THE PLACE!
BUT WE DON'T EVEN KNOW IF GUSTAVE'S IN THERE, STELLA!
AND WE ALSO DON'T HAVE PROOF THAT CORDIFER'S INVOLVED!
SO WHAT'S THE PLAN, THEN?
THREE OF US WILL GO AND SPEAK WITH CORDIFER TO TRY TO GET SOME CLUES. THE OTHERS WILL STAY OUTSIDE AS BACKUP.
SOUNDS GOOD! FLORA, WILL YOU COME WITH ME AND BLOOM?
YES!
MUSA, TECNA, AISHA—WE'LL LET YOU KNOW IF WE NEED HELP!
LET'S TRANSFORM BACK SO CORDIFER WON'T SUSPECT US!
YUP! JUST THREE REGULAR TEENAGERS WITH SOME HARMLESS QUESTIONS...
BZZZ

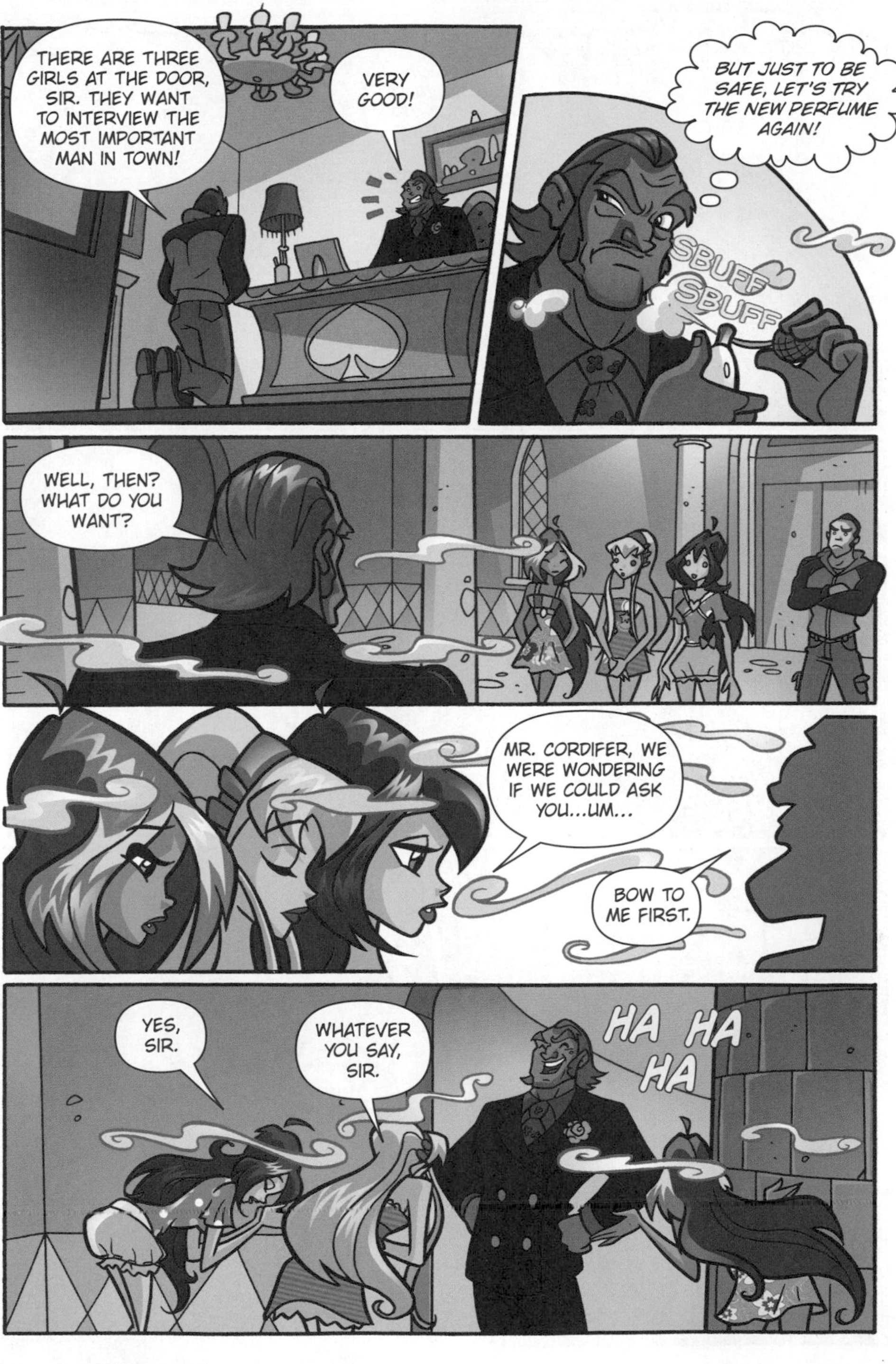
THERE ARE THREE GIRLS AT THE DOOR, SIR. THEY WANT TO INTERVIEW THE MOST IMPORTANT MAN IN TOWN!
VERY GOOD!
BUT JUST TO BE SAFE, LET'S TRY THE NEW PERFUME AGAIN!
SBUFF
SBUFF
WELL, THEN? WHAT DO YOU WANT?
MR. CORDIFER, WE WERE WONDERING IF WE COULD ASK YOU...UM...
BOW TO ME FIRST.
YES, SIR.
WHATEVER YOU SAY, SIR.
HA HA HA

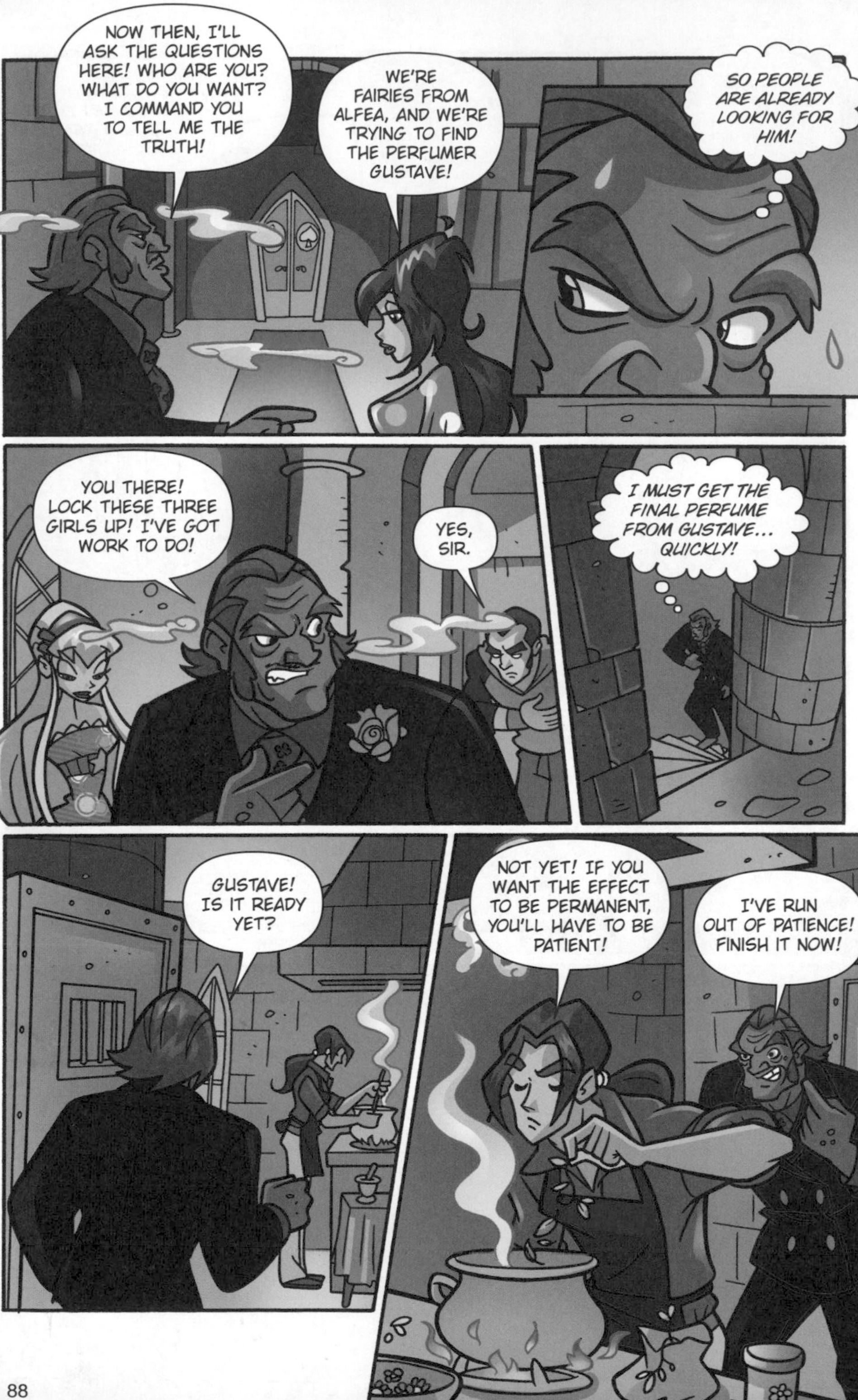
NOW THEN, I'LL ASK THE QUESTIONS HERE! WHO ARE YOU? WHAT DO YOU WANT? I COMMAND YOU TO TELL ME THE TRUTH!
WE'RE FAIRIES FROM ALFEA, AND WE'RE TRYING TO FIND THE PERFUMER GUSTAVE!
SO PEOPLE ARE ALREADY LOOKING FOR HIM!
YOU THERE! LOCK THESE THREE GIRLS UP! I'VE GOT WORK TO DO!
YES, SIR.
I MUST GET THE FINAL PERFUME FROM GUSTAVE... QUICKLY!
GUSTAVE! IS IT READY YET?
NOT YET! IF YOU WANT THE EFFECT TO BE PERMANENT, YOU'LL HAVE TO BE PATIENT!
I'VE RUN OUT OF PATIENCE! FINISH IT NOW!

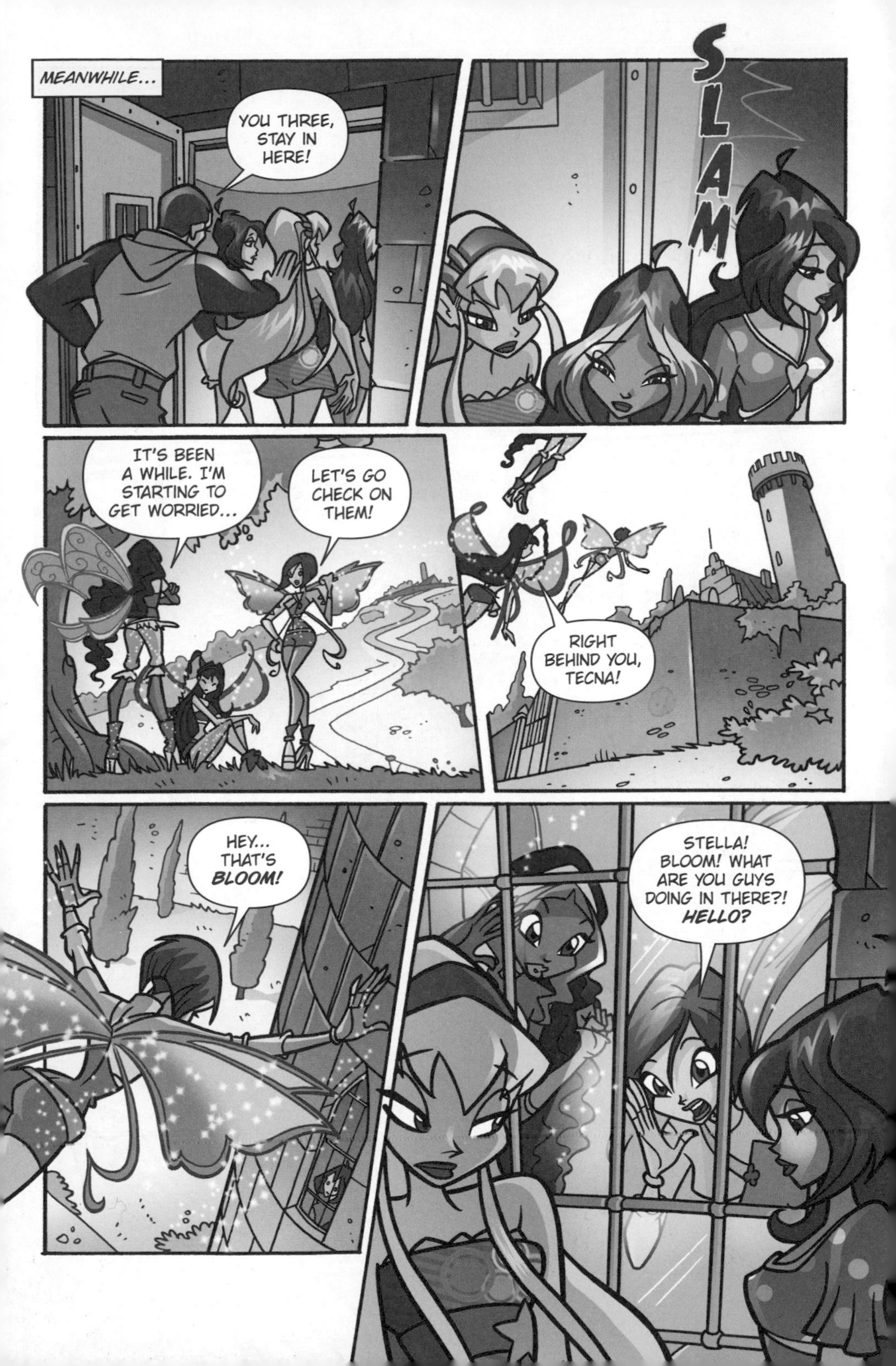
MEANWHILE...
YOU THREE, STAY IN HERE!
SLAM
IT'S BEEN A WHILE. I'M STARTING TO GET WORRIED...
LET'S GO CHECK ON THEM!
RIGHT BEHIND YOU, TECNA!
HEY... THAT'S *BLOOM!*
STELLA! BLOOM! WHAT ARE YOU GUYS DOING IN THERE?! *HELLO?*

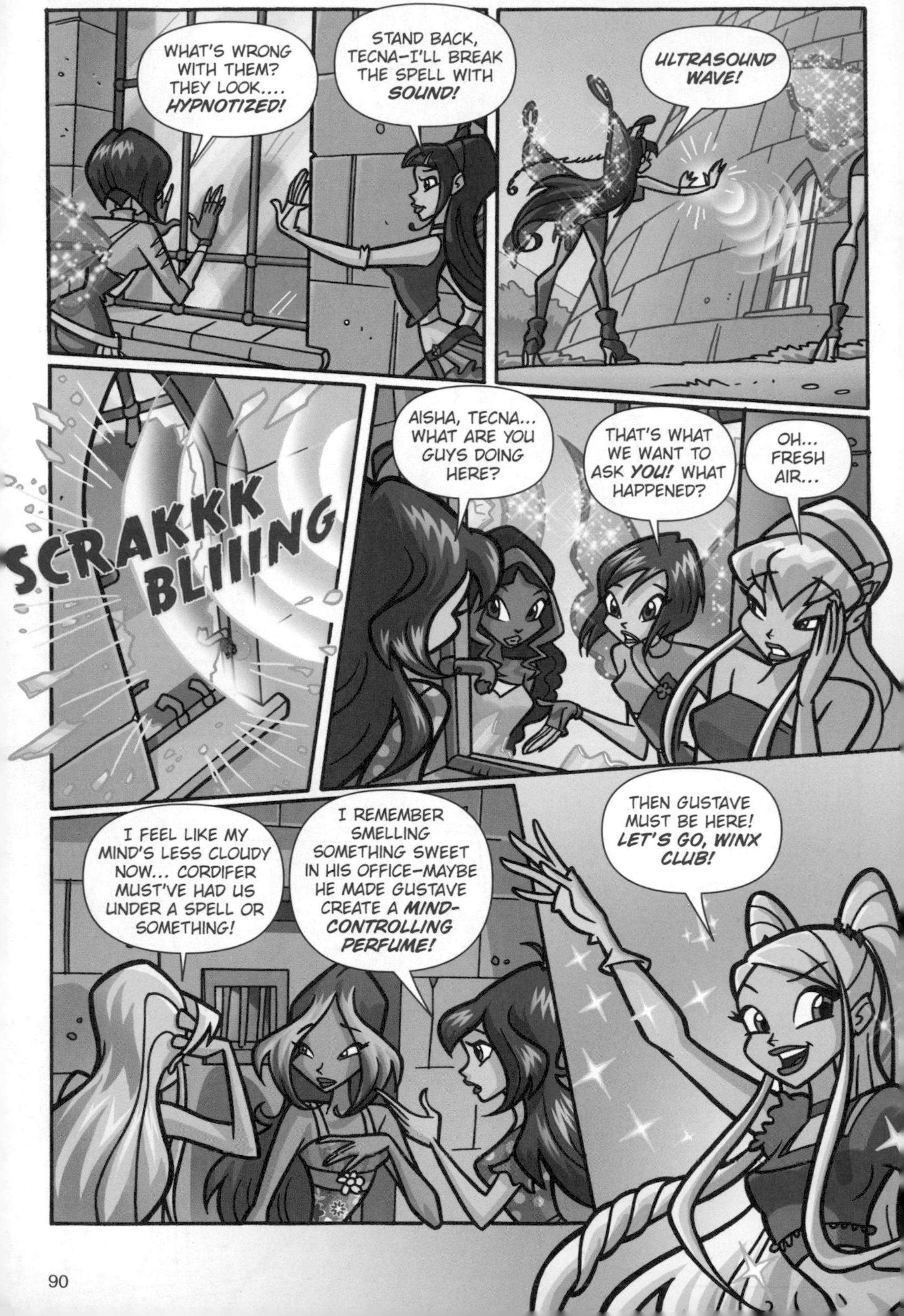
WHAT'S WRONG WITH THEM? THEY LOOK.... HYPNOTIZED!
STAND BACK, TECNA—I'LL BREAK THE SPELL WITH SOUND!
ULTRASOUND WAVE!
SCRAKKK BLIIING
AISHA, TECNA... WHAT ARE YOU GUYS DOING HERE?
THAT'S WHAT WE WANT TO ASK YOU! WHAT HAPPENED?
OH... FRESH AIR...
I FEEL LIKE MY MIND'S LESS CLOUDY NOW... CORDIFER MUST'VE HAD US UNDER A SPELL OR SOMETHING!
I REMEMBER SMELLING SOMETHING SWEET IN HIS OFFICE—MAYBE HE MADE GUSTAVE CREATE A MIND-CONTROLLING PERFUME!
THEN GUSTAVE MUST BE HERE! LET'S GO, WINX CLUB!

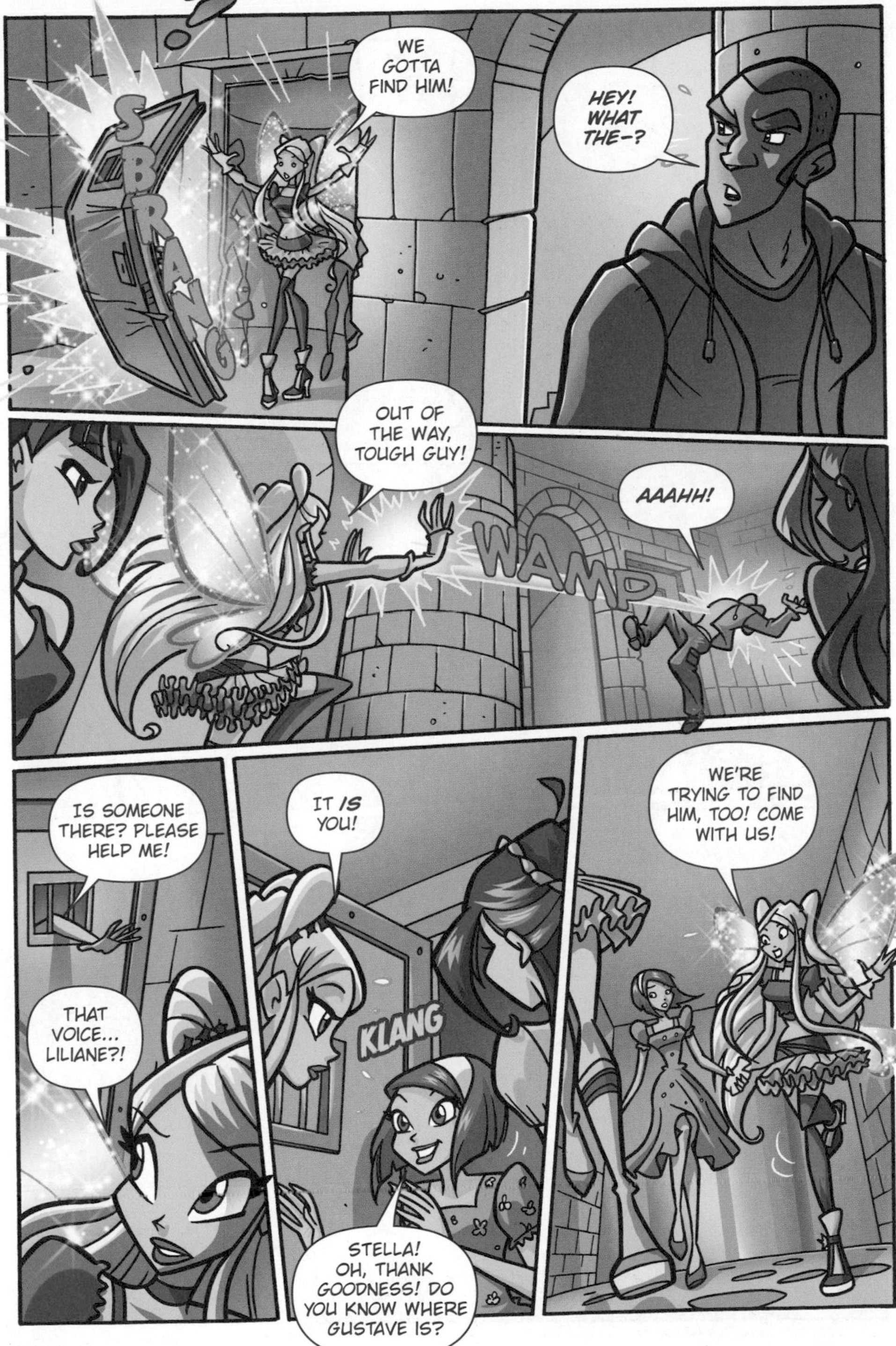
SBRANG
WE GOTTA FIND HIM!
HEY! WHAT THE–?
OUT OF THE WAY, TOUGH GUY!
WAMP
AAAHH!
IS SOMEONE THERE? PLEASE HELP ME!
THAT VOICE... LILIANE?!
IT IS YOU!
KLANG
STELLA! OH, THANK GOODNESS! DO YOU KNOW WHERE GUSTAVE IS?
WE'RE TRYING TO FIND HIM, TOO! COME WITH US!

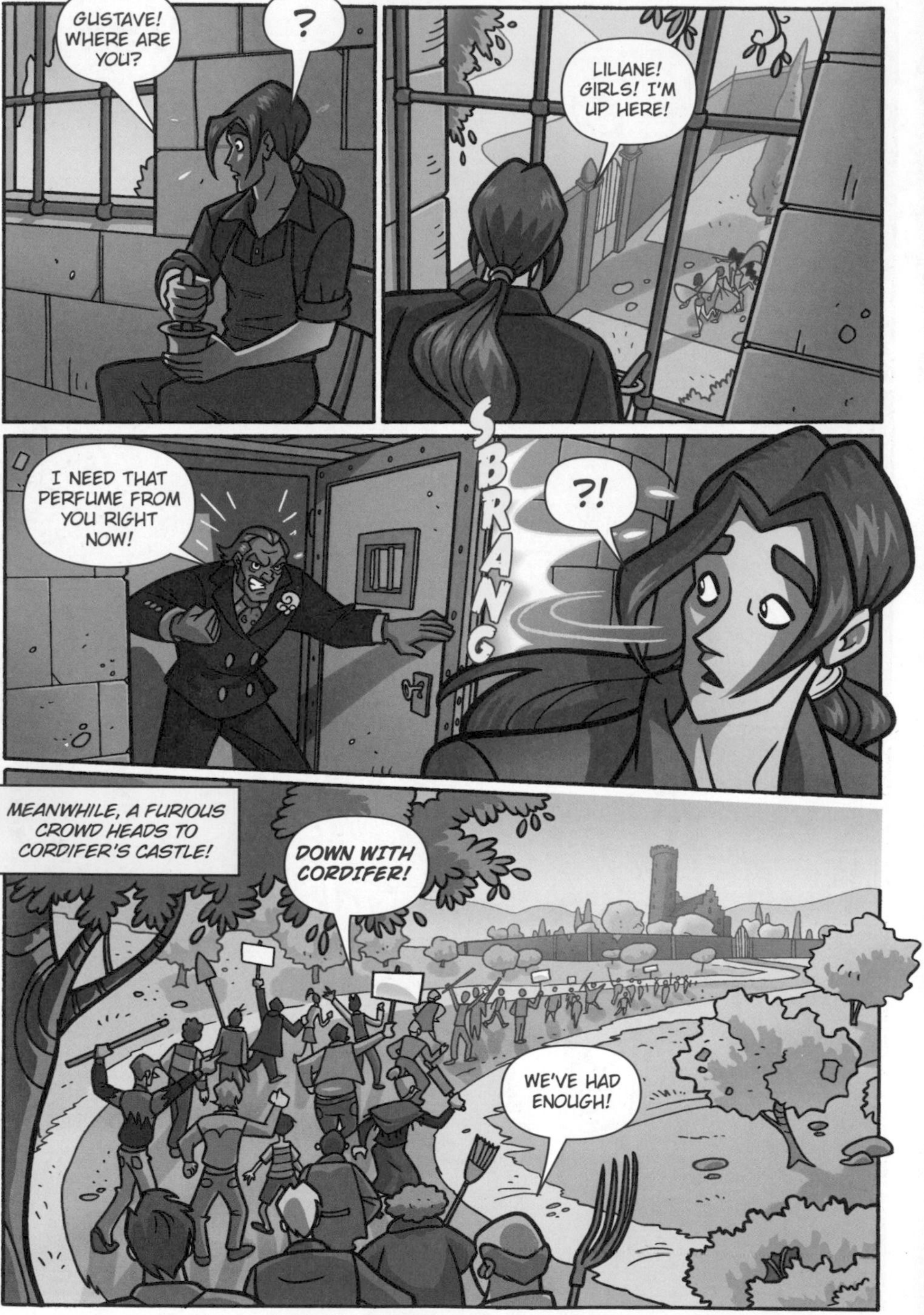
GUSTAVE! WHERE ARE YOU?
?
LILIANE! GIRLS! I'M UP HERE!
I NEED THAT PERFUME FROM YOU RIGHT NOW!
SBRANG
?!
MEANWHILE, A FURIOUS CROWD HEADS TO CORDIFER'S CASTLE!
DOWN WITH CORDIFER!
WE'VE HAD ENOUGH!

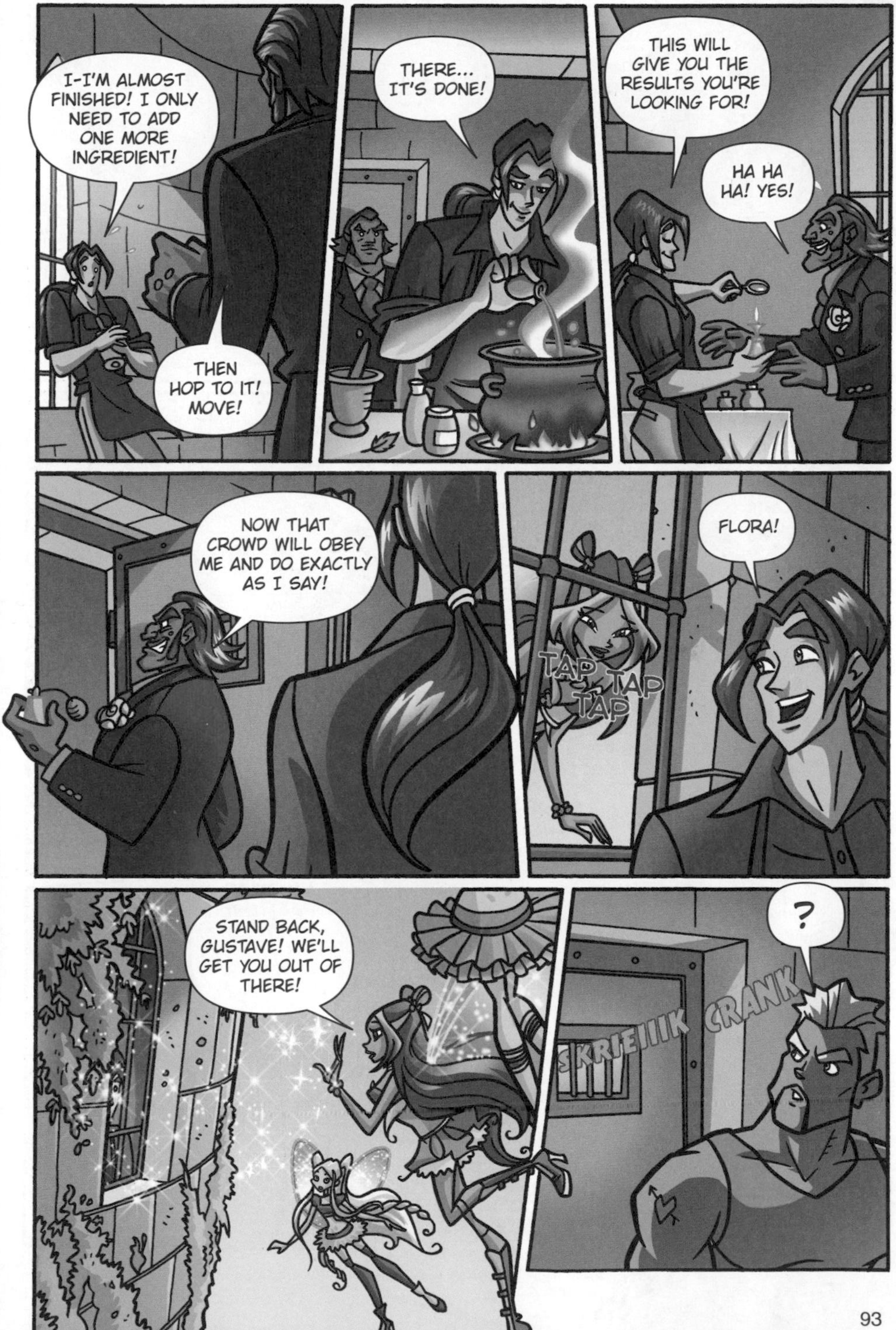
I-I'M ALMOST FINISHED! I ONLY NEED TO ADD ONE MORE INGREDIENT!
THEN HOP TO IT! MOVE!
THERE... IT'S DONE!
THIS WILL GIVE YOU THE RESULTS YOU'RE LOOKING FOR!
HA HA HA! YES!
NOW THAT CROWD WILL OBEY ME AND DO EXACTLY AS I SAY!
FLORA!
TAP TAP TAP
STAND BACK, GUSTAVE! WE'LL GET YOU OUT OF THERE!
?
SKRIEIIIK CRANK

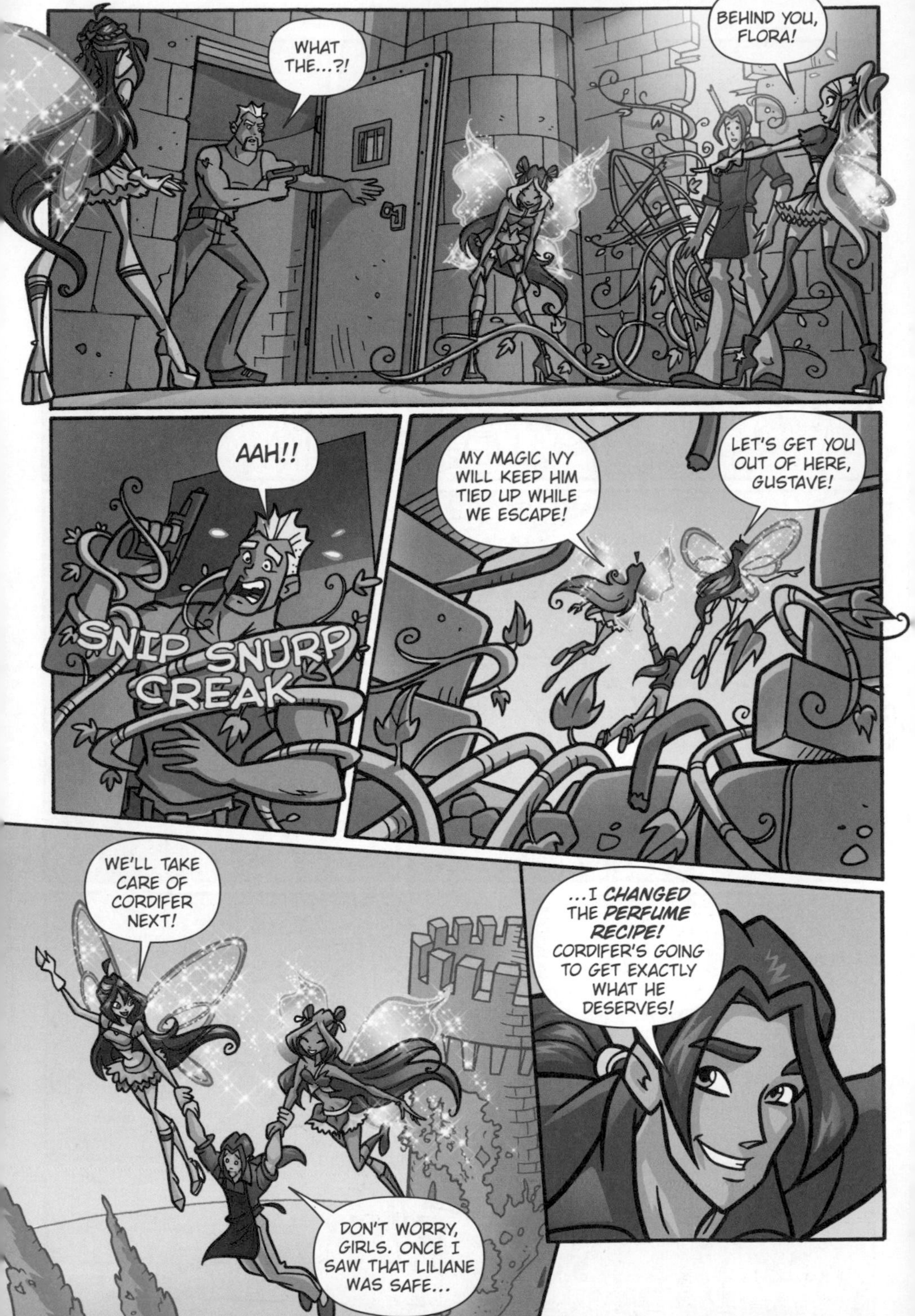
WHAT THE...?!
BEHIND YOU, FLORA!
AAH!!
SNIP SNURP CREAK
MY MAGIC IVY WILL KEEP HIM TIED UP WHILE WE ESCAPE!
LET'S GET YOU OUT OF HERE, GUSTAVE!
WE'LL TAKE CARE OF CORDIFER NEXT!
DON'T WORRY, GIRLS. ONCE I SAW THAT LILIANE WAS SAFE...
...I *CHANGED* THE *PERFUME RECIPE!* CORDIFER'S GOING TO GET EXACTLY WHAT HE DESERVES!

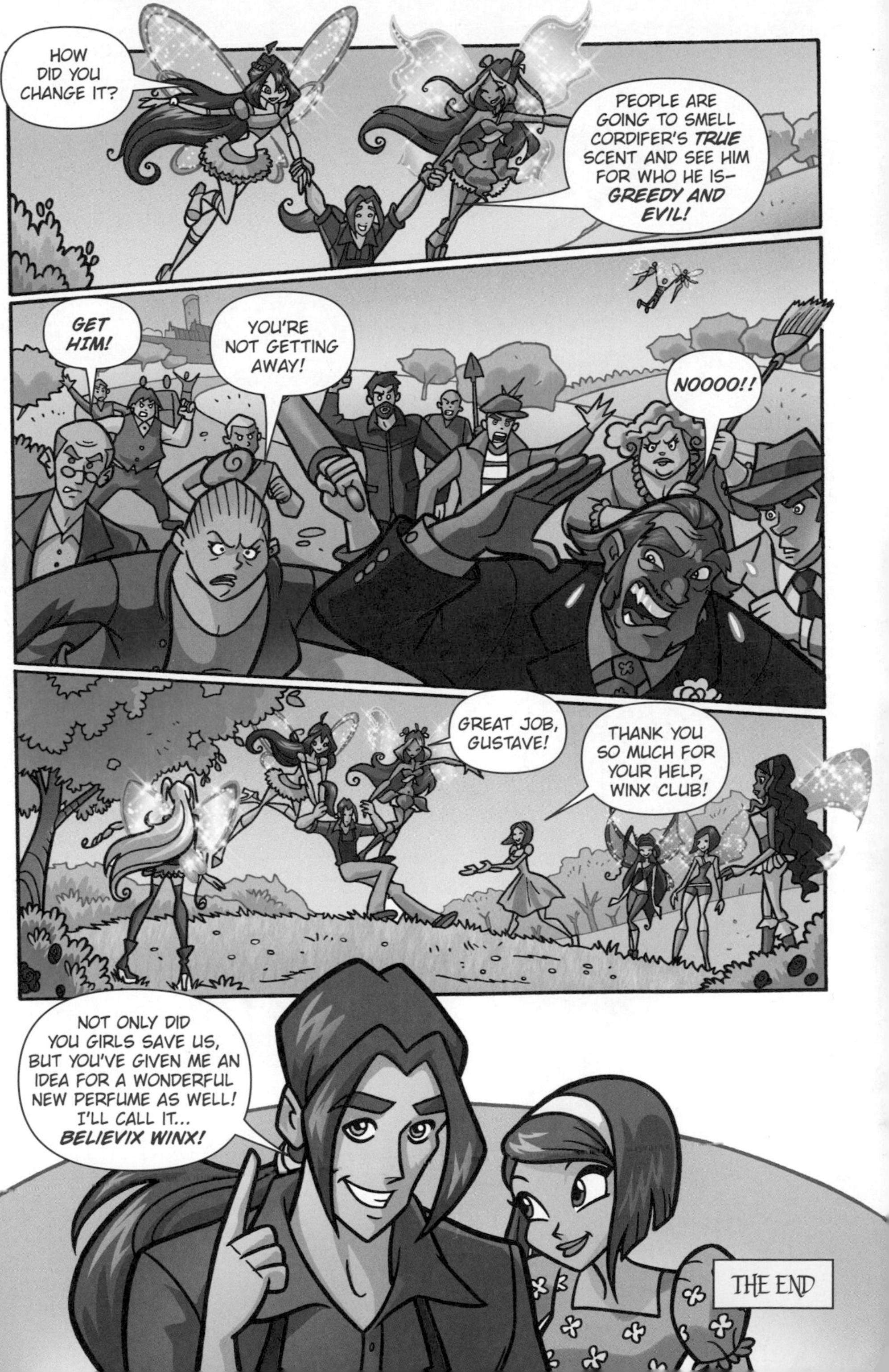
HOW DID YOU CHANGE IT?
PEOPLE ARE GOING TO SMELL CORDIFER'S TRUE SCENT AND SEE HIM FOR WHO HE IS— GREEDY AND EVIL!
GET HIM!
YOU'RE NOT GETTING AWAY!
NOOOO!!
GREAT JOB, GUSTAVE!
THANK YOU SO MUCH FOR YOUR HELP, WINX CLUB!
NOT ONLY DID YOU GIRLS SAVE US, BUT YOU'VE GIVEN ME AN IDEA FOR A WONDERFUL NEW PERFUME AS WELL! I'LL CALL IT... BELIEVIX WINX!
THE END

Now Available

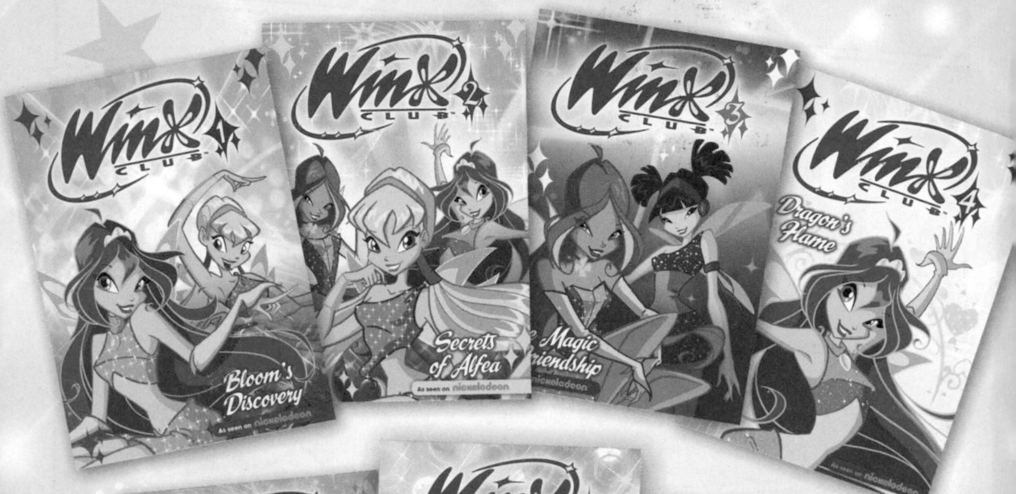
Winx Club 1
Bloom's Discovery
As seen on nickelodeon
Winx Club 2
Secrets of Alfea
As seen on nickelodeon
Winx Club 3
Magic of Friendship
nickelodeon
Winx Club 4
Dragon's Flame
As seen on nickelodeon
Winx Club 5
Fairy Dreams
As seen on nickelodeon
Winx Club 6
Time for Magic
As seen on nickelodeon
Winx Club 7
Adventures Away
As seen on nickelodeon

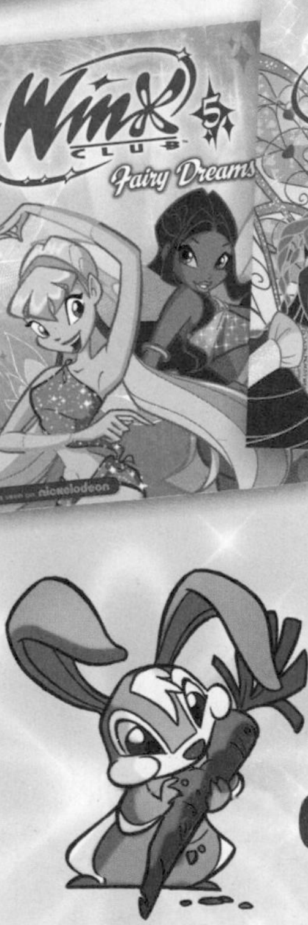

Look for MORE
Winx Club Adventures
COMING SOON!

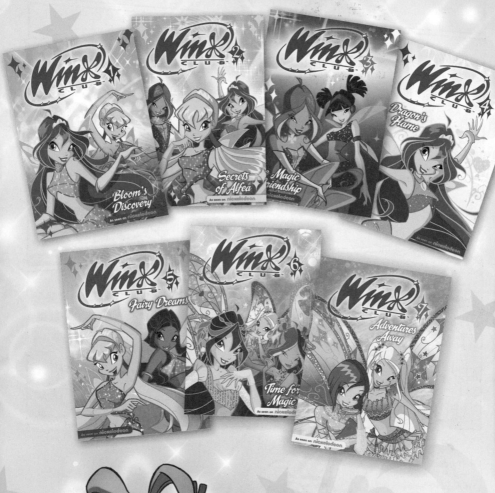